The Art

of the

Traditional
Short Story

The Art
of the
Traditional
Short Story

by
Lester Gorn
&
James N. Frey

BearCat PRESS

San Francisco

Hardback: 978-1-937356-28-6
Trade: 978-1-937356-29-3
Kindle: 978-1-937356-30-9

Library of Congress Control Number 2012936511

Publisher's Cataloging-in-Publication Data

Gorn, Lester H.
   The art of the traditional short story / Lester Gorn,
James N. Frey.
      p. cm.
   ISBN: 978-1-937356-28-6
   1. Short stories, American. 2. Short story.   I. Title. II.
Frey, James N.
PS648.S5 G67 2012
813—dc22
                          2012936511

Front cover photograph by Paula Melton

Book design by Frogtown Bookmaker

Published by BearCat Press: www.BearCatPress.com

*To
Winnie
and
Liza*

Listen, little Elia: draw your chair up close to the edge of the precipice and I'll tell you a story.

— *F. Scott Fitzgerald*

The destiny of the world is determined less by the battles that are lost and won than by the stories it loves and believes in.

— *Harold Goddard*

Introduction
James N. Frey

A traditional short story has a beginning, middle, and end; it features dramatic conflict and dynamic characters struggling to achieve goals where the stakes are high. Traditional short stories end with a strong climax that reveals dramatic transformations in the characters. Such stories have a hypnotic power that makes the reader dream the fictive dream. Traditional short stories are highly emotional, they will often make you laugh or cry, be frightened or terrified, and they usually say something important about human nature. The best of them will stay with you long after you read them, perhaps years. Perhaps a lifetime.

There is another type of short fiction that departs from the traditional form. Literature professors call this type *modernist*. Modernist stories are often plotless, non-linear, and are sometimes written in a stream of consciousness narrative that when done well creates a feeling of immediacy, and when done poorly creates a feeling of being lost in a labyrinth of incomprehensibility.

Modernism was born in the late 1800s, but did not bloom until after World War I. Modernist stories deal with themes such as alienation, isolation, despair, and self-destruction. These themes were engendered by the mass slaughter on the battlefields of the war. In modernist stories, characters are blown about by the winds of a fate they are powerless to control or even understand.

i

Modernism continued to grow in fits and starts during the 1920s and 1930s and into the 1940s, especially in academic and Bohemian circles. Meanwhile quality traditional stories were widely read in large circulation magazines such as *The Saturday Evening Post, Cosmopolitan, The Atlantic, McCall's, Collier's,* and *Esquire.*

After World War II, tens of thousands of returning soldiers wanted to write of their experiences and the government was providing a free college education to them; hence, the birth of university creative writing programs. Literature departments at these universities were hot on the modernist bandwagon, of course, and so writers who wrote modernist stories were selected for these new plum teaching jobs.

It was in these years that modernist fiction became known as "literary fiction" and literary reviews gradually stopped publishing traditional short stories because, well, they were too low-brow. Since modernist stories are by definition literary, by implication traditional short stories are obviously, well, not literary. Traditional short stories weren't exactly junk fiction either, but to the literati they were close. *Entertainments*, they were called derisively. Academics started to refer to traditional stories as "genre fiction," "popular fiction," or "romantic fiction," but no academic would ever call even the best of them literary.

In the 1960s modernism evolved into Postmodernism. Postmodernism is characterized by the use of even more self-conscious techniques such as metafiction, unreliable narrators, and fragmented narrative through-lines. Postmodern short stories are but a further development of modernism, not a radical departure from it.

Fans of modernist and postmodernist fiction accuse traditional short stories of being formulaic and moralistic, qualities that do not appeal to what they call "modern literary sensibilities." Traditional stories are also, they say, too *accessible*.

Fans of traditional short stories counter this by saying: If true, short story masterpieces such as Shirley Jackson's "The Lottery," Jack London's "To Build a Fire," Edgar Allan Poe's "The Tell Tale Heart," Willa Cather's "On the Gull's Road," Flannery O'Connor's "A Good Man Is Hard to Find," and hundreds of other great works written in the traditional form that will knock your socks off are not worth the trouble to read. What a bunch of bull!

The traditional short story has been around for several millennia at least, and is not going away any time soon. The form, according to psychologist Carl Jung, is hard-wired into our brains in structures he called *archetypes*. The form of the traditional short story is the modern incarnation of oral tradition heroic myths that predate the written word by countless thousands of years. Modernist and postmodernist stories have been around about a hundred years, give or take—about as long as the fictional rogue biography fad lasted in the 17th century and the closet drama fad lasted in the 18th.Writers who write traditional stories to be read and enjoyed by ordinary people have always suffered at the hands of the critics who see things through the lens of literary snobbery. Dickens in his day was scourged by literary critics who accused him of being a hack writer of cheap magazine serials. Tolstoy was ostracized by the Moscow literary elites for writing for the masses, especially his moral tales intended for the young. Emily Bronte's *Wuthering Heights* (1847) was excoriated for being, well, a dark, gothic horror novel on a par with potboilers like Ann Radcliffe's *The Myteries of Udolpho* (1794) and Matthew Lewis's *The Monk* (1796).

Oh, well.

Fans of modernist and postmodernist stories like to read them, they say, because they're lyrically written and replete with supposedly arresting philosophical insight and striking images. They make you think, they say. Fans of the traditional short story do not like modernist stories because, they say, they lack narrative drive and clarity, and don't induce the fictive dream. They're almost without exception boring.

This clash of sensibilities between traditionalists, who for the most part adhere to proven and enduring aesthetic principles, and the revolutionary avant-guard that smashes them to smithereens goes on and on and on.

It all comes down to a matter of taste, perhaps.

We hope you will not find any of the stories in this book to be boring—or inaccessible. This collection includes stories of crime and punishment, war, Nazi atrocities, the supernatural. There are two comic stories featuring an inept private eye, a love story, a sci-fi story, a story of a woman prison guard who is promoted to be a state executioner, an off-beat war story of soldiers temporarily taking over a civilian's house, and a couple of stories that are precariously perched on the borderline of just plain weird. All fourteen are in the traditional form and deal with both modern themes such as alienation and loneliness, and traditional themes such as love, loyalty, forgiveness, courage, honor, and duty.

One of the stories might be technically too long to be deemed a short story: It's called "Brothers." A literature professor might call it a novella. Our publisher's readers and the editor found it gripping and moving (one reader called it a tour de force), so we included it.

Let us know what you think of all these stories. We'll post all readers' comments on the Jamesnfrey.com website. You can write to us at: jnfrey@Jamesnfrey.com.

James N. Frey
Berkeley, CA
2012

The Art of the Traditional Short Story

Reflections on Humanity
The Chinese Lantern
An Early Education
Trespass

Reflections on Love
Paris Interlude
Brothers

Reflections on an Extraordinary Crime Stopper
How to Be a San Francisco Shamus

Reflections on Evil
A Letter from a Far Place
Where True Love Can Take You
Spanish Lesson

Further Reflections on an Extraordinary Crime Stopper
Murder Is My Specialty

Reflections on Fate
The Good-bye Room
Duty

Reflections on the Absurd
Bread and Circuses
There's a Stranger in Town

Reflections on Humanity

The Chinese Lantern
Lester Gorn

Russia: September 1941

Scharführer Felix Multcher maneuvered the mud-splattered, steel-gray Panzer through the shallow stream. With visibility circumscribed by the slanted rain, he was caught by surprise when the opposite bank loomed before him. Almost without thinking, he calculated the power needed to negotiate it with minimal jolting to the crew.

The tank treads took the rocky bank with scarcely a shudder, and Multcher's inner voice now reverted to the refrain: *Not too fast.* If the lead tank were to move too fast, the infantrymen sloshing through the creek behind them would be unable to keep up.

The tank started the uphill climb to the ridgeline. *Slow and easy.* Multcher's sleeve, stiff with dried mud, cumbered his sinewy wrist as he reached to the throttle.

Lt. Haeckel's voice came crackling through the earphones. "Slowly!"

Rankled, Multcher glanced toward the commander's seat. All he could see of Lt. Haeckel was his legs and torso—the lieutenant's head and shoulders were lost to view beyond the open turret. Lately, the lieutenant had constantly been finding fault. He reserved his approval for *Unterscharführer* Geist, a born

1

schleimscheiber, ass-kisser. Perhaps he thought the corporal could drive better.

Multcher's annoyance passed. Lt. Haeckel had been without sleep for thirty-one hours, so his irritability was understandable. Prolonged battle could grind down the best of them. As usual, the company had been called upon to lead the counterattack. Once again, the Lili Marlene II was in point position. Multcher rubbed his tired eyes. He and the lieutenant had been together a long time. The Lili Marlene II was the second tank they had shared. Other crew members had come and gone—killed, wounded, transferred.

Multcher peered through the waning light toward the crest. His blue eyes felt raw and watery. Fatigue lay heavily on his lids. He sternly warned himself to stay alert. The undulating terrain provided endless hiding places for T-34 tanks, and the Russians seemed to have an endless supply. Knock out one and two more popped up.

To fight off gloom, he resorted to the glorious truth: he was part of the greatest army in the history of the world. In less than eight months, the blitzkrieg had squashed Denmark, Norway, France, Belgium, the Netherlands, Yugoslavia, Greece! And that had been only the beginning! Since then, the army had piled up even greater glories! Three hundred thousand prisoners at Smolensk! Six hundred fifty thousand at Kiev!

Sgt. Multcher had a special stake in the victory to come. Before the war, his plow had unearthed a wallet containing 1,040 *Reichmarks*. The find made Multcher realize that God had chosen him to become rich. Over the years, there had been other signs of God's favor. Multcher had been received into the SS brotherhood and won the right to wear its collar patches. His brawny hands had proved to have a delicate touch, and he had been assigned as a driver to Lt. Haeckel's tank. Thus far, he had come through the war without a scratch. He had won a gold watch in a regimental lottery. On his last leave, Magda Poppelmann had let him undress her in the barn. To lighten God's task, Multcher spent every spare minute on perfecting a system to break the bank at fabled Monte Carlo. When the Reich reopened the casino after the war, he'd find out how many chips God was willing to stuff in his pockets.

The Lili Marlene II cautiously poked its nose over the crest, and the valley opened up to Multcher's view. The distance to the next crest was about 800 meters. The sergeant mumbled to himself. Their new, longer-barreled 75mm gun could penetrate a Russian T-34's armor at 1200 meters. So why fight in terrain that gave so little advantage to their increased firepower?

Even as he grumbled, his eyes studied the terrain and chose the likely locations of enemy antitank guns.

Suddenly, a hidden enemy gun opened fire. Its flat-trajectory shell swooshed past the Lili Marlene II, ripped into the slope and blasted its deadly fragments into orbit. That the round had been a near miss was confirmed when Multcher heard fragments clog-dancing on the hull. The next round would be armor-piercing, and the enemy gunner almost certainly would not miss. The sergeant glanced in the direction of the lieutenant. It was time to bail out.

"Multcher! Are you asleep? Reverse!"

Cursing, Sgt. Multcher reversed. Spikes churned mud. The tank slipped sideways. Multcher fought the skid. He would have to get back over the hump and nurse Lili into a hull down position before the enemy gunner could make his adjustments and fire again.

The diesel engine whined, the treads screeched. Multcher found traction. The treads bit into rock, spit mud and lumbered upward. *Come on, Lili! Up! Up! One last spurt! That's the girl!*

Over the hump, by Christ! Jubilant, Multcher nursed the tank into a hull down position and sat back in his seat—drenched in sweat, breathing heavily, ignoring the tremor in his right hand.

Lt. Haeckel's voice: "Geist! Traverse right!"

The turret and its 75mm gun started to revolve in a clockwise direction. Suddenly it stopped. Evidently the traversing mechanism had frozen up. It might need some grease. Sgt. Multcher turned in his seat in time to see Geist wrenching the hand wheel, stupidly pitting sheer muscle against the jammed gears. In the dim light, the gunner's fair face was tight.

Jumping from his seat, Multcher grabbed Geist by the shoulder and flung him aside. He glimpsed the gunner's stricken eyes as he snatched up the grease gun. The lubricant jetted from the flexible nozzle into the traversing mechanism. Multcher twisted the wheel. The gun did not budge. Baffled, he paused.

"Traverse, damn it!"

Standing over the wheel, Multcher glimpsed a bit of cloth caught in the gears. As his fingers touched it, he realized the cloth was the corner of a cleaning rag. Glaring at Geist, he tugged and twisted. The gunner shrank back.

Working the rag free, Multcher tested the hand wheel. The turret started to revolve. Too late!

From out of the murk, a shell hit the tank like a giant sledgehammer, dumping Multcher to the floor. The reverberations beat at his eardrums. Before he could shake them off, the tank was hit again. The very air took on force, hoisting Multcher's body high and slamming it down. A fuel tank blew up. Fire broke out near the ammunition locker.

Multcher, dazed, felt a great weight pinning him down. Smoke assaulted his eyes. His lungs burned. How come they'd been hit? Hadn't the hull been all the way down? Might they have been hit from the rear by friendly fire that had fallen short?

Pulling up one knee, Multcher tried to rise. Through the haze, he glimpsed Lt. Haeckel discard his headset and slide from his seat. The lieutenant's hands reached down. He lifted. The mangled face of Stinnes—the loader—flipped into view. Multcher stared at the crushed nose and empty sockets for a second or two, then tightly shut his eyes to deny the sight. He struggled to his feet.

A bubble burst in his ear. From somewhere, he heard moans. *Schutze* Koch was slumped over the machine gun, his leg afire. Snatching a coat from the rack, Multcher beat out the flames along Koch's thigh.

A hatch clanged open. Multcher looked up in time to see Geist lever himself upward and vanish into the patch of murky light. A stiff wind swept in to simultaneously fan the fire and diffuse the heat. Koch's smoking left leg again came ablaze.

Joining the lieutenant, Multcher tried to boost Koch through an open hatch. Half conscious, the machine gunner resisted the alien hands on his body. His legs bucked and kicked. Flames leaped upward from the left leg to his torso. He screamed. Multcher seared his hands as he and the lieutenant heaved Koch's body through the hatch onto the hull.

Pulling himself upward to the twilight, Multcher swung onto the hot hull. The wind whipped him with cold rain. Gulping air into his lungs, he spotted the red-orange muzzle flash of an antitank gun—probably the gun that had hit them. He took a moment to fix its location.

Lt. Haeckel brushed past him and leaped from the treads to the ground. Then, turning, he reached up his arms. As enemy bullets rattled off the turret, Multcher lowered Koch's flailing body. The machine gunner slipped from the lieutenant's grasp and plopped into the muck. Rain and mud smothered the flames licking at his leg and chest.

As Multcher jumped to the ground, a flare went up in the half-light. It rocked gently overhead, shedding glare on the infantrymen running for the cover of the firs and aspens fifty meters south. In a half-crouch, Multcher and Haeckel bundled Koch toward the swaying trees. The mire sucked at their boots. Tracer bullets—glowing red—ripped past them. Twenty meters ahead, the infantrymen stumbled into a minefield. The blast threw up clumps of mud, flesh, weapons.

The woods had taken on the appearance of a field hospital. Aid men, harassed by enemy fire, moved among the wounded. Screams and moans punctured the air. White-hot shell fragments thumped into bark. Ricochets whined. Frantic soldiers burrowed into the ooze, their faces at one with camouflaged helmets and field-gray uniforms.

As an aid man administered morphine to Koch, the small arms fire diminished, and Multcher heard the noisy static of a field radio. He saw Lt. Haeckel hurry to the soldier crouched over the set. Multcher followed.

The radioman shook his head. "Can't raise them, sir."

Peering toward the thicket sheltering the antitank gun, Multcher confirmed his earlier estimate of its position: 500 meters. If radio contact could be established, mortars or artillery could be provided map coordinates. Friendly tanks could be warned to steer clear of the ridge until the gun was taken out. The lieutenant could use the radio to direct the bracketing.

Removing a glove, Multcher squeezed ointment from a small tube onto his burned hand. A detonation shook the dusk and made him duck. He turned. Fire had ignited the ammunition stores of Lili Marlene II. Glancing at Lt. Haeckel, Multcher marveled at the officer's show of calm. Except for the sodden field uniform, he looked like the sternly resolute warriors pictured in the magazines at home.

Smoke and fire spouted from the Lili Marlene's slits and hatch edges. The wind joined the reek of hot metal, diesel fuel and burning flesh to the sweet, sickening gases of the maggoty dead inhabiting the forest. Contrary to radio reports, the

Russians had been able to halt their retreat and mount a counterattack. The area had changed hands several times.

As Multcher coughed and spat to get rid of the foulness, he saw Lt. Haeckel cock his head as if to listen. A moment later, from beyond the ridge, he heard the diesel hum of an approaching Panzer. Leadenly, he gazed toward the crest, willing the Panzer—*Untersturmführer* Kersten's, probably—to stay out of sight.

Kersten's battered tank climbed into view. As it started down from the crest, the enemy gun fired. A shell hit the Panzer, pinning it to the slope. Fire broke out. Flames fed flames. Multcher watched intently. The fire lit up the hillside. No hatches opened.

A hand grasped Multcher's sleeve. He turned.

"I got wounded," Geist said, pressing a gauze pad to his upper thigh.

Multcher felt like putting a fist into the gunner's sad, brave smile. From the day Geist had arrived as a replacement, Multcher had tagged him as a malingerer. Over Multcher's objection, Lt. Haeckel had picked the ass-kisser—he of the crinkly eyes and curly hair—to be the gunner. It was Multcher's secret opinion that the SS—eager to expand—had made a mistake when they designated Geist as a racial German. How could a mongrel from Rumania—or Hungary or the Ukraine—be a racial German? Yet the lieutenant seemed to go along. And now the foreigner's sloth had brought disaster.

Geist fidgeted under Multcher's stare. "If I'd been hit three inches higher, I might have lost my manhood."

"Not your manhood," Multcher said. "Just your Rumanian prick."

Geist shrank back. "I'm sorry, Sergeant, about the gun."

"You should be," Multcher said. "Especially since you're going to be brought up on charges. Dereliction of duty."

"It could have happened to anybody, Sergeant. The last time I had any sleep was at 0500 yesterday."

"Your negligence has cost lives," Multcher said. "There is no defense. *Ordnung muss sein.* Things must be in order."

Geist appealed to Lt. Haeckel. "Cleaning the breech, I could hardly stay awake."

The lieutenant did not take his eyes from the burning tank. "We'll see."

Multcher scowled. Never before had Lt. Haeckel failed to support him on a disciplinary matter. Were there no limits to what Geist's shit-friendly smile could accomplish?

"A court martial will decide," Multcher told Geist.

Turning, the lieutenant regarded him sharply. "We'll talk about it, Sergeant, in due time."

Multcher stiffened. *"Zu befehl, Herr Untersturmführer.* As you command." His deference had a defiant edge.

Lt. Haeckel chose to overlook it. Hunching into his coat collar, he blew on his hands. "It'll be almost an hour, Sergeant, before the darkness forces that damned gun to cease fire. We can't wait until then. I'll lead the detail to silence it. Round up some men and weapons. Be ready to go in five minutes."

"Zu befehl, Herr Untersturmführer." Again, the exaggerated courtesy escaped a reprimand. Turning, Multcher hurried back to the improvised field hospital.

"By my count," the senior aid man said, "we have thirty-four men here." He twisted a stick to tighten the tourniquet on a patient's leg wound. "Except for me and the radioman, every one of them is wounded. The less seriously wounded are giving critical care to the others." He gave the stick another twist. His patient groaned. "And the only available weapons are rifles. No Panzerfausts, no shaped charges or grenades."

Multcher reported back to Lt. Haeckel.

"So be it," the lieutenant said. "The two of us, then."

8

Geist, sitting on a nearby stump, lifted his head. "I'd like to go with you, Lieutenant."

"Your wound won't slow us down?"

"No, sir."

The lieutenant glanced at Multcher.

"We could use a volunteer up front," Multcher said deliberately. "Someone who ain't scared shitless by mines."

"Count on me," Geist said.

Lt. Haeckel looked from Geist to Multcher and then back to Geist. "All right."

The detail moved out with Geist in the lead. Multcher fell in about ten paces behind the lieutenant. Their boots squished in the muck as they made their approach along the lip of a ditch. They avoided the ditch itself. Almost certainly, it had been mined. They made steady progress. Soon, the thicket took on definition against the leaden sky.

A cluster of flares probed the dusk. Instinctively, Multcher threw himself into the muck, using his elbows to keep his rifle clear. The bluish glare picked out puddles of rainwater. Multcher felt the chill wetness penetrate his coat. His hand was swollen. It hurt. He cursed.

The flares came to earth and sputtered out. Clambering erect, Multcher again fell in behind the lieutenant. The detail resumed the trek.

Shortly afterward, the antitank gun resumed firing. Its nest was close now. The muzzle blast lit up the thicket. Again and again, the gun's lordly *kwump* proclaimed high explosive or armor piercing missiles on the way. Multcher looked back toward the ridge. Two more Panzers had come ablaze. The valley resounded with their knell. The gun was deadly.

The gun stopped firing. Ahead, Geist halted and raised his hand. With the lieutenant, Multcher went forward. Geist pointed into the ghostly light. The sergeant was able to make out the silhouette of an embankment, perpendicular to the thicket.

They ran to the embankment in a crouch, then crawled along its base. As they reached the thicket, they heard the clunk of entrenching tools and the damp thud of mud sliding from a shovel. There were four of them: flat peasant faces, baggy field uniforms. Two were chopping at the semi-frozen earth, trying to dig a slit trench. A third stood directly behind the gun, peering into the distance and sipping from a tin cup. The fourth was off to one side, taking a piss in the underbrush. His stream plashed into the shrubs.

To use guns would risk alerting nearby enemy soldiers. Lt. Haeckel gestured with his dagger. Multcher and Geist nodded. Assigning individual targets, the lieutenant looked at Multcher and pointed to the enemy gunner, then looked at Geist and pointed to one of the soldiers digging the trench. Again, they nodded.

Slowly, noiselessly, Multcher placed his rifle atop a bush, a meter's remove from the muck. Then he drew his dagger, checked to be sure Geist was in position, and waited for Lt. Haeckel's signal. In that brief interval, he regretted having consented to take Geist along on the mission. He'd give three-to-one odds that the Rumanian would mess it up.

As the lieutenant made his move, Multcher sprang forward. In six steps he was atop the enemy gunner. An upward thrust planted his dagger in the gunner's back, and he rode the man down to the ground, feeling the warm blood gush over his hand. The man's tin cup clattered onto a rock. As Multcher pulled the blade free, he saw the lieutenant's left arm hook the head of the soldier taking a piss. The lieutenant jerked the head upward, then whipped the dagger in his right hand across the throat. Multcher nodded to himself. No vacillation there.

He heard a cry. Whirling, he saw Geist under assault by the two remaining enemy soldiers, armed with mattocks. Multcher leaped forward, his dagger poised. He caught a whiff of onions as his blade sliced into the man's chest. The peasant grunted; the body obligingly sagged. At that moment, the lieutenant fell upon the last survivor. The man bellowed. It took repeated thrusts to bring him down. Despite the screams, nobody came running. Either there were no enemy troops nearby or the soldiers within earshot had no stomach for hand-to-hand combat.

Stepping around the bodies, Lt. Haeckel looked out over the gun barrel to the burning tanks on the ridge. Then, turning, he punched Multcher lightly on the arm. "Good work, Sergeant."

Before leaving, they searched the site. As expected, they found some explosives protected from the rain by a ragged tarpaulin. To deny the enemy a chance to reclaim the explosives and the gun, they decided to destroy them. In magnanimous mood, Multcher let Geist set off the charges.

The detonations drew an immediate response from the enemy. A flare split the gathering darkness. They hit the dirt. As the flare flickered out, they arose and headed back to the aid station.

Geist, still abashed by his performance, eagerly took up the point position for the return trek. All went well until his foot tripped a wire at the lip of the ditch. The blast threw his body parts ten feet into the air.

Another flare lit the landscape. Multcher dove into the ditch simultaneously with the lieutenant. He skidded through the mud and came to rest alongside some discarded shell casings. He took stock. Not a scratch! As always, God had watched over him. He no longer felt clammy, and the pain in his hand was gone.

Rolling over on his back, he stretched luxuriously and looked up at the flare. It swung back and forth, bathing the ditch in flickering violet light.

Beautiful, he thought. Like a Chinese lantern.

An Early Education
James N. Frey

This morning I read a small article in the paper about the latest milestone in the life of Henry X. "Hex" Saunders. I'd known him almost forty years ago when we were both students at T. Aaron Levy Junior High School in Syracuse, New York. For a short while I even thought of him as a friend.

We were both in the ninth grade, but he was a year older. He'd flunked the fourth grade. He had trouble reading and, except for auto shop where he was a standout, he was an indifferent student. He was dark and tall and naturally athletic, solidly built, wore a cocky grin most of the time, and had deep-set black eyes that could send a chill down your spine if he stared at you hard. Rumor had it that he'd kicked a guy's eye out in a fight and he'd taken on a high school wrestler and nearly killed him. We half believed it.

I was slightly built at the time and somewhat timid. I was the fourth man on the track team and rebellious at home (never home on time, wouldn't clean my room, that sort of thing). Despite that fact, I got on well with my love-to-party stepmother, who was not really married to my father. My father drove big tractor trailers long haul for Boss-Linko Trucking and was hardly ever home. When he was, he was too busy with his model trains to bother much with me. I was quite a good artist, winning a few prizes for paintings of cars (particularly '56 Ford Crown Victorias, the most beautiful machine ever crafted by the hand of man), and might have made it big in that field on the commercial side had I pursued it. It was the rebelliousness in me that drew me to Hex Saunders.

His mother had left the household years before and he was living with an alcoholic stepfather in a cramped, musty, attic apartment. The stepfather's work took him out of town often. He was a pot-bellied, surly man with a red-veined face and a nasty temper. My friends and I were all afraid of him, but Hex would joke around with him and tease him, put him on edge just for the fun of it. It reminded me of taunting a zoo animal by poking him with a stick through the bars. At times there were unexplained bruises on Hex's face, bruises he didn't want any of us asking about. The zoo animal, we figured, had snapped back.

Hex would have me and my other friends over to the attic apartment for poker games, which he almost always won, and he served us our first taste of bourbon, our first puffs of cigarettes, our first look at a *Playboy* centerfold. Hex knew how to do it with girls and he gave us all instructions on how and what to touch, fondle, suck, and whisper in their ears. He sold us our first Trojans.

Though he was exciting to be around, he made me uneasy. He would often speak of enemies. Unnamed enemies. Out of the corner of his mouth, under his breath, he would make dire threats against his teachers; he'd say he'd bash their brains out with a baseball bat, that kind of thing. And how much fun it would be to electrocute the gym teacher. He said they were all against him, that they'd put listening devices in his bedroom, that they searched his locker on weekends and that was why he cleaned it out every Friday.

He had a cat he would kick if it got in his way. He never mistreated any of us as long as we kept losing our allowances to him at poker. He was probably cheating, though none of us were ever clever enough to catch him at it.

One day I was walking with him on Canapy Street after school. We were going to buy baseball cards at a grocer's on Thurman Avenue. It was a crisp fall day. The elms and oaks and sycamores were turning, dried leaves crunched beneath our feet, and the sweet-acrid smell of burning leaves filled the air. Ahead of us there were two other boys. They were a grade or two behind us and smaller. Both lugged books and notebooks; one carried a violin case. They wore lace-edged skullcaps. Hex said, "Hey! Look, Jews! Let's beat the shit out of them!" And he sprinted toward them, laughing loudly, falling on them, hitting and kicking them with a terrible fury.

I was stunned, and for a moment stood frozen. The two boys cried out, but Hex kept kicking and punching in a frenzy.

Finally, finding my courage, I ran up to them to try to stop it, just as the kid with the violin case ran down a driveway between two houses and Hex took off after him. I helped the other kid collect his books. His face was a bloody, swollen mess. Through his tears he kept saying he'd got him one good one and I kept saying sure he did. I told him to get the hell out of there, then I went down the driveway where Hex was kicking the other kid and calling him a "dirty Jew." I managed to drag Hex off the kid, saying he'd had enough, that we had baseball cards to buy and we didn't have time to be fooling around. He took a few last kicks like a glutton, having gorged himself, wanting just a few more spoonfuls. We left the kid on the ground sobbing, curled up with his arms around his violin case, blood running out his nose all over his white shirt.

I'd never witnessed an anti-Semitic attack like this. T. Aaron Levy Junior High was about half Jewish and half Christian and there may have been some serious friction, but I, personally, was not aware of it. There was a wall of separation, but it was not a high one. You were expected to date within your own group,

14

and most of us did, but when you were the one who picked the players for the baseball game after school, your teammates expected you to pick the best players, no matter. My Christian friends and I had often gone to the Jewish Community Center to play basketball after school with some Jewish kids and were warmly welcomed. At holiday time all the kids sang both Christmas and Chanukah songs. We always had a Christmas tree and a menorah in the main hallway; everyone treated each other's icons with respect, as far as I could tell.

We had a few black kids at T. Aaron Levy Junior High too, and they were accepted. One was captain of the football team, another the student body president. I rarely heard racist or anti-Semitic epithets. On the whole, it was a good place; we all got along. We were proud of it.

The rest of the day after Hex attacked the two Jewish kids I was frightened because I thought I'd be blamed. I was relieved when the police didn't show up at the house that evening. My father, who was home and irritable after taking a load of chinaware to California, did not like visits from the police and would have taken a strap to me.

The next morning I went to school trembling with fear, thinking the police would be waiting for me at homeroom. But they weren't. Hex didn't seem particularly worried; he was grinning his usual cocky grin. He told me to stay cool, that he could handle it.

Our first class was English. It barely got started when the door opened and Mr. McNeal, the guidance counselor, and Mr. Carlisle, the civics teacher, came in, flushed with anger. They were the biggest men on staff—both in their thirties and both at least two hundred pounds. One took me by the arm, the other took Hex by the arm, and they jerked us out of our seats and escorted us into the hall. I'd never been that scared in my life.

The two Jewish kids were waiting in the hall, bruised and bandaged, one with a cast on his arm. They backed away as if

Hex were a snake that might strike, even though Mr. McNeal had a tight hold of him. Mr. McNeal asked which of us, Hex or I, had done it. The two Jewish kids looked terrified, but they both pointed to Hex. Mr. Carlisle let me go and told me and the two Jewish kids to go back to class. Mr. McNeal and Mr. Carlisle each took hold of one of Hex's arms and led him away.

Hex looked more puzzled than frightened. For that moment, his cocky grin was gone.

The doors to the classrooms at T. Aaron Levy Junior High were recessed into the wall about three feet so the doors could come open without hitting someone coming down the hall. I slipped into the recess and watched as Mr. McNeal and Mr. Carlisle took Hex into the boy's lavatory at the other end of the hall, no doubt to administer a beating.

I was relieved they weren't dragging me away too, but still my heart beat fast. Something terrible was going to happen to Hex, I was sure of that.

I went back to my class. Although the English teacher didn't ask me what the trouble was, I could tell she was curious. The kids were all curious, too, but I didn't say anything. I tried to look busy taking notes on the lecture.

After about ten minutes the door opened and Hex came back in. He looked a little disheveled and winded, but he gave me the thumbs-up sign as he took his seat. I assumed they must have given him a stern lecture, sentenced him to detention or something like that, then let him go. Taking him into the boys' room must have been just to scare him.

But a while later, out in the hallway, someone screamed and soon we heard an ambulance siren. The intercom came on and we were all told to stay in our seats: there was an emergency.

I looked over at Hex. He was slouching back in his seat with his hands behind his head like he owned the world.

By lunchtime everyone was talking about it. One of the kids who caught a glimpse of the two teachers being taken away in the ambulance said they looked like ripe tomatoes that had been stomped on. Hex wasn't talking, but he was grinning ear to ear. He went outside to smoke behind the gym. Later, we heard that Mr. McNeal had broken ribs, a fractured jaw, and a broken pelvis, and that Mr. Carlisle had fractured ribs and a broken foot. Both men suffered multiple bruises, contusions, concussions, and abrasions.

Rumor had it that Hex had urinated on them.

The next day Hex's stepfather showed up at the school. He said the Jew-loving teachers had gotten what they had coming and he found the whole situation amusing. He threatened to have Mr. McNeal and Mr. Carlisle arrested for assault if they tried to get the cops to arrest Hex. No charges were ever brought.

Years later, I ran into our principal, Mrs. Dawson, long after she had retired. She was an old woman then, but thinking of the incident brought back the fear. You could see it in her eyes. She said she had two sons of her own; she wasn't going to push it. There was no telling what Hex Saunders might do, she said.

I remember how, after the beating, when it was clear he had escaped punishment, Hex took on the aura of the invincible conqueror. He stopped doing homework, came late, left early, and often heckled the teachers in class. He got OK grades and never drew detention.

My friends and I never had much to do with Hex after the beatings. But Hex didn't mind; he had legions of new friends. He would take them to Mr. McNeal's house after school while he was still recovering. They had great fun making up verses to chant beneath his window.

> *McNeal, McNeal, McNeal*
> *thought he was tough,*
> *thought he was bold*
> *Until he tried a lad named Hex*
> *and got himself knocked cold.*

Later, at Nottingham High, Hex became a football star as outside linebacker and ended up with a scholarship to college. The sportswriters all said he was a "vicious hitter." Once he left for college, he never came back to Syracuse that I know of.

Mr. McNeal quit teaching and moved to Rochester and went to work for Kodak in the shipping department. Mr. Carlisle didn't come back to teach until the following year, but his heart wasn't in it. He became a regular at a dive called Wanda's, I heard. He had a stroke a few years back, that's all I know.

The two Jewish kids transferred to private school and I don't know what became of them.

After high school I became a firefighter. I had this stupid vision of carrying kids from burning buildings on my back. I never did anything like that in the twenty-seven years I was in the department. I did get my lungs seared twice, pretty bad. I'm on disability now. I still paint pictures. Mostly cars. Mostly '56 Ford Crown Victorias, the most beautiful machine ever crafted by the hand of man.

Funny how even after all these years I sometimes wake up in the middle of the night and it all comes back to me, that Jewish kid on the ground holding onto his violin case, blood gushing out his nose all over his white shirt.

As for the article in *The Wall Street Journal* this morning: It said that Henry X. Saunders was promoted to CEO of an oil company and is living with his wife and four children in Pasadena, California. It said he was a graduate of the University of Colorado where he had been second-string All American, and that he was born in Syracuse, New York, where he received his early education.

Trespass
Lester Gorn

Fighting along the river south of Constanza had been fierce, so it was no surprise when word came down that the 414th would stay put in the city for awhile and let the rear area gold-bricks carry the load north.

The men scattered, mostly in pairs or clusters of three or four.

The captured city offered a wide choice of accommodations. Its civilians had prayed ceaselessly for relief from the pounding of U.S. planes and artillery, but most of them had finally acknowledged God's indifference to their plight and holed up in the dark, wind-swept hills to the east. It would be a day or two before they found the strength to advance one leg after another for the trek home.

Half the Eyeties who had chosen to remain in Constanza now were buried in its rubble. Their sweet stink held sway over the reek of overflowing sewage and uncollected garbage.

An upthrust human arm poked from a heap of broken jars, dishes, mirrors, toys, framed pictures of FDR, Fiorello La Guardia, Caruso and the Pope. Dogs scavenged at garbage cans. Two shivering kids huddled over a fire in an overturned oil drum.

At night, the Eyeties who'd stayed put and made it through the city's firestorm burrowed into their houses. In daylight, some of them ventured forth to goggle at smoldering rubble and beg passing G.I.'s for rations. Italians rarely looted. They were too law-abiding or too scared.

G.I.'s didn't loot at all. They simply helped themselves to whatever they wanted. What had been paid for with blood was theirs.

Seeking snug quarters, Private First Class Boz Menke and the Perfessor—Sergeant Louis Palmieri—sleepwalked past the shell-pocked mortuary that housed Regimental Headquarters. Helmets, field packs and the impedimenta that flapped from their web belts bulked large in the dusk, and the damp and cold collaborated with muck-heavy boots to slow them down.

Still, their forward movement was steady. Sleep-heavy eyes could sense potholes in the torn-up road, and the two did not need words to mutually reject slogging an extra mile to a more prosperous quarter.

A charred, two-story apartment house won their approval. High explosive shells had stripped walls, ceilings and furnishings from three or four contiguous rooms on the building's second floor, but the first floor looked unscathed.

Settling into a tidy apartment on the ground floor, the two put on clean, dry fatigues and then put in eleven hours of sack time made rapturous by the bedroom's clean white sheets and feathery comforters. At noon, they scraped the dried mud from their boots and went scouting for food, *vino* and women. The city proved bereft of qualified women, but the two did liberate some bread, cheese, olives, wine and a cut of beef.

Arriving home, they broke up some chairs and built a fire on the tile floor of the living room. They straightened a coat hanger for use as a spit. The pantry yielded sauces and spices. In no time at all, the beef was being barbecued to a fare-thee-well. Smoke eddied upward toward the vent they'd hacked in the ceiling. As the room warmed up and the air filled with good smells, Boz and the Perfessor doffed their coats and took their ease by the campfire.

In repose, the craggy Boz conjured up a welterweight prizefighter: big hands, big shoulders, broad chest. Few people south of Market in San Francisco would have recognized him as the tightly-wound teenager who'd won the jitterbug contest at Mission High two years in a row.

Similarly, few people in Albany, New York, would have recognized the Perfessor as the glib, dapper, seemingly surefooted careerist he once had been.

During the depression years after high school, Louis Palmieri had bided his time as assistant advertising manager of the John G. Myers Department Store—essentially a gofer. He had gotten his big break fourteen months before Pearl Harbor, when Franklin Roosevelt called the National Guard to full-time active duty. Louis' boss had been a civilian-soldier in the National Guard, enabling him to make like a warrior and ride a horse like Tom Mix once a week. Roosevelt's call-up had forced him to hie himself off to the Cavalry at Fort Knox, Kentucky, where he would ride a tank instead.

Louis' dizzying reign as advertising manager and resident Don Juan at John G. Myers Department Store had lasted four months, at which time General Hershey (impresario of the national lottery) decreed that Louis' winning draft number had earned him a free ride to Fort Dix, New Jersey, a training camp so overwhelmed by incoming recruits that it was unable to supply them with rifles, coats, gloves, boots, barracks, cooks, leak-resistant tents or potbellied stoves. There, in a single winter, Louis had uncovered his true talent: to adapt, improvise, scrounge.

Now, Boz and the Perfessor sprawled before their campfire, sampling provolone and Strega while languidly contemplating a faded, framed print identified by the Perfessor as a Raphael.

The talk was not confined to the dismal prospects for choice tail.

Boz had heard that the regiment wouldn't be moving out until after the engineers restored electricity. With luck, the engineers would fuck up as usual, and Boz and the Perfessor would be in Constanza long enough to confer C-rations and cigarettes on Eyetie poontang returning from the hills. Meanwhile, Boz would have time to cogitate postwar plans to introduce Italian style bedrooms in the States. As soon as he got back home, he'd organize a platoon of artists to go around painting satyrs and nymphs on every ceiling in the Mission.

The Perfessor had heard things, too. One thing he'd heard was that the postal people had gotten religion. On the alert for looters and black marketeers, they'd taken to checking money orders as well as packages addressed to the States. So naturally, the Perfessor was leery of sending home his $1400 in poker winnings. He'd sweat it out until word came down that the backsliding had begun.

It was shortly after Boz and the Perfessor uncorked the second bottle of Strega that Boz found the secret compartment behind a bookcase. Having run out of firewood, he'd started to feed books to the flames. The removal of a four-volume set of Mussolini's speeches had revealed a locked compartment about thirty inches square built into the wall. "Hey!" Boz said. "Jackpot!"

After he and the Perfessor had combined their muscle power to tug one end of the heavy bookcase away from the wall, he pulled at the knob. The compartment door did not budge. He pushed, twisted, yanked. No dice.

Boz and the Perfessor ogled the secret door as they replenished their wineglasses. Could it be that a big-time thief or Eyetie bigwig had chosen this modest apartment to stash illegal funds or valuables? Gold? Rubies? Diamonds?

Unpocketing his Swiss Army knife, the Perfessor poked a narrow blade into the lock and pushed back its tongue. The spring resisted, so he abandoned the lock and pried at the door edge. The blade snapped in half.

Boz lost patience. One blow from his rifle butt smashed in the compartment door. Quickly, he and the Perfessor forced aside the splintered panels.

The cache proved to consist only of books, neatly stacked. They gawked. Why would anyone trouble to hide books? Boz' head tilted in thought. He brightened. "Porn, maybe. Dirty pictures." Pulling out a volume, he leafed through it. To his annoyance, it contained no pictures, dirty or otherwise. With a sweep of his hand, he toppled one stack to the floor. Then, kneeling, he started to go through the books one by one: turning them over, shaking them by their covers, fanning their pages.

The Perfessor plucked a fat volume from the heap and turned to the inside cover. "Hmm," he said. "*Ex libris dottore Federico Moscone e Rosa Moscone.*"

Boz looked up. "Since when do you read Italian?"

"You don't have to know the language to figure this one out. 'From the library of Dr. Federico Moscone and Rosa Moscone.'" The Perfessor fingered the raised lettering on the book cover. "Rococo."

"Rococo." Boz nodded sagely. "So it's the books themselves are valuable."

"Afraid not, Boz." Dropping to his knees, the Perfessor sifted through the jumble. "They're neither leather-bound nor old nor rare."

"Why put them under lock and key, then?"

"Because they're subversive, I guess."

"Huh?"

"They're on Mussolini's shit list," the Perfessor explained, "along with anybody who reads them."

"Like communists, you mean?"

"Yeah. Even if the doctor's not a commie, he's a subversive. His wife, too, probably."

"What makes you think so?"

"I recognize some *verboten* names," the Perfessor said. "Radical writers, politicians, labor leaders."

"Yeah? Who?"

"Nobody you'd know, Boz."

"Who says?" Boz bristled. "A fucking know-it-all. Just cuz I din't go to college— Like always, you make like I'm ignorant."

"'Like always?' When?"

"All the time."

"Tell me one time. Just one."

"I'll tell you shit! You want I should keep track? Carry a notebook? Put everything down?" Boz's tone turned surly. "I know a lot more than you think I know."

"I don't doubt it."

"You'd be surprised," Boz said. "Historic events, dates, writers. Ask me anything. Put some names on the table."

"Forget it, Boz. You got nothing to prove."

"Fucking well told, nothing to prove! Go ahead, ask."

The Perfessor sighed. "All right, Boz." He took a breath. "Voltaire. Zola. Vanzetti."

Boz scrunched his face into thinking mode. "Zola," he mused. "Vanzetti." He gazed afar. "Know them from somewhere."

"Indubitably. Vanzetti, for sure. Executed with his friend, Sacco, for murder—or more likely for his anarchist ideas."

"Oh," Boz said. "That one."

"Yeah. Italian immigrant. Spoke broken English."

"I remember him now. "

"Uh-huh."

"Really," Boz said.

"Sure."

24

"You don't believe me."

"Course I do."

"No. If you believed me, you'd ask what I know about the man." Boz looked the Perfessor in the eye. "'If it had not been for these things, I might have lived out my life talking at street corners to scorning men.'"

The Perfessor's jaw dropped.

"'I might have died unmarked, unknown, a failure. Now we are not a failure.'"

The Perfessor lifted up his jaw. "Fucking unbelievable."

Boz grinned. Idly, he glanced down at the loose pages in his hand. "Hey! This one's in English!" He examined the mutilated book. "The doc's a subversive, all right."

"Let's see." The Perfessor scrutinized the pages. "Gene Debs. Some woman named Mother Jones. And a marked passage quoting Mark Twain." He read the quotation aloud: "'Man has no more occasion to love and honor king and Church and noble than a slave has to love and honor the lash, or a dog has to love and honor the stranger who kicks him.'"

For a moment, the two were silent.

The Perfessor said: "Nice stuff."

"Yeah." Boz reclaimed the mangled book and picked his coat from its hanger. "I wonder," he said, cramming the book into the coat pocket, "where the doc is right now."

"In the hills, likely," said the Perfessor.

"Rosa, too, I guess."

"Who?"

"The doctor's wife." Scooping up some books from the pile, Boz started to restack them inside the compartment.

"Hey!" the Perfessor said. "What are you doing?"

"Putting them back."

"Slow down, Boz," the Perfessor said. "We'll freeze."

"No sweat," Boz said. "Constanza's got fuel to spare. Other things, too."

The Perfessor weighed Boz's tone. "What other things do you have in mind?"

"A little surprise for our host—some leather-bound books, say, to replace the burned ones."

"Great idea," said the Perfessor, seemingly without sarcasm.

"And maybe a better print for the wall," Boz said.

"Wonderful," the Perfessor said. "I'll saddle up Rosinante for you."

"Fine. Do that."

"To avoid enemy territory, you'll have to ride due west, across the Mediterranean. A fer piece."

"I don't mind, if Rosinante doesn't."

"To Spain. Where the windmills are."

"So long as it's rear area." Boz gazed into the fire. If he was confounded by the references to Rosinante and windmills, he showed no signs of it. "Come to think of it," he said, "why settle for a print? Might as well do it right. Should be easy to scare up an original, a rich town like this."

"Why stop with books and a painting?" the Perfessor said. "Requisition a carpenter, rebuild the compartment."

"Good thinking. A mason, too, to repair the floor and ceiling."

The Perfessor poked a knife into the spitted beef. Carving out a chunk, he wolfed it down. Juice splattered his upper lip. "Could be, Boz," he said pleasantly, "you'll wind up with a section 8."

"Good deal! Loonies are shipped home." Boz plopped some olives into his mouth. "Which reminds me," he said. "What's 'rococo'?"

When the doctor and his wife came in from the hills, they found their street aswarm with American troops.

26

The 414th was preparing to pull out. Motors roared. Fumes assailed the eyes and nostrils. Soldiers piled aboard truck beds. Tailgates clanged.

Guiding Rosa through the milling crowd, Dr. Federico Moscone—slight, grizzled, disheveled—squeezed her hand reassuringly, but he could not help flinching when accosted by two burly soldiers at the apartment house entrance. One—dark-faced—wore three upside-down V's on his upper sleeve. A sergeant, the doctor believed. The other—pale skin under stubble—had only one such V. What one V signified, Federico did not know.

"Who are you?" the sergeant demanded in English.

"We live here." The doctor, too, spoke in English. "We have been away and now we have returned."

"What's your apartment number?"

He knew he should answer promptly, but he was confused by the question, and by the noise and the turbulence about him, and he was very tired. He and Rosa had not eaten for two days. He put an arm around Rosa's waist to stop her from trembling. "It's all right, Rosa." He addressed her in English, so the sergeant wouldn't suspect a deception of some kind. "They mean no harm."

"'Rosa,'" said the pale-faced soldier. "That's the password." He held out his hand. "Here's your key."

As in a dream, he accepted the shiny new key dangling from the soldier's fingers. Before fleeing to the hills, he had hidden his old key under a dead potted plant in the hallway. He could not understand where the new key had come from. Nor did he understand what the soldier meant when he said "Rosa" was the password.

Turning away, he guided his wife down the rubble-strewn, sour-smelling hallway toward the apartment. Rosa's bent shoulders felt thin. She stumbled once but did not fall.

To Federico's relief, the new key worked.

The first thing he saw as the apartment door opened was the far wall. He gaped in disbelief. The washed-out Raphael print had been replaced by an original painting: an airy, vibrant Chagall. Even at a distance, he instantly recognized Chagall's fanciful ox and floating lovers. Incredible!

The painting, he knew, was the property of Giuseppe Antonio Ferrero, the puffed-up little *il duce* of the Constanza branch of the *Unione Fascista Famiglie Numerose*, whose annual ceremonies bestowed medals, plaques and certificates on strutting home-grown peacocks adept at keeping their wives endlessly pregnant. Giuseppe Ferrero somehow had acquired the Chagall after its owners, the Paolo Levi family, had been shipped off to what reliable partisans swore to be a German extermination camp. No doubt Ferrero's respect for the painting's monetary value exceeded his aversion to so-called Jewish art.

The doctor stood before the Chagall, drinking it in. His heart sang. It would have to be stored in the secret compartment, of course, but they would take it out now and then to look at. And at war's end, when the nation established justice under law, he and Rosa would be able to enjoy it day and night until they located Signor Levi's heirs.

From afar, he heard his wife's voice. "The smells."

He sniffed. How could he have missed the smells? Smoke, charred wood, freshly cut lumber, stain, varnish, tanned leather. Turning, he looked around. The table had been sanded and freshly stained, and many of the tiles in the middle of the floor had been replaced. He knelt. Yes, there had been a fire here, but the restoration had been exacting, and the new tiles came close to matching the beauty of the old ones. Similarly, the chairs replacing the ones around the table came close to a perfect match. Incredible!

Federico's attention shifted to the bookcase. His heart skipped a beat. One end of the heavy bookcase had been moved from the wall. The set of Mussolini's speeches seemed to be intact, but books stacked adjacent the set were unfamiliar. Rising, he went to the bookcase. Some old books, he saw, had been replaced by others bound elegantly in leather. He saw, too, that the Mussolini volumes did not occupy the same space they had occupied before. His heart pounded as he approached the new door—extravagantly paneled—that had replaced the compartment's old one. One twist of a knob and the door opened. Anxiously, he checked out the compartment. As far as he could tell, the hoard was intact.

In a daze, he walked into the kitchen. There, he found his wife standing wordlessly over a table heaped high with bread, cheeses, olives, tea, coffee beans, wine, C-rations, Hershey bars and a baked ham. Dumbfounded, Federico struggled to make sense of it all. The key. The Rosa password. The two soldiers at the entrance.

Saints.

He caught himself. Bizarre, to beatify the marauders. Where had he misplaced his common sense?

In the street outside the living room windows, the uproar took on a newly charged tempo. Federico rushed to see what was happening. The troops were moving out. A motorized column jounced over the ancient cobblestones, its wheels spitting ooze onto cracked and broken sidewalks.

Twenty paces from the house, an American half-track pulled a dead horse from the road. A neighbor, Signora Urbano, kept pace with the moving carcass to hack away a haunch. Blood splashed her gloves and neat wool coat. She paid no heed. The loss of two sons in the North African campaign had numbed her to such things.

Rosa's voice: "Such generosity, the Americans. So kind."

Yes. Generous and kind—no denying it. And—truth to tell— he coveted their bounty, for himself as well as for Rosa, even at the expense of his neighbors. Wartime, he told himself, justified a greed normally indefensible.

He fidgeted. Why, then, did the sight of C-rations and Hershey bars on his kitchen table make him uncomfortable?

He sighed. What he truly wanted was to be spared clanking tanks and muddy slit trenches and mangled bodies and wailing children and Rosa's trembling and falling-down buildings and the sight of Signora Urbano flailing at a bloody carcass. He wanted to again be admired and adored by grateful patients streaming hour after hour through a shiny-clean, well-equipped clinic where gunshot wounds and amputations were a rarity.

He wanted his city back.

He caught himself. Enough!

To wail about war's inevitable fury was to give way to a shameful self-pity. Obscene, to resist gratitude for gifts so imaginatively bestowed—and for the decency that had inspired them.

His shoulders lifted. He would get his city back in due time, and—thanks to the so-called enemy—it would be a city that no longer feared a knock on the door.

As he turned to rejoin Rosa, Federico glimpsed—or thought he glimpsed—two soldiers wave at him from a truck rounding the corner. Gathering his senses, he waved back.

Too late. The truck had vanished from view.

Reflections on Love

Paris Interlude
Lester Gorn

Everywhere, the fatherland's flags celebrated the occupation of Paris. Blood-red swastika banners draping the facades of public buildings made a mockery of the ubiquitous monuments to France's historic victories and conquests. Posters proclaiming the virtues of "Work, Family, Country" had displaced the Republic's effete "Liberty, Equality, Fraternity."

Ironically, Paris' street signs still paid homage to French writers, artists and revolutionaries. Museums, galleries, salons and bookstores abounded, and *bouquinistes* along the quai still pinned up rare maps, pictures and sketches—or what passed for rare maps, pictures and sketches—to snare preoccupied passersby. Deprived of art, France could not live. With art, France could not die. Or so the French told themselves.

Actually, defeat had struck deep. The conquerors inundated streets, hotels, parks, cafés, theaters, monuments. They censored books, magazines and newspapers. Masterworks not hidden from the *boche* ended up in trash heaps or private collections. In once-grand stores, half-empty shelves and display cases attested to the country's rapid shift from consumer products to war materials, and to the avidity with which visitors in uniform snatched up perfumes, cosmetics, jewelry, tinned delicacies, stockings and lingerie for shipment home. Although sequestrations, petrol rationing and the shift of skilled mechanics to war industries had diminished the cars, trucks and buses that claimed the streets and alleys, mechanical breakdowns still clogged traffic and incited horns and curses.

Plus ça change, plus c'est la même chose.

Changed or not, Paris still qualified as the tourists' favorite city.

Especially because it was now theirs to do with as they liked.

Walking across traffic-choked Pont Neuf, Lt. Kurt Haeckel spotted a lush green finger of land jutting out into the Seine below. He paused a moment to gaze at a bronze *Vert-Galant* heroically riding his steed atop a suitably grand pedestal, then descended a steep stone urine-spattered staircase and walked past a docked *vedette* to the waist-high metal fence enclosing a tiny park shaped like the forward deck of a flower-bedecked ship, its prow about fifty meters ahead.

Unlatching the gate, Kurt started along a pathway toward the prow. The late afternoon sun filtered through leafy willows to speckle flowerbeds luxuriant with violets and pansies. Flowering trees puffed white clumps blushing pink. All of the benches were occupied. Except for one matron who murmured a polite *bon jour, monsieur* as Kurt passed by, park patrons avoided looking at him. The larks and pigeons, though, were unafraid. They did not take wing at Kurt's approach. They simply stepped aside.

Reaching the prow, Kurt stood at the metal fence and looked out over the Seine. *Vedettes*—sightseeing boats festive with fluttering pennants—passed in review, crammed with soldier-passengers dreaming of an out-of-nowhere encounter with a rosy, busty, eager demoiselle. Now and then, a solitary barge lazied down the river, sometimes with no visible pilot. Across the water, a brood of bicyclists sped noiselessly past the Louvre, gloomy with the grime of centuries. Built-up grime also darkened the noble facades of the tall-windowed apartments alternating with the stately domes, spires and battlements of public buildings.

Kurt breathed deep of the garden's fragrance. The park was magic. Although it could not bestow contentment on one such as he, it eased the self-consciousness and tension that burdened him whenever he left his billet and ventured into a public place. If only regulations permitted wearing civilian slacks and a sports shirt during his ten-day leave! It would help with the heat, too. Christ, it was hot! In peacetime, they said, the French virtually abandoned the city during August. No wonder!

Unpocketing a handkerchief, Kurt wiped the sweat from his face and neck as inconspicuously as he could. To publicly display vulnerability of any kind was unbecoming an SS officer.

He consulted his guidebook. The park, he learned, actually was one end of Ile de la Cité, a boat-shaped island married to a succession of bridges over its close-to-two-mile length. Two thousand years before, a Celtic tribe—the Parisii—had decided the island was a good place to settle down and fish and chase women. Their descendants and invading Franks, Romans, and others had expanded outward and built a city.

Kurt scanned the nearby benches. One young couple—heads tilted downward—seemed to prefer their books to each other, and their shaded bench could easily accommodate an additional person.

He addressed the young man. *"Permettez?"*

The two looked up, startled. Kurt had a glimpse of the girl before she ducked back into her book. Mid-twenties, slight; white blouse over a knee-length pleated skirt.

"Mais certainement, monsieur," the young man said.

No problem. Kurt sat down. A minute later, it became apparent that still waters hid turbulent depths.

35

Glancing at his watch, the polite young man stiffened and shook his head, as if he'd just realized the lateness of the hour. Then he gathered himself together and moved off, his measured pace disavowing flight.

Clearly, the two readers were not a couple—the young man had left without so much as an *au revoir*. Kurt stole a quick look at the girl's profile: a bold undulating line from brow to chin.

Kurt turned his eyes to the placid Seine. A barge pushed by. A fat man sat on deck, alone, smoking a pipe. A small swastika flag fluttered from an improvised flagpole atop the cabin. Protective coloration?

Although Kurt fought off the temptation to doze, he yielded to what he believed to be a dignified languor.

The gathering dusk summoned him to sit up straight. He suppressed a yawn. People were leaving the park. Perhaps they did not want to risk after-dark unpleasantness with a German patrol. He glanced sideways. The girl had turned slightly, so Kurt now was able to see her more fully: dark eyes, tawny skin, tangled black hair. No getting around it, French girls were pretty. Underneath, though, French girls—rosy or not—were said to be like the factories and office buildings they worked in. Rub one and the dirt would come off.

Not this one, though. She evoked spring, sunshine, sparkling water splashing over pebbles. Covertly, Kurt studied her. Curious, that his Stygian presence had not frightened her off. Curious, too, that she seemed oblivious of his scrutiny and—despite the waning light—intent on her book. On the bench beside her, one corner of a small, unwrapped cardboard box protruded from under a folded green sweater. Was it fanciful to wonder if the box contained contraband of some kind—possibly an explosive? At his billet, there were constant briefings on incidents of sabotage—infrequent, but growing. Could it be that the girl was bent on a nighttime operation? Or that she was a courier, waiting to pass off the box to an accomplice? Perhaps the accomplice already had made his appearance and been scared off.

She closed her book. Unhurriedly, she scooped up her belongings, then rose and started away. Her stride was brisk, in keeping with the tart set of her mouth but alien to the rest of her.

He caught himself. The rest of her? To be titillated by a full skirt atwirl over fine brown legs was understandable, but that did not give him license to indulge infantile daydreams.

Paris was seductive. Soft. Even its light was soft. You sank into it. Adrift. If you did not resist, you'd have no more resolve than a child.

He watched the girl as she neared the gate. Suddenly, she veered toward a section of railing in deep shade. Although he could not see her clearly, it seemed to him she was fumbling with the cardboard box, perhaps preparatory to hurling its contents over the rail into the river. Rising, he hurried forward. Her back was toward him—she was unaware of his approach. And, yes, the box was open and she was reaching inside.

"*Mademoiselle?*"

As she turned, he got his first close view of her face. Fright glinted in her hazel eyes and trembled at her lower lip, but there was nothing tart about her mouth. Nothing at all. So much for first impressions.

"May I ask what you are doing?" he asked in French.

Anger pushed fright aside. Tilting the open box close to her breast, she screened its contents from view. "You already have. Asked."

"Well, then," he said. "Tell me, please."

"No. Why me? I've done nothing wrong."

"Then you can't object to showing me the box."

"But I do object." She stared at a cluster of people—three men, four women—who'd paused on the path to watch the encounter. The cluster broke up under her glare, and its component parts moved on toward the gate.

"I must insist," he said.

"By what right?"

Her audacity stunned him. He looked at her.

She handed over the box.

He recognized its contents immediately: crematory ashes.

"My brother loved this place," she said. "He would have wanted his ashes scattered here, law or no law."

He scanned the park. The dusk had deepened. The last of the dawdlers had cleared the gate. "No policemen in sight," he said. "What's stopping you?"

She eyed him quizzically, as though trying to reconcile his words with his uniform. Then she nodded to herself and, taking the box from him, started scattering ashes over the flower beds.

He was momentarily shocked to see her using her hand to do the scattering. He had always thought that ashes were disposed of by using a scoop of some kind, or by pouring the ashes directly from the container. Now, though, his squeamishness seemed foolish. Why should the touch of a brother's ashes be abhorrent?

The girl worked steadily at her task, like a farm worker sowing seed or scattering feed to chickens. Kurt, looking on, caught himself dwelling on the gentle curve of her buttocks. A flush of guilt forced him to look away. Apostates attending last rites were not entitled to voyeur privileges.

"Jacques was twenty-four years old," the girl said. "A lieutenant. Like you."

Kurt flinched.

"No, no," she said quickly. "You people didn't kill him. He died in an auto accident."

"Oh." He took in the full measure of her grief.

She used her forearm to wipe sweat from her eyes, then scattered the last of the ashes over the ground. That done, she turned the empty box upside down, tapped it smartly with her palm, then stepped toward a public trash bin. Halfway there, she faltered. Peering at the inside of the box, she examined it for residue.

"Maybe you'd feel better if you took it home and burned it."

"Oh, no. I couldn't possibly." She eyed the trash bin. "Well, maybe." She watched a squirrel scamper across the path and climb a tree. As the squirrel explored the tree's upper foliage, she reached a decision. "Yes. More—respectful to take it home."

Handing Kurt the box, she dusted off her hands, then picked her sweater off the fence, retrieved the book propped atop a crosspiece and made one last survey of the flower beds. As she turned away, her shoulders straightened in a visible effort to throw off sadness. She made no move to take back the box.

Walking with him toward the staircase, she detected his covert scrutiny of her book. She said guardedly: "'For Whom the Bell Tolls.'"

He nodded. "Hemingway."

"Yes." Surprise did not dislodge wariness. "You've read Hemingway?"

"Yes."

She brandished the book. "This one?"

"No. This one's new. I read Hemingway in the early days, before it became *verboten*—and before I realized he was the enemy of my country."

She was unable to hold back her reply. "I'd think that would be all the more reason to read him."

He gaped at her.

"I could lend this one to you, if you like."

"Why would you do that?"

She threw off all caution. "Better, I guess, than having you confiscate it. Or burn it."

He said stiffly: "I am not a policeman, *mademoiselle*."

"No," she said. "Merely SS?" She hesitated. "The SS also burns books, *n'est-ce pas?*"

"Sometimes."

"Have you?"

Dumbfounded by her impertinence, he stalled for time. Then: "No."

She did not let up. "Would you?"

"Would I burn books, you mean, if ordered to? Yes, I suppose I would."

They became mired in silence. Then she said: "I didn't mean to badger you."

"Odd," he said, "I had the impression my embarrassment gave you pleasure."

"You're mistaken." She considered. "Well, maybe. Some."

He gazed at her. Suddenly, out of nowhere, desire surged through him—a desire different from any he had ever known. He liked this girl. He liked her open-eyed look and her straightforwardness and her courage. And, yes, the sway of the small breasts under her blouse.

A strange weakness invaded his limbs, accompanied by an irrational fear that the girl could read his thoughts. Casting about for an impersonal something to say, he fell back into Hemingway territory. "I've been told the protagonist of your novel is an American who volunteers to fight in the Spanish Civil War. On the Loyalist side."

"Who told you that, Lieutenant?"

"A friend."

"A German friend?"

"Yes."

"How did he know?"

"Somehow he managed to get hold of a copy."

"So you could have read it if you wished."

"Yes. It was my duty to refrain."

She considered. "Your friend didn't refrain."

40

"No."

"Yet you remained friends."

He nodded.

"And you did not report him."

"No."

She broke step to look into his eyes. "Even though it was your duty."

"Yes."

Reaching the staircase, they started up the steps to the street level.

Then she said: "Did you like him?"

"Who?"

"The early Hemingway. Whatever Hemingway you read."

"In some ways. Mainly, I guess, I admired his prose—no flourishes. One- and two-syllable words. Simple, clear declarative sentences. And characters who stand for things."

"What things? Besides masculine swagger?"

"Is that what you see? Swagger?"

"Add it up. Hunting, fishing, bullfighting, sailing, boxing. And war."

"No credit for commitment and courage? Or for a refusal to whine or indulge in self-pity?"

"Hmmm." She considered. "Odd, that I glossed over such virtues."

As the two reached the top of the stairs, they stepped out into Pont Neuf's hurly-burly of honking horns and auto backfires and workmen repairing the roadway and people hurrying home to beat the blackout. Soon, they became aware that they were the targets of numerous glances—some of them masked, some hostile, some carefully neutral. Turning, they walked to the parapet and leaned on their elbows to contemplate the shadowy Seine.

He watched a *vedette* as it approached the bridge. "Is it acceptable, I wonder, to ask if we're going to see each other again?"

"How stiffly you ask! Is that you?" She sobered. "To fraternize, Lieutenant, is to invite constant slights and slurs. Not that the majority truly are devastated by our defeat. They're hard hit, though, and it's patriotic to care, so they do."

He nodded. "I should not have asked," he said, handing back the empty box.

"Whether you asked or not didn't actually matter," she said. "I'd already decided."

"So I thought."

"Tomorrow," she said. "Lunch."

He stared at her. "Lunch?"

"Yes. Noon."

"Lunch at noon."

"Yes."

"You'd already decided to see me again if I asked?"

"Or even if you didn't."

"You're impulsive," he said.

"More like intuitive, I think. Are you free?"

"Yes."

"Good. Do you know Les Deux Magots?"

"I've heard of it." He hesitated. "Luncheon there may not be a good idea. Too popular. Too—public."

"Bourgeois Paris is a small town, Lieutenant. Secrets don't keep. I often run across a friend or neighbor at out-of-the-way places. Better to meet openly—and in daylight."

"I'm an enemy soldier. You don't even know my name. Are you sure you want to do this?"

"You're stuck, Lieutenant. You can't back out now."

"I warn you—Embarrassment may be the smallest part of what you're letting yourself in for."

"Believe me, I understand the risks involved." She paused. "What I don't understand is what you're doing in that SS uniform."

He said stiffly: "You mustn't believe that all SS officers—"

She cut him off. "Whatever I 'mustn't believe,' Lieutenant, tends to be high on my beliefs list."

"I can believe that," he said wryly. "Still, it won't kill you to remember that apples come in many kinds, sizes and colors."

"Notwithstanding, apples are apples." She looked him up and down. "Your uniform simply doesn't fit, Lieutenant, and there's no way in this world it can be made to fit."

⚜

Les Deux Magots did not turn out to be a wise choice.

During the two decades before the war, Les Deux Magots had been a favorite hangout for young writers and artists, including such expatriates as Ernest Hemingway and Scott Fitzgerald. Now the café attracted multitudes who longed to absorb the Lost Generation's vibrations, or at least to breathe the same air as the current literati. Daily, German officers opted to mingle with French businessmen and secretaries for lunch and people-watching on the café's terrace, where sunlight and aperitifs and laughter approximated the surface gaiety if not the lightheartedness of an earlier era.

Kurt and Odette were midway through chicken with *frites* and a reasonably priced Chardonnay when Kurt was hailed by Wernher von Blucher. "What luck to run across you," Wernher called in German.

Kurt quashed a frown. Having decided that popularity would greatly enhance his chances for rapid promotions, Wernher was making an all-out effort to efface the hauteur that had claimed his eyes and mouth at birth. He had chosen to overlook Cadet School quarrels with Kurt and make repeated overtures of friendship. Only yesterday, he'd offered to introduce Kurt to some girls from the Folies Bergère. Now he was steering his latest acquisition—pert, perfumed, bubbly—to Kurt's table. "Mind if we join you?" Almost before the words were out, the two were seated and exchanging introductions.

Bubbly's name was Marie. She had met Wernher at a party. She thought him twenty thousand leagues removed from the *boche* she'd heard about all her life. To hear her parents tell it, Germans were boors. Cruel, too. In World War I, they had raped Belgian nuns and bayoneted babies. The Germans of today were even worse.

Marie brushed a possessive hand over Wernher's sleeve. "It's truly unjust to paint all Germans with the same brush."

Startled by Marie's paraphrase of a remark he'd made the day before, Kurt glanced self-consciously at Odette. She dismissed his concern with a brushing motion of her hand.

Wernher, across the table, was intent on the menu. He weighed his choices carefully before ordering *noisettes d'agneau* and a vintage Burgundy. That freed him to report on his Paris peregrinations. Like Kurt, he spoke proficient French.

"Marie has been showing me the city," he said. "Today, we walked down the Champs Elysées and through the Tuileries to the Louvre."

"A productive morning," Kurt said.

"Not as productive as yesterday, Kurt—the Tuileries slowed us down. Yesterday morning we were able to cross off the Eiffel Tower, the Trocadero and Napoleon's Tomb. The afternoon—Notre Dame and the Pantheon. And Sacre-Coeur."

"Don't forget the restaurants," Marie interjected. "Lunch at Le Procope, dinner at La Tour d'Argent."

"Yes. Half the list, thanks to you." Wernher patted Marie's hand. "By the time my three-day leave is up, I'll have seen virtually everything worth seeing."

"*Wunderbar*," Kurt said.

Something about Kurt's tone nettled Wernher, but the waiter's arrival with the Gevrey-Chambertin '35 gave him the opportunity to overlook it.

Reverently, the waiter opened the Burgundy and poured a sampling. Wernher sipped and nodded approval.

"I do not mean to offend," he said to Odette and Marie. "Paris is charming, but I must say the dirty streets and the sidewalk excrement are deplorable. The dingy buildings, too."

"Perhaps after the war," Odette said, "the city will get around to sandblasting the buildings and scrubbing the streets. They've talked about it for years."

Wernher looked at her. "'The city?'" he said. "'They?'"

Kurt said quickly: "Whoever's in control at the time."

Odette sipped from her glass. "Naturally, I assume it will be my countrymen in control."

"Under Occupation supervision, of course."

"No." Odette was able to keep her voice steady. "The assumption was—is—that the city will be ours again."

Wernher set down his glass. Its muted thump savaged the hush.

"A natural assumption," Kurt said. "No doubt most Parisians share it. If Berlin were occupied, Berliners would feel the same way."

Wernher said stiffly: "I will not have such talk at my table."

Odette paled.

Looking from Odette to Wernher, Kurt ran his finger over the rim of his glass. "May I remind you, Lieutenant, this table is not yours."

Wernher reddened. In the seconds he took to rev up an angry retort, however, he was preempted by a real-life drama that played out in full view of the lunch crowd on the terrace.

An old flatbed truck crammed with eight or nine families of deportees labored past the café, followed by a police car. The limited space of the truck bed made it necessary for the passengers to stand. The lucky ones clutched the wooden supports at the sides of the truck. The others clung to each other and kept their balance as best they could.

Suddenly, a Renault sedan pulled away from the curb, directly in the truck's path. There was a screech of brakes. The truck swerved. Detainees at the sides clung to the supports to keep from falling. Most of those in the middle were packed so close together that they managed to stay upright on their own. A few lost their footing and slipped down onto the truck bed, out of sight. A man wearing a white long-sleeved shirt and a striped tie fell over the tailgate and struck his head on the pavement. From within the heaving, struggling crush came screams, shouts, whimpers.

On the terrace, movement had ceased. Food and drinks were ignored. Waiters stood stock-still. Pedestrians stopped in place. All eyes were fixed on the street spectacle. As the truck stopped, the Renault that had instigated the imbroglio speeded up and vanished around a corner. The police car skidded to a stop less than ten meters from the back of the truck. Two gendarmes—clean-cut, smartly uniformed, immaculate—leaped out, pistols unsheathed and ready.

At that moment, a boy of about eight jumped from the truck. Resolve etched grim lines on his wan face. Skirting the injured man on the pavement, he started running at an angle toward the nearby Saint-Germain Metro entrance. The *flics* blocked his way. Halting, the boy backpedaled. Closing in from either side, the *flics* pinned his arms and hustled him back toward the truck. The boy resisted fiercely. One *flic* said something to the boy and gave him a comforting pat. The resistance subsided.

Once the boy was aboard, the gendarmes turned to the man on the pavement, now struggling to his feet. Shaking off their assistance, the man staggered to the tailgate. Willing hands reached down and hauled him into their midst. Less than two minutes later, the crowded truck and its cargo were gone, and the traffic had reclaimed its lunatic normalcy.

Pedestrians dispersed. The café's sounds and movements resumed. Silverware clattered. Waiters rushed platters of *andouillettes, moules,* and *coquilles Saint-Jacques* to their assigned tables. Ice cubes floating in tall glasses struck middle C's. A cork pulled free with a hollow pop.

Talk resumed. Although few diners seemed shaken, nearly everyone was excited. Much of the speculation concerned the Renault that had forced the truck to stop. Almost certainly, the incident had been staged to give the deportees a fighting chance to escape. If so, the scheme had utterly failed. The ensuing chaos and confusion—and the quick reactions of the *flics*—had assured the triumph of law and order.

"The driver must have been a Jew." Wernher paused while the waiter placed his entree before him. "It's the kind of sleazy stunt a Jew would pull. On a crowded street, nobody dares shoot for fear of hitting innocent civilians."

Odette shifted in her chair. Kurt avoided her eyes.

"Note," Wernher said. "It's French police—not the Gestapo—carrying out the deportations. Quite willingly, it appears." Cutting into a lamb cutlet, he ate with relish. "Nor do I detect anger or regret in witnesses."

Marie said, "I can't help feeling sorry for that boy, though. At his age, it must be a terrible shock to be yanked from your home and shipped to the east."

Avoiding a direct comment, Kurt confined himself to the pragmatic. "Why ship them east? Why not put them to work here in France?"

Odette, silent until now, spoke up. "Can't you guess?"

"No." Kurt shook off a presentiment of disaster. Already, diners at neighboring tables had picked up on the tension and were trying to eavesdrop. "It doesn't make sense."

"It makes sense if their exile has no end."

Kurt's breath caught. Irritation tainted the tenderness that welled within him. Odette had treated a vile rumor as though it had substance. Was there no limit to her recklessness? He said quickly: "It's possible, I guess, some deportees will put down roots and elect to stay on."

Wernher did not seem to have heard him. "My country has a manpower problem," he told Odette. "Our young men are serving in the armed forces, yet our production goals must be met." His politeness had steel at its core. "Are you suggesting, *mademoiselle*, that we've no moral right to require parasites and agitators to work where they're most needed? Or worse: that we're sending them off to so-called death camps?"

Odette suppressed a tremor. "At the moment, Lieutenant," she said, "I'm suggesting you've no right to turn what has been a pleasant lunch into a political interrogation."

"I've every right, *mademoiselle*," Wernher said, icily polite. "It's you who have no rights. In Roman times, you would be a slave. Under the Reich, you may live as you please, so long as you behave responsibly. You're even free to have lunch at Deux Magots — within certain limits." Pushing back his chair, he stood up, ramrod straight, and signaled the waiter. "I am not welcome here," he said to Kurt. "Nor am I comfortable with the slander to which I have been subjected." As the waiter arrived, Wernher pressed some currency into his palm, then gestured toward a vacant table near the sidewalk. "You will arrange my move to that table." He looked at Marie. "Come, my dear."

Compliantly, Marie picked up her purse and her half-full glass.

"Not the glass, dear. We'll get another." Pivoting to face Kurt and Odette, Wernher drew himself stiffly erect, clicked his heels and bowed. Then his body unwound a notch, and he offered his forearm to Marie. She took it.

Kurt watched them go with dread. However unpleasant the last few minutes, the worst was yet to come. In less than twenty-four hours, his idyll had reached its end. He saw it in the expectant faces of those who'd looked on from nearby tables. And he felt it in his gut.

His gut proved reliable. Odette's voice was unsteady, but there was no mistaking its finality. "Yesterday, Kurt, you wondered whether I knew what I was letting myself in for. I thought I did."

He did not speak.

"I kept telling myself you are not your uniform, and the uniform is not you, and I know in my bones and heart it's true. And my heart tells me ours is a bond that could grow—over time—into something we'd both cherish—and that too I know to be true." She paused. "But when I tell myself the uniform will not poison our days—that, I know, is a lie."

What she'd said mirrored his own thoughts—or, rather, articulated thoughts too fuzzy or too heavy on the tongue for him to express.

"I've always believed," Odette said, "that hate destroys the hater. I still do, but now the very sight of a swastika in our streets makes hate irresistible." She blinked back tears. "What's bizarre is that I do not even see a German when I look at you. I see what a Jewish friend calls a *mensch*."

Tears. For him.

"I long to embrace you before I leave, Kurt, but I'm too sensible for that. I worry about what people will do to me after the war." She stood up. "May God watch over you."

She turned away.

He watched her as she threaded through the terrace tables to the sidewalk. Wondrous, her tears. Impossible that he had known her for less than a day. Unbelievable that he could feel about her as he did. He loved the fall of her dark hair. He loved her hesitations, her silences, her forthrightness. He loved her smell. He loved her sun-browned legs and the tender slope of her backside.

He loved her love of freedom. He loved her recklessness. He loved her refusal to indulge false hope.

He loved her un-Germanness.

Brothers
Lester Gorn

The merchant came riding out of the afternoon mists, his huddled body swaying with the horse's every labored step. Moisture gave a cold sheen to the mare's skin; rivulets dripped from her flanks onto the dirt road. As the merchant passed through Yung Chang's outskirts, he saw that its streets had been abandoned to the fog. Lamplight gleamed from within Sung Ho Inn, but the windows revealed only a few moving shadows.

At the hitching post, the merchant clambered down and tied up his horse. Flexing stiff fingers, he flailed his arms at the chill and the solitude, then unlashed his pack from behind the saddle and shook moisture from it.

Footsteps sounded on the sidewalk planking. A woman approached. Hunched into a dark cloak, she angled her torso away from the merchant, enlarging by inches the space between them. Scuttling past him, she vanished into the mists.

The merchant slung the pack at his shoulder and entered the inn.

Even as the innkeeper served him hot mulled wine, the merchant felt the weight of the inn's dank silences. Clasping the steaming cup, he looked around the room. The two men playing *yet-pang-mang-i* by the open charcoal fire did not so much as acknowledge his presence. Nor did the men at nearby tables, brooding over their wine cups. One clutched a cold pipe. Plain black robes contrasted with the merchant's embroidered blue robe and its tasseled sash.

The merchant unslung his pack. Some loose toys—two bird whistles and a flute—dropped onto the counter. When the merchant picked up the toy flute and blew a few notes, the card players looked up. One tugged at a wispy beard to bring indulgent lines to his mouth and jaw. The other exposed a smiling yellow tooth. The gloom could be dented, it seemed.

The merchant displayed a sealed scroll to the innkeeper. "I've a letter to deliver. Where can I find a man named Da Tsung?"

Inexplicably, the innkeeper tensed.

With a bound, the yellow-toothed man crossed the room, wrested the scroll from the merchant's hand, and hurled it into the brazier. Falling short, the letter smoldered on half-burned coals.

The bewildered merchant took a step toward the brazier.

"Don't."

The merchant faltered.

"Sir," the innkeeper said. "If you deliver the letter, you will sell no toys in Yung Chang. If you so much as speak to Da Tsung, you give up your right to walk our streets in safety."

Scanning the room, the merchant found every face set against him. "Why?"

No one spoke.

"I promised I would find him."

"Promises do not apply to beasts."

"No man is a beast."

"This one is."

"A good man, I was told. What has he done?"

"Done?" the innkeeper said. "I'll tell you what he's done—!"

The bearded man took command. "Nothing!" His glance rebuked the innkeeper for his indiscretion. "He's done nothing. He doesn't exist." He let his mouth get fat with smile. "You will not be blamed. Others came with letters. They were not blamed. The letters simply vanished."

"This one won't vanish." Deliberately, the merchant stepped to the brazier and plucked the scorched scroll from the coals. Although its red seal had softened, the wax had not run. The merchant seized his pack and headed out.

"Sir!"

The merchant stopped.

"You've proved your courage," the innkeeper said. "Now prove yourself sensible."

"A man cannot be both sensible and honorable."

"Honor pushed too far," the innkeeper said, "can end in the grave."

"The grave? Come, now."

"I myself would not go so far. Others might."

"I promised I'd deliver it," the merchant said doggedly.

The yellow-toothed man blurted: "Who did you promise? Who's the letter from?"

"No one!" The bearded man interposed his voice and body between Yellowtooth and the merchant. Flushing, Yellowtooth retreated to his chair. A stare pinned him there. Satisfied, the Beard recited the litany: "No one writes to Da Tsung. He doesn't exist. Hence the letter doesn't exist."

"If the letter doesn't exist," the merchant said, "why the uproar?" He strode to the door. No one tried to stop him.

Outside, the merchant made his way to the hitching post. There he paused, uncertain. A youth walked by, his footsteps hollow on the wet planking. Leaving his horse, the merchant hurried after him. "Boy!"

The youth halted.

"I'm looking for someone who lives here in Yung Chang."

"Yes, sir."

"A man named Da Tsung."

The youth stiffened. He spat and started to turn away.

Reaching into his pack, the merchant came up with some toys. The boy turned back. He eyed the outstretched hand, then searched the mists for danger. Not until the merchant sounded a sweet trill on a flute did the youth build the boldness to snatch the toys.

Picking up a stick, he used it to draw a crude map in the dirt. "Take the road north about two *li* until you reach the creek." He used the stick as a pointer. "West along the creek about a hundred *ma*. If you keep to the north bank—"

A horse whinnied. The youth peered toward the inn. He fled.

Through the mists, the merchant detected Yellowtooth and the Beard, armed with clubs, bearing down on him. He bolted. The road was firm under its mud coating, and the booted pursuit bounced echoes off shops and dwellings. The echoes pounded at the merchant's back. Sprinting down an alley, he sighted a shelter formed by some stacked lumber. He was breathing hard, and the chance to hide and rest was enticing. He hesitated. Rain began to fall. He crawled into the hollow.

Atop the lumber pile, a cat had trapped a mouse. As Yellowtooth and his cohort entered the alley, the cat pawed the mouse, let it go, then pounced. A loose board teetered. To prevent its clatter from calling attention to the hiding place, the merchant inched forward and held the board steady. Alarmed, the cat scrambled off. The board bounced noisily, despite the merchant's grip. The bearded man, alerted, stalked to the lumber pile, the club swinging gently at his side. Eyes glinting, he came within inches of his quarry.

The merchant, rigid, held his breath.

The Beard moved on.

Exhale.

An hour later, the merchant trudged along the creek north of Yung Chang. The rain was heavy now, and he was drenched.

At the bend, the creek overflowed, and the merchant was forced to higher ground. There, he came upon a shanty half-hidden by some stunted apple trees. A pig and a few chickens wandered about a vegetable garden, poking through weeds. An old horse shivered in the wet.

The merchant knocked on the shanty door. Nobody answered. He knocked again, the worn wood vibrating beneath his knuckles. No answer. Turning away, he heard a distant chopping sound. He stood still, head cocked. The sound came again, from the woods to the east. Crossing the creek, the merchant picked up the trail.

He reached the clearing in time to see a woodsman deliver a final blow of his axe to a log. The movement was fluid: the axe an extension of hands powered by massive shoulders. The log's severed portion—about the size of a man's torso—flew through the air straight at the intruder. So intent was the merchant on the woodsman that he failed to duck. The chunk plummeted end over end past his ear.

A tree trunk of a man in his early forties, the woodsman was big, strong, vital. Sadness permeated his every fiber. The oppressive rain seemed his natural element. Sighting the stranger, he took a belligerent stance—jaw thrust forward, eyes glinting malice, fingers tight on the axe handle. "All right," he said in a thick voice. "You have had your look at me. Now go!"

"Da Tsung? You are Da Tsung?"

Confusion blurred the hard mouth. "You dare speak to me?" The words were slurred, stilted. "No fear of—consequences?"

"No one tells me who to talk to."

"A stranger, eh? Lost your way?" Visible gladness came, only to be checked by doubt. "You know my name." Then, quickly: "No matter. What's a name? Lost, not lost—what difference?" The words poured out, tumbling: "Come up to the cabin. A cheerful fire to get you dry. Wine I made myself, and good fresh pork. The head meat goes good with wine. I'll lend you a horse, too, if you like, to get to Yung Chang." He hurried into his jacket. "Wouldn't expect a woodsman to have a horse, would you? No ordinary woodsman, mind. A good position once."

"Oh?"

"Enough of bragging." Shouldering his axe, Da Tsung herded the merchant toward the shanty. "What's past is past. Dead."

"Not entirely." The merchant waited a dramatic moment. "I've brought you a letter."

Da Tsung stopped short. "Who would write to me?"

"They tried to stop me. All the others gave up. Not me." The merchant savored his triumph. "I promised your brother I would deliver it."

Da Tsung went taut. Rage flamed in his eyes. He grabbed up the merchant in his big hands. "You are not of the village. You do not share their dishonor. Yet you come all the way out here in the rain to torment me with a letter from the dead?"

Vainly, the merchant struggled. He managed to reach the scroll and flourish it in proof. Heedless, Da Tsung flung the man from him. The flailing body slammed into a tree trunk. The letter dropped from the merchant's hand. Arms and legs made swimming motions.

Pulling erect, the merchant floundered off through the brush. At a safe distance, he paused to vent his pain and fury. "The risks I took! Beast! They're right! Unfit to be with humans!"

Da Tsung took a threatening step. The merchant fled. Impassively, Da resumed walking toward the shanty. He wavered. Turning back, he picked up the scroll and stuffed it unopened into the pocket of his soaked jacket.

Late that afternoon, Da brooded over wine at the shanty table. He tried to ignore the scroll jutting from the jacket by the fire. The letter could not be from his brother! They were set on tormenting him! And yet . . . For fifteen years they had been content to ostracize him. Why now did they hire a stranger to stoke the fire? And the stranger's outcry: "The risks I took!" How could such outrage be feigned?

Da went to the brazier. His hand reached to the jacket pocket in an almost furtive way. Returning with the scroll, he sat down on the bench by the table. Then his manner turned casual. Putting aside the scroll, he tossed off the wine and refilled his cup. Idly, he fingered the rough, smudged indentations of the red wax seal. He got up a second time to put some fresh charcoal on the fire. But there was nothing casual about his fingers when he finally broke the seal and uncurled the scroll. It took only a glimpse of the calligraphy to drain the blood from his face. Dumbfounded, he dropped the letter to the tabletop. It wasn't possible! The burning charcoal shifted in the brazier, but neither the noise nor the shooting sparks caused Da Tsung to stir.

At dawn, the crowd had assembled in the town square, about fifty meters from Sung Ho Inn. Sadness and revulsion had deepened as Chao Tsung was escorted by two guards to the executioner's block. The sun's first rays sought out colors in the gloom—robes of red and yellow and blue—and licked at individual faces.

Li Mu, a stocky woodsman, could not keep his voice from quavering. "Courage, Chao," he called.

Jui Hseuh was rapt. The pretty barmaid had worn her best pink dress for the occasion. "Farewell, Chao," she said to the young prisoner as he passed by. Her voice caught.

"Be of good heart, Jui Hseuh."

The site was ringed by guards, their swords at salute. On reaching the block, Chao Tsung exchanged glances with his brother. Dressed in a scarlet ceremonial robe, Da Tsung was impassive. A knife was at his belt, a huge axe at his side.

A guard gave Chao Tsung a bowl of wine. He drank. Wine dribbled out of the corner of his thin, sensitive mouth. Overhead, a falcon wheeled. Chao Tsung wiped his lips with his sleeve before kneeling at the block, his neck at its edge, his head poised over the woven basket. The escort withdrew.

Stepping forward, Da Tsung stood over his brother.

The crowd shouted its abhorrence.

"Shame!" the innkeeper yelled.

"Shame!" yelled Jui Hseuh.

"Your own brother!" yelled Yellowtooth.

"Beast!" shouted the Beard.

The drums rolled. Da Tsung raised his axe. The crowd grew still. Da did not falter. The axe swept down. Its arc was blurred . . . .

Da Tsung's arm swept down, the arc blurred. The fist thudded onto the shanty table, causing the wine cup to jump and the wine to spill. With his sleeve, Da wiped the wine drops from the scroll. The drops left a bloody smear. He shuddered. Tears started to his eyes.

Stumbling to a storage chest, he pulled out some saddle-bags. He gathered bread, sausage, wine, spare clothing. Last to be packed in the bags was a live chicken.

It was almost dark when the yellow-toothed man left the Sung Ho with a fat friend. Outside, the two met Jui Hseuh returning to work. Wine made them gallant; they outdid each other with sweeping bows. It was then that Da Tsung passed the inn on his horse.

Involuntarily, the barmaid nodded to him. Da was startled. After a moment, he returned the nod.

Yellowtooth turned severe. "To speak to Da Tsung is improper."

"I didn't speak," said Jui Hseuh.

"You nodded. It is the same."

The barmaid appealed to Yellowtooth's friend. "After fifteen years, what harm to nod?"

"You've no call to set yourself above the town."

"Serve you right," Yellowtooth said, "if we let everyone know."

Jui Hseuh resorted to a not-so-secret weapon. Tears.

The friend turned on Yellowtooth. "Now look what you've done." Then, to Jui Hseuh: "Don't cry, little lady."

The barmaid huddled her tiny shoulders. "I didn't mean to. It's my nature to be kind."

At that moment, an alley fifty *ma* away exploded some boys out onto the road. They were having a mock battle with poles, sticks and wooden swords, and their battle cries were fierce and bloodthirsty.

One by one, the boys caught sight of Da Tsung. They stopped fighting. Only the horse's slow hoof beats could be heard. One boy called: "Murderer!"

Others joined in: "Monster!"

Da Tsung did not seem to hear, but suddenly his hand darted toward an axe protruding from the saddlebags.

"Look out!"

"He's got an axe!"

The urchins scattered. Da Tsung smiled faintly. As he rode on, the kids reassembled.

"A close escape."

"Lucky we ran."

"Give him half a chance, and he'd have been down off that horse swinging his axe at everyone in sight."

"Our blood spewing in torrents."

One boy was puzzled. "What did he do?"

"Uh?"

"I mean, why do we hate him? Who did he ever kill?"

Silence.

Then, resentfully: "How should I know?"

Day flows into night.
Night flows into day.
Day has no end, as night and time have no end. All are one.
The land is one, too. It is misshapen by storms and enveloped by heavy, swirling mists. It disgorges flying snakes to plague, leopards to strike and gash. Even as one tries to snatch a few hours of sleep, the trees dance and groan and mock.

Dusk.

Da rode past the ferry tied to the riverbank and reined in at the open campfire.

The ferryman—old, bent, ugly—was baking a large river turtle. Oddly, the empty shell as well as the scooped-out turtle meat was spitted on the pole above the flames.

"Can you ferry me across?"

"You're late," the ferryman said.

A curious remark. The ferryman could not have been expecting him. What he probably meant was that the ferry did not operate after dusk. Opening the saddlebag flap, Da seized the live hen by the legs and drew it, squawking, into the firelight.

The ferryman made no move to accept it. "Watch the turtle shell."

"Why?"

"The way it cracks will tell your future."

Obviously, the man was a bit cracked himself. Not once had he looked up.

The shell cracked. The sound was ragged, like that of a boulder wrenching loose from a mountainside. The long wide split sprouted several lesser cracks. A gnarled finger traced one. Placing his palms on bony thighs, the ferryman boosted himself erect. "You must cross now, Da Tsung."

Da started. How had the old man known his name? Had their paths crossed before? No. The ferryman was not someone easy to forget. There was something strange about him — Da had sensed that from the beginning. "Do you not want the chicken?"

Striding to the riverbank, the ferryman fumbled with a rope tied to an exposed root.

After Da guided his skittish horse aboard, the old man cast off and poled into the current. Soon, the inky river closed about the ferry. The mists thickened and blocked the chinks of light. Wraithlike forms rose from the river surface. Wild birds screamed overhead.

The ferry hit some rapids. Water surged against the sides, battering, wrenching. Old timbers groaned. The ferry yawed. Creaking sounds mounted to screaming pitch. The horse shuddered.

Off the prow, water dripped. The dripping sounds swelled into moans of woe and lamentation. In vain, Da told himself that the moans were imaginary. He looked back at the helm. Only the old man's torso could be seen. The fog swirling around his shoulders had devoured his head.

✦

Water slides into land.
Shore slides into forest.
Shore, forest and water are one, fused to past and present.

With a screech, the ferry lurched onto the opposite bank. Snorting, the horse pawed frantically at the slippery deck. Da grabbed the halter and yanked at his head. Resisting, the animal reared. Da felt an odd satisfaction. Striking out with his fist, he beat the horse into trembling submission. It was then he became aware that the ferryman was watching him. He stirred self-consciously. "Fool of a horse."

"We are all fools, Da Tsung," said the ferryman.

The remark stayed with Da as he rode through the night and into the somber morning. Fools, he thought. All. Who but a fool would be riding through a dark funnel of twisted oaks and jagged stumps to seek a reunion with a brother long dead? He slowed his horse to descend a slope. Yes, his brother was dead, but someone had written a letter in a hand remarkably like Chao's. Someone had gone out of his way to lure him to Lung Tan Jan, said to be five days south of Yung Chang. And that someone had alerted the ferryman to his coming.

Loose rocks made the horse's footing unsure. Da Tsung decided to dismount and lead the horse down the slope. As his foot left the stirrup, he felt a broadsword at his throat.

"Careful," said the lean young bandit.

Before Da's boots touched ground, the bandit's hands had searched the pockets of his robe.

"I've no money," Da said.

"If you're a liar, you may live. Money buys life." Flinging aside Da's axe, the bandit ripped open the saddlebags. The chicken burst from the pouch, wings furiously beating. Disgusted, the bandit worked himself up for the kill. "No money. A tired nag."

"The axe, the bags, my boots. They're worth something."

"You might better beg."

"If I beg, you will think me a worm. It is easier to kill a worm than a man."

The bandit noticed the scroll protruding from Da's jacket pocket. "Give me the paper."

Da regarded him dully. The bandit reached for the letter. That was the move Da had been waiting for. His stiffened hand slashed down on the bandit's exposed wrist. As the wrist bone broke, the fingers opened and the broadsword fell. The bandit sagged to a sitting position on the ground. He raised his crippled wrist to plead helplessness.

"If you sit still," Da said, "you will live. Stillness buys life." He gathered his belongings. Repacking his rations and clothes, he tucked the axe in place behind the saddlebags, then went after the chicken. He trailed it through the stumps and back toward the bandit. As the hen, clucking, paused to peck at the earth, Da bent and reached out both hands. Suddenly, the bandit's boot kicked into his groin. Agony whipped through him. He plucked the broadsword from the ground. The bandit tried to roll away. The broken wrist caught beneath his chest. Groaning, he scuttled sideways. Da's boot stamped down, pinning the wriggling body in place.

Da raised the broadsword high. The blade glanced off an overhead limb, deflecting it. Water pattered down. As Da pulled back his arm to start the stroke afresh, a drop of water landed on his wrist. It burned. Da faltered. It seemed to him that he could hear water trickling all about him, unnaturally loud. Even as he fought to repel the sound and the burning sensation, a new sound merged with the old. Faintly, Da heard the irregular thump of a distant axe. He shivered. Before his eyes, the bandit's face seemed to become the face of Chao Tsung.

Hurling the broadsword into the brush, Da remounted. As he spurred his horse forward, the thump of the axe grew louder. The axe blows rang and clanged all about him, a demoniacal din. He clapped his hands to his ears. Instantly, the din stopped. Only the dripping oaks could be heard in the eerie silence.

Eventually, Da came to another river, screened by aspens. Searching for a fording place, he did not know surcease. He found himself unable to look away from the dripping trees.

Fifteen years.

Outside the office window, a branch dripped.

Quietly, Da opened the office door. Unnoticed, he stood watching the district magistrate sign the official document and hand it over to the stolid, chunky Li Mu.

The magistrate said: "You'll be paid as soon as the job is done."

Da Tsung stepped forward, the scarlet robe over his arm. "By what right, sir, do you assign tomorrow's execution to Li Mu?"

"Just for tomorrow. You don't want tomorrow. You couldn't."

"As official executioner, it's my duty to conduct all executions in the district. I intend to do my duty."

"Your own brother?" Li Mu said.

"I know your game, Li Mu." Da brandished the robe. "I won this robe in open competition with you and all the other candidates. I do not intend to allow you to usurp my position."

Li Mu reared back, then spit in Da Tsung's face.

Da made no move to wipe away the spittle. Instead, he turned to the magistrate in mute appeal. In the ensuing hush, only the drip-drip of the branch outside the open window could be heard.

Shrugging, the magistrate took back the document from Li Mu and crumpled it up.

Outside, the branch wept.

Water churned off the horse's flanks as the animal pulled free from the muddy river bottom. Guided by the tallest reeds, Da Tsung maneuvered the horse through the marsh to the river's opposite bank. The drip-drip of water, joined to the thump of the distant axe, pursued him as he rode toward a ravine sheltered from the wind.

A hare hopped along the bank. With one vicious sweep of his axe, Da Tsung cleaved it. Reining in, he dismounted and secured his horse to a birch. He flung the carcass onto a log in the hollow. Not until he stumbled on a tree root was he jarred out of his trancelike despair. The axe blows and the trickling sounds became weaker as Da brought his violence under control and set about routine tasks. Gathering some kindling, he struck a flint on a stone to start a fire. Then he began to skin the hare.

Da stopped. He stared down at the bloody carcass and the stained knife. He looked away. Water dripped from the driftwood scattered along the riverbank. Da's face contorted. The carcass fell to the ground. Stamping out the fire, Da ran to his horse and started the hard ride up the mountain slope through ragged oaks. The sounds persisted. Axe blows. Dripping water.

Two hours later, as Da Tsung neared the mountain crest, the sounds had taken on timbre. They seemed nearer, too. At times, they came in upon his ears like waves, battering, relentless. Anguish rode his back and shoulders. His body resembled a stuffed and lumpy sack about to fall.

The horse climbed the last rise to the crest. Unexpectedly, the sun broke through the clouds. The sounds ceased. The cold ground steamed in the sun. The mists lifted. A lark sang.

Da Tsung roused. The oaks no longer hemmed him in; they were at a friendly distance. Below, in the valley, a sparkling river wound through a verdant countryside dotted here and there by farms. The sun coddled Da's back, and he could feel its opiate flowing to his every muscle. A squirrel poked his head out from behind some ferns. A hare nosed a wildflower.

Leaning forward, Da stroked his horse's face and neck before starting down into the valley.

Da Tsung rode along the valley floor.

Oaks had given way to firs. Lush meadows smiled green under an azure sky. Cowbells gave music to the air. Birds— babblers, sun birds, yellow-throated bulbuls, fly catchers—winged from tree to tree, showing off multicolored plumage. Ahead, the sun glinted on a pristine lake.

So languid were the hours that Da Tsung was surprised by the coming of night and his arrival at Lung Tan Jan, a village on the lake's southern shore. A full moon gave lustre to the inn, high on a hill. The glow seemed to come from inside as well as outside the inn, whose liquid lines merged with a smudge of spruce.

As Da dismounted, he could hear laughter, hearty shouts, clinking glasses. Taking a deep breath, he started down the path through a terrace fragrant with orchids and narcissus. The encounter he dreaded was at hand. Still, he could not but marvel at the beauty around him. Leaves rustled underfoot; iris and peonies overgrew the path. A tiny stream overflowed an embankment to splash on the rocks below.

The dining room was crowded. Nobody noticed Da in the doorway, numbed by tension and the crowd's good spirits. Patrons at the polished teak tables ate, drank and joked with an élan no longer known in Yung Chang. The woman serving them — the sole woman in the room — clearly enjoyed their open affection.

Near the unused fireplace, a contest of strength was in progress. A man obscured by the crowd was trying to lift a heavy table from the floor with one hand. Having knelt, he grasped the table leg at its base. The encouraging shouts took on fervor as he succeeded in raising the table a few inches. The crowd shifted, unblocking the view of the contestant, a handsome man wearing a white apron over an orange robe.

Da Tsung paled. Chao! Alive! The nose, the chin, the brow. Fifteen years older, but unmistakably Chao. Da stood transfixed. Impossible!

Chao caught sight of Da. He dropped the table to the floor with a crash. Then a volcanic joy: "Is it really you?"

The room hushed. All eyes were on Chao as he ran to Da and embraced him. "At last! After fifteen years!"

Chao's mouth. Chao's fair skin. There could be no doubt.

Aglow with love, Chao jostled Da toward the woman and caught her around the waist. "Mei-Mei! Now I am truly content. My wife and my brother under my roof, together."

Da's eyes found Mei-Mei's. He knew at once that she was aware of his shock. And he knew he would have to deflect her curiosity if future options—whatever their nature—were to be protected. With heroic detachment, he studied her. Unlike Chao, who had retained his boyish good looks, Mei-Mei had built what must have been an adolescent prettiness into the open-eyed woman he now saw before him: strong, thoughtful, warm.

Chao Tsung hurried to the bar. Pouring wine, he summoned helpers. "Wine! Wine for everyone!"

Alone with Da, Mei-Mei probed. "A joyous occasion."

"Wonderful."

"Odd, you've not said a single word to my husband."

"He hasn't given me a chance."

From behind the bar, Chao lifted a cup in toast. "To my brother!"

"To your brother!"

"A long life to him!"

"A long life to both brothers!"

Chao used a tray to bring some wine to his wife and brother. "Drink!"

He proffered two brimming cups and took one for himself. "Never a brother so dear."

Mei-Mei drank before speaking to her husband. "Da has had a long trip, Chao. He may be tired."

"Tired?" Chao scoffed. "You don't know him. The strongest man in Yung Chang." He gestured an invitation to Da to lift the heavy table. "Show her!"

"In a while." Da watched his brother return to the bar to pour more wine. Didn't Chao realize that *in a while* was the first and only thing he'd said to him?

Chao's friends basked in his exuberance. "For years, Chao, you've been saying your brother would turn up. We didn't believe you. But it's come true."

"If you want something enough," Chao said, smiling, "it comes to be."

For Da, Chao's open childlike smile evoked memories of his brother's passage from childhood to an innocent manhood. To drift with such memories was sweet, but the drift ceased with an inescapable thought: Chao was a ghost! He had to be! No other explanation would hold.

"You don't go in for displays of strength?"

Da became aware. He tried to smile at Mei-Mei. "You make me sound solemn."

"Or is it that you don't want to make Chao look weak? You needn't be concerned about that, you know. If you succeed in lifting the table all the way, nobody will be happier than my husband."

"No man is happy to be second best. Either in physical strength or in affairs of the heart."

"You are blunt where delicacy is called for."

"So are you."

"It can get you in trouble."

"Trouble is my fate."

"Not solemn, perhaps, but serious. Very."

"All middle-aged men are serious. They feel death brushing close."

"Close or not, death is unknowable and irrelevant. It's life that's worth serious thought. Are you married?"

"Is that what 'life' is to you? Marriage? No, I'm not married. And I don't really know any more about the heart's affairs than most men. Less, perhaps."

"That seems doubtful." Mei-Mei caught herself. "Yes, I'm blunt, too. Unseemly. And with a man I've just met."

"With a brother-in-law."

"A man I've just met. Shameful."

"Why, I wonder, is honesty admirable in a man and shameful in a woman?"

Mei-Mei laughed.

At a nearby table, a patron frowned at her merriment. Apparently he thought it excessive. Even Lung Tan Jan, it seemed, had its fools.

Chao returned. "Already good friends."

"Your brother's a thinker," Mei-Mei said.

"We don't get many thinkers around here. He'll be good company for you."

"I see you in him," Mei-Mei said.

"I'm no thinker."

"He's another man, yet he's you." She considered. "I guess that doesn't make sense."

Chao grinned. "One man in two bodies."

Da pondered. He could not reconcile ghostly imaginings with Chao's wholehearted grin, particularly since he'd not given credence to the supernatural since childhood. The death of his parents by a bandit's sword had set him to wondering about ghosts, regarded as real by virtually everyone in Yung Chang. Writings and meditation forced on him by the lonely years had reinforced skepticism. Now he tried to remember all he ever had heard about ghosts. Could ghosts marry? Have children?

Of one thing he was certain. Chao did not suspect himself to be a ghost. Did Mei-Mei? Was it possible to live with a ghost and not suspect?

"For years," Mei-Mei was saying to Chao, "they've gotten comfort from your unfailing optimism, and now they've found it has substance."

"And they're happy for me."

"For you and for themselves."

Chao turned to his brother. "Ready to try the table?"

"Don't expect too much," Da said. "I'm not the strong man you once knew."

"The Da Tsung I once knew could lift two such tables—one in each hand."

One patron, listening, was dubious. "We'll be satisfied with one."

Another nodded. "Let's see."

Going to the table, Da knelt on one knee. Excitedly, the crowd gathered around him. Bets were offered. Money passed from hand to hand. Mei-Mei watched closely as Da grasped the table leg at its base. The crowd hushed.

Da flexed his fingers. If he failed, Chao would be less awed and perhaps less wary of questions. Affecting exertion, Da lifted the table a few inches, to about the same height as that achieved by his brother. He invited a tremor to his hand and forearm. With a grunt, he gave up and lowered the table to the floor.

The crowd sighed.

"I knew he couldn't do it."

"No man can."

Chao Tsung was undisturbed. "He's tired from the trip. Wait until he's rested. You'll see." He touched Da's arm. "Let me take you to your room."

"My horse hasn't been fed, Chao."

Chao summoned a boy. "See to my brother's horse. And bring his pack to the guest house."

"As you say."

Chao banged on a table to attract attention. "Everybody!" The patrons quieted down. "Tomorrow night we'll celebrate! You're all invited! I'll provide a pig. A whole pig! And my finest wines!"

A cheer went up.

Da waited for the cheer to die down. "Good night, all."

A clamor of hearty good-nights.

"Rest well, Da," Mei-Mei said.

"Thank you."

Chao guided Da out the rear door. The two men started across the courtyard to the guest house. "I take it," Chao said, "that you too have prospered over the years."

"What makes you think so? No, I've not prospered."

"Good! I've prospered for us both. Life's been good to me. I live in a virtual paradise, and it is you who made it possible."

Unexpectedly, wrath stirred in Da. "How did I make it possible?"

Jarred by his harshness, Chao swallowed hard. "Have I hurt you in some way? Do you think I gloat at my good fortune? That I act toward you as a rich man to a poor one? Please! Never would I hurt you. When I said 'Good!' it was because I welcome the chance to show the depth of my gratitude. Were it not for you, I never would have escaped Yung Chang. The wish to share my plenty comes from a loving heart. To share is a privilege!"

"Why now, after fifteen years?" The wrath had sinew now; lean, sleek. "Why didn't you offer to share before? Why didn't you so much as inform me you were still alive?"

Chao flung open the door to the guest house. Moonlight spilled into the room. Striding inside to a desk, he picked up a half-written letter and thrust it into Da's hand. "I dared not visit Yung Chang. I couldn't risk capture. So for fifteen years I've sent you letters, to let you know I made it safely to Lung Tan Jan. This very afternoon, I was writing you again. Every time I met a merchant or a priest traveling in your direction, I gave him a letter. Some reported back that you were dead. I refused to believe them. Others said they couldn't find you. Still others claimed they'd delivered a letter through a friend."

"I have no friends. Everyone turned against me."

"Because you helped me escape."

The damning rejoinder—"Because I killed you."—trembled on Da's lips, but he could not utter it.

"No matter," Chao said. "All that is over now." He tossed the letter into the fire pan and touched a paper match to it. "No more letters! You're here to stay!"

"To stay?"

"To stay." Chao used the match to light a lamp. "The fifteen years have been hard ones for you. Rest! Sit, dream, fish."

Da gaped at him.

"To loaf the days away is impossible for you?" Chao's sadness gave way to amusement. "Work, then. You're a woodsman. Winter comes, and there is much wood to be cut. Work as much or as little as you please. But stay, as I stayed. Start anew, as I started anew." He gave his brother a parting hug. "Few men enjoy each waking hour. I do. So will you." The door closed behind him.

Da slumped into a chair. To have uttered the virulent words would have defiled Chao's love. To what end? Ghost or not, Chao was convinced that the execution had not taken place. He believed he had escaped, and his gratitude was boundless.

The window, Da saw, looked out on the rear of the inn and afforded a clear view of the dining room. Snuffing out the lamp, he carried a chair to the window. Sitting, he gazed across the courtyard. Chao, he saw, was riotously happy. He shouted and sang. Da watched Mei-Mei move from behind the serving counter to her husband. Touched by Chao's happiness, she tenderly filled his cup . . . .

Fifteen years.

Jui Hseuh, the barmaid, tenderly filled Da's cup.

Although it was afternoon, the Sung Ho was jammed. A celebration was in progress. Among those eating and drinking at nearby tables were Li Mu, Yellowtooth and the Beard.

"Celebrate!" Da shouted. "Eat! Drink!"

So taken was Jui Hseuh with Da Tsung's brawling exuberance that she neglected to serve wine to Chao. Noticing that his brother's cup was empty, Da seized the bottle and filled Chao's cup to over-flowing. "Drink! Drink to my new position!"

Chao took a tentative sip.

The chunky Li Mu spoke to Chao from an adjacent table. "Why don't you drink?"

"I'm drinking."

"That's no way to drink." Li Mu drained his cup and held it upside-down.

Da intervened. "My brother's a gentleman. He thinks wine should be savored."

"That's not why he doesn't drink."

"Besides, lovely barmaids make him nervous."

Jui Hseuh, serving bread rolls, brought off a demure fluttering. "It's me who's nervous. The only girl among so many men."

Li Mu would not be diverted. "Maybe Chao doesn't drink because he's unhappy with your new position. A scholar. Squeamish."

Chao said evenly: "It's just that I'm unused to drinking." He picked up his books from the table. "I'm due at the tutor's, Da. I must go."

"Stay a while longer." Amiably, Da got up and walked over to Li Mu. "He who ridicules my brother ridicules me." Collaring Li Mu, he heaved him ten ma to the open doorway and out into the street.

The inn rocked with laughter. Returning to the table, Da grinned at his brother. Chao smiled weakly. Jui Hseuh hovered over them, replenishing their cups and plates.

Unconsciously, Chao tore the heel from a bread roll. His hands went to a second roll, twisted it. Da noticed. "Separating a head from a body?"

Startled, Chao looked down. Aghast, he thrust the pieces away.

Jui Hseuh fluttered in pretty concern, increasing Chao's embarrassment.

"Li Mu is right," Da Tsung told his brother. "You're not happy with my victory." He held up his hand to still Chao's protest. "Someone has to do the job, Chao. I can do it better than anyone else. One clean, swift blow." He gestured toward the men at the other tables. "I won. They lost. Now they celebrate with me because they know I deserved to win. Look at them! Butchers! Two strokes, three. Think of the pain the condemned would suffer at their hands."

Jui Hseuh gave Da glib support. "The condemned will be grateful to Da. He can make it easier for them."

Da placed his hand atop Chao's books. "The extra money will come in handy, too. It'll be easier for you to complete your studies."

Fervently, Chao clasped Da's hand. His voice shook. "You went after the job to help me complete my studies, and now you ask my pardon for taking it."

Jui Hseuh was surprised to discover tears running down her cheeks. They seldom came unbidden . . . .

At the window of the darkened room, Da Tsung sat watching the revelry reach its peak.

One patron was playing a flute. The others formed a circle around Chao Tsung, and they clapped their hands in unison as he danced, legs stamping, arms snaking high, fingers joined and shaped like a cobra's head. Dancing closer and closer to Mei-Mei, Chao gestured a plea for her to join him. When Mei-Mei shook her head, he seized her around the waist and drew her inside the circle.

Self-conscious, she tried to pull away. But Chao's grip and the insistent handclaps made her acquiesce, and soon she was caught up in the rhythm.

Da, looking on, could hear the crowd's appreciative cries. A rare woman, Mei-Mei: head thrown back, cheek flushed, hips and breasts sensually alive beneath the loose gown.

He caught himself. Mei-Mei was a married woman. More than that: she was Chao's wife. A ghost Chao might be, but he also was his brother, whose every breath he cherished. In no way was Chao responsible for the hell in which Da had languished for so long.

Still. Chao was a ghost. What could a ghost bring to the carnal darkness? Mei-Mei's marriage was built of straw and sympathy and sisterly affection. By what right could a ghost ask fidelity?

Chao had to be a ghost! With his own hands, Da had delivered the death blow. With his own eyes, he had seen Chao's head drop into the basket.

Da heard the beating of his own heart. Every fourth or fifth beat seemed to coincide with a chopping sound. Da's fists bunched. He wrenched his gaze from Mei-Mei and, leaning back, closed his eyes. The chopping sound receded. Da's hands relaxed, and he fell into an uneasy sleep.

He awoke early. Need and habit impelled him to find something to do. He went outside. Just beyond the courtyard wall, he came upon a woodpile. At its base were some thick branches that needed to be cut and split. He hesitated. Mei-Mei and Chao had been up late; noise would disturb them. He scanned the three outbuildings to the east of the inn. The largest one had a slanted roof and clean lines, elegant in the dawn's pale light; that one would be Mei-Mei's. She would be sound asleep, her long hair strewn about the pillow, veiling the sweet profile; one outflung hand touching the body beside her.

He went back to the guest house and got his axe.

Stripping to the waist, he went to work. The axe rose and fell; one branch after another felt his power. The chips flew.

At the instant he sensed Mei-Mei's presence, he knew why he had decided to go ahead, and the knowing troubled him.

"Good morning," Mei-Mei said.

"Good morning." He wondered how long she had been standing there, holding teacups and a steaming teapot on a tray. He became conscious of his naked chest. "I hope the noise didn't waken you."

"Some tea?"

Clearly, it had. Da put on his jacket before hoisting himself to a sitting position atop the woodpile. He did not look directly at Mei-Mei until she served the tea and started to leave. "There are two cups."

She colored. "I thought maybe my husband was out here with you."

"Since he isn't—" Da gestured an invitation to join him.

"To sit with you alone is improper."

"I thought we'd agreed not to conform to a false and foolish decorum."

She handed up the tray. Climbing up onto the woodpile, she attempted vainly to maintain her grace. Da Tsung was charmed but could not restrain a smile.

Mei-Mei's annoyance lasted until the absurdity of the attempt hit home. She laughed.

Da Tsung joined his laugh to hers. Then, wonderingly, he listened to his laughter.

"Something wrong?"

"It's just that I'd forgotten what it is to laugh. It's the first time I've heard that sound in fifteen years."

"You cannot be serious."

"Just as it's the first time in fifteen years I've been alone with a woman."

"How is that possible?"

"Certain things happened."

"What things?"

"Things better forgotten."

"In my husband, too, these frightful memories he cannot talk about."

Da sipped the tea. "Chao's never talked about the trouble he got into?"

"He's talked in a general way about being arrested, and your arranging his escape."

"But he never told you how he got away?"

"No. I'd like to know. Please." She waited. "Once, he started to tell me, but a quiet came over him. A gravity of spirit, like yours. He couldn't get it out."

"Like me."

"Yes. But Chao, at least, has had peace since Yung Chang. I've tried to make him forget. Maybe I can help you forget, too." She faltered. "What I mean is—"

"I know what you mean." Da's matter-of-fact tone eased her constraint. "You're already helping me forget."

Chao Tsung approached, carrying two fishing poles. "Breakfast on the woodpile? Why not?" Putting down the poles, he perched himself beside his brother. "You look rested, Da. Not so tense."

Mei-Mei stirred. "I'll get another cup."

"Don't bother," said Chao. "I've already had tea."

"Going fishing?" Da asked.

"If you'll go with me."

Da glanced at the woodpile. "Much wood to be cut."

"Work if you must," said Chao drily, "But don't try to do it all on the very first day."

On the nearby road, a procession neared the inn. Taoist priests in ceremonial robes were trailed by supplicants carrying a huge pig on a rack. The pig was dressed in flowers, plaques and banners.

"Festival time," Da said. "I'd forgotten."

Chao nodded. "The seventh month of the lunar calendar."

Mei-Mei said: "Why not take Da into town for the celebration?"

"Another time. Tonight we're having our own celebration here at the inn."

"The seventh month," Da said, "when the gates of the underworld are opened and the spirits come to earth and eat their fill and enjoy themselves."

Mei-Mei said lightly: "If the spirits are still hungry tonight, they're welcome to come out from town and eat some more."

Chao smiled. "They might get a stomach ache."

"A ghost," Mei-Mei said, "can't get a stomach ache."

"Why not?" Chao said. "Remember the goddess Tchi-Niu? She lived with a man named Tong-yong and had a child. If ghosts can have a child and can enjoy feasting, they must be able to feel a stomach ache."

"Hardly," Mei-Mei said. "A stomach ache hurts. If a ghost can be hurt, he can die. But a ghost is already dead."

"Not dead," Da said. "Dangling in space, maybe, between life and death."

Mei-Mei considered. "Your dangling ghost can be hurt. Can he also bleed?"

"One way to find out," Da said tersely. "Wound one."

"That," said Chao, "wouldn't be very hospitable."

Suddenly uneasy, Mei-Mei slipped down from the woodpile. "If you two are going fishing, I should make you a lunch."

"We'll catch our lunch," Chao said.

"You may not be lucky."

Chao watched Mei-Mei go. "I've been lucky every day for fifteen years."

Da nodded. "How did you meet her?"

"My luck started with the escape." Chao spoke without signs of strain. "For five days I ran and walked, scarcely pausing for sleep." His voice went husky. "Until at last I came down into the valley."

Entering the inn, Chao did not permit himself to stagger, but he nested into the chair like a spent quail. It was through half-closed eyes that he first saw the pert, pretty waitress.

Mei-Mei was lingering at the table of a big, brooding man, twenty years her senior. "More fish, Mr. Su?"

"No. I've had enough."

"Dessert? An earth melon? Cherries?"

"No."

The place was quiet. The afternoon light was soft and made few shadows. At a table by the window, a man dozed. Smoke wisped from the pipe in his hand.

At the bar, Him Lai—Mei-Mei's father—served wine to Kee Fong, a friend. He set the cup down slowly. The blotches on his pale hand evoked the grave.

Kee Fong said: "If you're not careful, Mei-Mei will marry Mr. Su."

"Never! I'll not permit it."

"You once swore you'd never let her wait on tables."

"That was different. When her mother died, she had no one. It can be lonely out here, away from town."

"Still, a girl of good family—"

"Times change. She could not bear to sit all day. I had no choice."

"The fact is, she gets what she wants from you."

"Not this time. When she marries, it won't be to Kao Su. Her marriage will be arranged as her mother's was arranged, and her mother's mother's before her." He eyed his daughter with exasperation. "With so many young men around, why is she taken with Kao Su?"

"You know why. He's miserable. He needs looking after. Mei-Mei is a born nurse."

Partly to escape his friend, Him Lai moved around the counter and went to his daughter. "If you're through serving Mr. Su—"

"All right, Father." Mei-Mei's petulance did not become her.

Walking back to the counter, Him Lai noticed the young man sitting alone near the door, staring across the room at Mei-Mei. So intent was the stare that it transcended the stranger's obvious fatigue. Covertly, Him Lai watched his daughter cross to the youth's table. If she sensed his admiration, she did not show it. After taking his order, she paused at the counter to mouth "sweet and sour pork," then hurried back to Kao Su.

Kao Su used his napkin to scrub his hands, one finger at a time.

"Why not try the hung shao beef, Mr. Su?"

"I must leave now."

"Will you be coming back tonight?"

"Possibly"

"I'll bake some buns especially for you."

Negligently, Kao Su pushed back his chair. As he got up, his elbow toppled a plate. It shattered when it hit the floor. "Sorry."

"No harm done."

Kao Su left. Mei-Mei knelt to gather the pieces.

Joining her, Chao knelt to help.

"Don't trouble," Mei-Mei said.

"No trouble." Detecting a broom against the wall, Chao hurried to fetch it.

Mei-Mei saw the exhaustion in his face and movements. Her eyes softened.

At the service bar, Kee Fong said: "If Kao Su marries Mei-Mei, he may change. In time, you may get accustomed to him."

"Small chance." Him Lai kept his eyes on Chao and his daughter. "Before I die, I intend to see to it that Mei-Mei and my inn are in good hands." Picking up a rag, he left the bar to wipe down the unoccupied tables. His work carried him table by table to the young man with the broom. "Thank you for helping my daughter."

"It is nothing, sir." Chao pushed aside a chair to sweep up some shards.

Mei-Mei looked at the two men. Taking the broom from Chao, she searched the floor for fragments. The search kept her within earshot.

"Are you a merchant?" Him Lai asked.

"No. Just traveling."

"You must miss your family."

"I miss my brother, sir. He's my family."

Him Lai blurted it out: "I can use a man to help around here."

Chao looked at Mei-Mei. Wordlessly, she proffered the broom. Accepting it, he resumed the sweeping.

"You're not very subtle," Mei-Mei told her father.

Him Lai managed a weak smile.

"Transparent, one might say." Mei-Mei laughed.

Relieved, Him Lai joined in.

Chao was perplexed and a bit hurt.

Da Tsung toyed with a pocketknife. "Did he ever fill your order for the pork?"

"Eventually." Chao smiled. "He never tired of boasting how he trapped me into staying."

"With Mei-Mei as bait, it couldn't have been difficult." Da hefted the knife, then put it in his pocket. "He's dead now?"

"Yes. About a year after we were married."

"Have you never had children?"

Chao's face darkened. "Our one disappointment."

"Forgive me. I shouldn't have asked." Da saw Mei-Mei approaching with a straw bag. He affected a jovial air. "Our lunch packed?" He took the bag. "Very compact." He tossed the bag into the air, then caught it as it fell.

Mei-Mei was bemused. "How strange the closeness of brothers. A few weeks ago, Chao threw a book up in the air the very same way."

"Mere coincidence," Chao said. "Something any two men might do. I don't remember it happening."

"I remember it clearly. Two weeks ago. Just after your birthday."

Da tensed. "Your birthday," he said to Chao, "isn't until the ninth moon."

Chao was unruffled. "To me, my true birthday is the seventh moon, the anniversary of my escape from hell. Truly, I was reborn then."

Mei-Mei looked Da up and down. "Why are you so quick, Da, to pounce on a misunderstanding?"

Chao's dismay overran his astonishment. "He didn't 'pounce,' Mei-Mei. How can you say such a thing?"

"Perhaps I should go fishing, too," Mei-Mei said to her husband, "in case you need help in satisfying your brother's curiosity."

"Really, Mei-Mei. This is unlike you."

"So many questions."

"We've not seen each other in fifteen years. What could be more natural?"

Mei-Mei looked into Da's eyes. "Even if I didn't have housework to do, I know I can't be constantly with my husband, fending off shadows. So please remember: scarcely a day in fifteen years that Chao did not express a longing to see you again. I hope you'll do nothing to blight his happiness."

"How could he?" Chao asked. "Why would he want to?"

"I don't know." She handed the fishing poles to Da. "Have a good day."

Chao looked after her with perplexity. "Never has Mei-Mei been so unreasonable. Women! There's no understanding them."

"Let's not try, then."

The two men talked little during the trudge to the lake and while fishing from its bank. The day's grandeur made voices intrusive. The lake glinted in the sun, doves and orioles gathered along the shore. Wildflowers swayed gently in the breeze.

At mid-morning, Da waded out to cast his line into a shady spot under the bank. Unexpectedly, he stepped into deep water, and his feet went out from under him. Flailing arms and legs churned the surface. The fishing pole floated clear. Sputtering, Da shambled after it, only to become entangled in the line. Chao, on shore, laughed uproariously. Da glared at him. Then a grin broke through.

By noon, sun and sky and lake had done their work. Da was content. He set about gathering fallen branches for the fire.

Chao was humming to himself as he cleaned and prepared the fish. "I've been thinking, Da, it would be good to repair my old boat. A skiff."

"What's wrong with it?"

"Leaks, mostly."

"I work well with wood, Chao. Repairs shouldn't take long." Cupping his hands to protect a spark, Da blew gently on some twigs. The spark caught, and flame spread to laced branches. Satisfied, Da turned to his brother. His glance met Chao's knife as it cut into the carp's underbelly. He froze. Vainly he tried to fend off dread. A phantom axe hammered at him from afar. His peace disintegrated.

Forcing calm, he took out his jackknife and tossed it end over end into the air. Deftly, he caught it by the handle.

"A bit dangerous," Chao said, intrigued.

"Not really." Again Da tossed and caught the knife. The hammering was muffled now.

"Let me try." Chao put the fish in the frying pan and positioned the pan over the fire between two parallel logs. Then he took the jackknife. On the first attempt, he threw the knife only a short way into the air.

"Higher," Da said.

Chao tossed it high. The sun glinted on the blade as the knife wobbled downward.

"Careful!" Da shouted.

Startled, Da clumsily snatched at the handle. He missed. The blade glanced off his palm.

Despite his satisfaction, Da winced. "You hurt?"

"Just a scratch." Chao covered the palm with his handkerchief.

"Let me see."

Chao withdrew the hand. "It's nothing."

"Won't hurt for me to take a look." Grasping the hand, Da pulled aside the handkerchief. The cut was small. It bled.

"Let's eat," Chao said.

Slowly, Da folded the handkerchief and tied it back in place. So the cut bled. Where had he gotten the idea that ghosts couldn't bleed? That Chao could bleed did not change the known facts. If Chao was not a ghost, then memory—the execution, the ostracism, the solitary years—was myth. Absurd. Da watched Chao, at the fire, using a flattened stick to turn the fish in the pan.

A patent absurdity. One might as logically conclude that he himself, and not Chao, was the ghost.

Sitting under a pine, Da watched a fat duck turn stately as it pushed off from shore and glided through the water. Overhead, a hawk soared toward clouds streaked a gossamer pink. The mountain summit to the north was suffused by light. Somewhere nearby, water trickled.

At first, the trickling seemed at one with the day's harmony. Gradually, Da became aware of its pulsations. A muscle in his temple seemed to draw the pulsations inward. The lake surface writhed as if its depths swarmed with monsters. Da rubbed his temples, but the throb did not ease. Madness!

No. Not madness. The truth could prove him sane! The pain would ease once Chao grasped the truth and shared its burdens. He had to push Chao to recall details of the escape! *I hope you'll do nothing to blight his happiness.* Forgive me, Mei-Mei.

"Pardon?" Chao said.

Da looked at him.

"I thought you said something."

"No."

"Something about Mei-Mei, I thought."

What he had to do was make it easier for Chao to recall the dim details—to lead Chao naturally, even if painfully, to that fateful morning.

Da steeled himself. "A beautiful day."

"Magnificent."

"Like the day I won the competition."

"Competition?"

"In the woods at Yung Chang."

"Oh."

The voice low, the game wary.

"Not so beautiful, that morning," said Chao. "At least it didn't seem so to me."

Da felt a rush of compassion. He forcefully put it down. "The sun warm, as today. The branches still, as today."

Excitement mounted in the spectators as the contest in the clearing neared its end.

Da Tsung stood to one side with other competitors. Chao was with him. All eyes were on Li Mu, whose bulk made him a crowd favorite.

Raising his axe, Li Mu delivered a blow to a log resembling a man in size and shape. The axe struck the log's narrow "neck," but the "head"—bound in scarlet cloth—failed to sever. It took Li Mu a second blow to send the head flying. The crowd applauded. The district magistrate nodded approval.

"Only two blows!" said the Beard.

"The best yet," said Yellowtooth.

The magistrate scanned a paper before making the announcement. "The last competitor. Da Tsung."

Leaving Chao, Da Tsung stepped forward. Another prepared log— the head wrapped in scarlet—was placed in position. The crowd hushed. Da lifted his axe.

Chao, in the crowd, watched the axe come down. He flinched at the splintering sound of the axe striking the neck. The single blow severed the head.

As spectators shouted acclaim, the magistrate marched forward. Ceremoniously, he draped a scarlet robe over Da's shoulders. "I hereby designate you the district's official executioner."

Amidst the clamor of congratulations, Da made his way to his brother. He threw his arm about Chao's shoulders. "Wine!" he shouted to the crowd. "To the Sung Ho Lo Inn! Wine, to celebrate my victory!"

But there was no exuberance in Da a week later as he awaited the dawn that would bring his first execution. Unable to sleep, he had gotten up early and put on the ceremonial robe. Now he idled at the window.

Chao, too, had been unable to sleep. He, too, had gotten up early. Now he was at his desk, practicing calligraphy.

"Another hour," Da said. "Another hour and a man's life will end."

Putting aside his brush, Chao went to his brother. "The man stole his neighbor's cow. His life will end with or without you." He paraphrased what Da himself once had said. "Only you have the muscle—" he touched Da's bicep—*"and skill—"* he touched Da's head—*"to do the job properly."*

Da relaxed somewhat.

But tension assailed him anew as the thief was escorted to the chopping block. To the crowd, Da looked calm. The crowd could not hear the thudding of his heart.

And his tension heightened when the thief ripped free from his escort and bolted through the crowd for the nearby wood. Spectators stood on tiptoes to get a better look. Some hoped the thief would make good his escape. Some were outraged on principle: the thief was draining dignity from the occasion. Others were depressed by the possibility that the execution, lacking a key participant, would not occur, and that this premier demonstration of Da's craftsmanship would have to be postponed—a deprivation all the more acute because they had been forced to leave warm beds well before dawn.

The guards on the periphery of the site had closed their ring immediately. Now, as they constricted the circle, the thief darted frantically back and forth. Inevitably, he reached the moment when he realized escape was impossible. He stopped. His body sagged. Two guards closed in, seized the thief by the armpits, and dragged him to the block. A wetness appeared at his crotch. At the last moment, he regained the strength to kneel by himself.

Da stepped forward, axe at the ready. He singled out his brother in the crowd. Chao managed an encouraging smile. He gestured toward his bicep, then toward his head. Da nodded. Then, pivoting, he lifted his axe and brought it swiftly down.

Chao closed his eyes against the sight, but he could not avoid hearing the sickening whap.

The job done, Da went to join his brother. The crowd opened up before him.

"Well done, Da!" called Li Mu.

"Such power!" said Yellowtooth.

"And precision!" said the Beard.

One man, a tailor, felt constrained to voice a contrary view. "Only a pig would kill an unarmed man."

Da froze.

Vainly, Chao tried to press his brother to walk on, out of earshot.

"A pig," the tailor said.

Li Mu confronted him. "Someone has to do it."

The tailor did not budge.

"You presume," said the Beard, "to question the wisdom of the authorities?"

"A necessary evil," said Yellowtooth. "Better it be done right."

"An unnecessary evil," the tailor said. "Better it not be done at all."

Da said nothing.

Later that morning, Chao encountered the tailor on a busy street. He was nearing his tutor's house when the man challenged him.

"Da Tsung is a pig!"

Chao kept on walking.

"Brother of a pig!"

Chao halted. "My brother," he said stiffly, "is a good and honorable man."

The tailor replied with a slap. Chao slapped back. A crowd gathered. There were cries and shouts.

"Kill him, Chao!"

"Knock the lout on his ass!"

Fists pounded Chao about the face and chest. Step by step, he backed toward a crumbling wall. His flailing hand touched a loose rock. His fingers closed on it. He lunged. The rock thudded into the side of the tailor's head. The man dropped.

Dismayed, Chao stared down at the sprawled body. A hush fell on the crowd . . . .

The trial was brief. That Chao had killed the tailor could not be disputed. The magistrate had no lawful alternative to execution at dawn the next morning. As the sentence was pronounced, Chao's stance took on the frantic quality evinced by the condemned thief when the circle closed about him. There was one difference. The thief had found no succor. Chao's eyes found Da Tsung in the courtroom crowd. Da nodded encouragement, and Chao walked erect to his cell.

Within an hour, the two were reunited.

A guard opened the cell door. Da entered. The brothers embraced. Da cupped his brother's face. The cuts and welts sustained in the fight would do no permanent damage. Da dropped his hands. "Listen closely, Chao. At dawn, when you're escorted to the block, I'll be there, waiting."

"You?"

"I'll raise my axe. Just before it starts to come down, when the officials least expect an escape attempt, I'll stumble and call, 'Go!' Your eyes will be facing the ground, and you won't be able to see the axe as it's raised, but you'll hear me stumble. That instant is critical. I'll have to call 'Go' softly, for your ears alone, so you must be alert." He knelt on the floor, eyes down, in simulation of the position taken by the condemned at an execution. "When you hear me call 'Go,' you are to spring aside—" Da sprang aside. "Seize the knife at my belt—" Da grabbed at an imaginary knife at Chao's waist. "And break for the woods."

"I won't be able to make it through the guards, Da."

"I've greased many palms. I'll grease more. The guards will put on a show of stopping you, but they'll let you pass. You must not use the knife unless you're forced to. Once in the woods, you'll be pursued. Put at least five days between you and the town before you allow yourself a full night's sleep."

"But will they let you officiate at the execution? Won't they suspect? What will they do to you for letting me escape?"

"I'm not letting you escape. You're taking me by surprise. The guards, too. My punishment will be as nothing compared to yours." Da handed his brother some money. *"For your journey."*

Chao hugged his brother to him. He tried to hold back tears until he saw that Da's eyes too were moist . . .

They sat cross-legged beneath the pine, full plates in their laps, the fish uneaten.

"I wasn't sure I'd make it past the guards," Chao said, "but you acted sure and that gave me confidence. That's why I made it. Still, all that is better forgotten. What's past is past."

"What's past is not past." Unexpectedly, Da's tone hardened. "Not for me."

"Da, don't spoil the day."

"The truth is, Chao, I have lapses of memory." Even as he voiced the pretext, Da knew it to be thin. No matter. It would do. It would have to do.

"Seems to me you remember every last detail."

"Everything except the escape itself. I don't remember key moments. To lose a piece of the past is to lose part of oneself. You can help me remember. Please."

"Shadows." Chao shuddered. "So that's what Mei-Mei meant." He picked at his plate. "Why make ourselves miserable? The escape happened as planned. Isn't that enough?"

"No."

"I can't talk about it, Da."

"You must."

"We're alive. That is what's important. It is better that you not remember."

"That's not for you to judge." Da's voice was cold. "You once needed my help, Chao. I gave it. Now I need your help. I need to know!"

Sweat broke out on Chao's forehead. He licked his lips. "At dawn," he said tonelessly, "the guards arrived at my cell and escorted me out into the light. Perhaps I was not so sure, after all. Something might go wrong. You couldn't risk calling 'Go' too loudly. What if I didn't hear the signal? What if I sensed your stumble too late?"

The sweat fell from Chao's brow to his eyelid. He did not blink . . . .

The crowd had assembled in the town square.

The prevailing mood was one of sadness and revulsion. The mood deepened as Chao Tsung was escorted through the crowd toward the executioner's block.

"Courage, Chao," called Li Mu.

"Farewell, Chao, " said Jui Hseuh, stricken.

Chao smiled at her. "Be of good heart, Jui Hseuh."

Upon reaching the chopping block, Chao was given a bowl of wine. When he drank, wine dribbled from the corner of his mouth. He wiped his lips with his sleeve. Glancing at the knife at Da's belt, he exchanged a long, loving look with his brother before he knelt.

Da Tsung stepped forward. The crowd screamed its abhorrence.

"Shame!" screamed Jui Hseuh.

"Shame!" screamed Yellowtooth.

"Beast!" the Beard shouted.

The drums sounded. The crowd grew still. Da Tsung raised his axe. As he started to bring it down, he suddenly stumbled and mouthed "Go!" Chao Tsung sprang aside. The axe smashed harmlessly into the block. Grabbing the knife from his brother's belt, Chao darted through the stunned crowd. Several guards made a token attempt to stop him, but they fell back when he brandished the knife. Within seconds, Chao vanished into the wood.

Uproar. Hubbub. A shout: "After him!"

The guards started in pursuit.

The sun glittered in a sublime sky.

Chao wiped the sweat from his face and neck. "If you can't remember, Da, I am to blame."

"No."

"It's because of what they did to you for helping me."

"Enough, damn it!"

Chao recoiled as if struck.

Da vainly tried to hold on to a soothing rage. Must Chao always be so noble? Always, he made a showdown impossible! How could one heap hurt on dumbfounded hurt? He heard himself say: "I remember now. You brought it back for me."

"All of it?"

The heartbreaking gladness.

"All?"

How pathetic could Chao get? Da felt the rage dissolve. Now that he'd had a chance to consider, rage was foolish and a showdown folly. He had needed to hear Chao's story, and he had heard it. What good would it do now to pound Chao with the truth? Never had he intended to hurt for hurt's sake. If Chao was a ghost, he was the most loving ghost alive.

Alive.

If.

He pondered.

Was it possible Chao's version was true and his own version false? That in some way he, Da, had died and been shipped to a living hell? That it was he who was the ghost?

No. It could not be. Fifteen years of ostracism was no myth.

"You remember it all clearly?"

"A few details, I remember differently."

"What details?"

Words strangled in Da's throat. Finally: "Nothing of consequence. Our memories differ slightly. A natural thing."

To hide his emotions, Da took his plate and Chao's to the fire. As he scraped the uneaten fish into the frying pan, he was struck

91

by a new thought. Chao's fifteen years of innkeeping was no myth, either. Nor was Mei-Mei a myth, nor her father. He put the pan back on the fire. If Chao's ghost had lived fifteen years as an innkeeper, then another ghost could have lived fifteen years as an ostracized woodsman. It was preposterous to reason that the ostracism could not have occurred if he had not killed his brother. The ostracism itself might be imaginary. It was even possible that a ghost mas-querading as Da Tsung successfully had sought a pretext to avoid following through on the showdown.

Da stood motionless. He glanced back over his shoulder. Chao was intent on the fishing poles—untangling lines and baiting hooks. Stealthily, Da took out his jackknife and opened one blade. With his back to Chao, he deliberately pressed its sharp edge against his own finger.

It bled.

When Chao and Da got back to the inn, Mei-Mei and the servants—two strapping women—were moving hot buns from the oven to the adjacent racks. Cookies, dumplings and bean cakes were cooling on the table. A pig was roasting over an open fire. Some smoke had bypassed the overhead vent, but the kitchen was spacious, light, and awash in good smells.

"Luck was with us, Mei-Mei." Chao displayed the string of carp. "See?"

"A fine catch." She kept working, but Chao's falsely cheerful tone did not escape her. "What happened to your hand?"

"Just a nick."

Wiping her hands on her apron, she unwound the bandage. "How did you do it?"

"Tried to catch a jackknife by the handle," Chao said sheepishly.

"Whose knife?"

"Caught it, too, the first time."

"It's not like you to throw a knife about." She caught sight of Da's cut finger. "You, too?"

"It would seem so."

Chao was perplexed. "When did you do that?"

Sensing tension, the servants vanished.

"Childish games," Da said to Mei-Mei. "We were intoxicated by sunlight."

"And the aftermath is what made Chao sad?"

"No. Memories. Unavoidable shadows. But no more. No more memories, no more shadows. I promise."

Stiffly, she brushed some flour from her apron.

"It's over," Chao said. "We got rid of it at the lake."

"You got rid of it."

"Yes."

"Rid of what?"

"Da just said. Memories. Shadows."

"How?"

"Does it matter?"

"It might."

"You'll just have to take my word, Mei-Mei. Our word. The sadness is over. Really over."

Da, looking on, was as confused by Chao's firmness as by Mei-Mei's reaction. She flushed. Her stiffness seemed to drain away. She was a reed. Pliant.

"You're not to worry any more," Chao said. "You're not to pry."

"All right, Chao."

Even eagerly submissive.

"You look tired," Mei-Mei said.

"I am, a little," Chao said. "Don't know why. It's you who's had a hard day."

"Tonight will be wearing. Why not get a little rest?"

"Good idea. How about you?"

"I've still a few things to finish up. You go ahead. I'll be there as quickly as I can." Her eyes, unguarded, shone. Then she became aware of Da's pointed inattention. The flush deepened on her cheek.

Taking the fish from Chao, Da plopped them into a huge wooden tub. Sterile, Chao might be. Impotent, no. Neither in the kitchen nor the bed. Da felt a twinge. To soften its import, he emptied a bucket of water into the tub and set about cleaning the fish. When he looked up, Chao and Mei-Mei were gone.

The twinge renewed itself and sprouted thorns. He hacked at the fish scales. In slipping away without a word, Mei-Mei may have intended a message. *Keep off.* He felt the thorns snag his skin. Jealousy took hold.

To throw off its grip, he tried to bring Mei-Mei down to brutish plane. Again he saw her shining eyes, and in retrospect they were feverish. Right now, Mei-Mei was in the bedroom. She was stripping the silk gown—or the gown was being stripped—from sluttish flesh.

He grimaced. Useless. Mei-Mei was no slut and he could not make her one. If he saw her eyes as feverish, it was because he longed to see them so—feverish with lust for him. If he saw the gown being stripped away, it was because he burned to do the stripping—to revel in the small frivolous bouncing breasts and the sweet elegant cleft. He saw her pouring herself upon him: touching, fondling, devouring; scissoring legs propelling her tender greedy mouth to new angles and vantage points. He saw his own mouth on hers, his chest pummeling scented breasts as Mei-Mei's elegant hips thrust upward to receive him—

Enough! He had no right. Obscene. Infantile. Despicable.

Even as Da scourged himself, he rejoiced. The stirring at his groin proved him alive! For fifteen years, self-discipline had blocked every carnal thought. He had come to believe abstinence could shrivel passion. Now he knew better. To sleep was not to die.

His fingers tightened on the knife handle. Neither he nor Chao was carnally dead even if one or the other was a ghost. He smiled. Where, then, was death's terror?

He became conscious of the blade scraping the fish, and of still another cause for celebration. The sight prompted no imaginary sounds — no axe blades, no trickling.

He was on his way to becoming whole.

Virtually the entire community turned out for the reunion party. Affection for Chao, reinforced by curiosity and lavish food and holiday wine, brought people from as far as six hours away. The walls seem to bend outward to contain the tumult, just as the table seemed to sag under the weight of its repast.

Da felt it his duty to keep moving among the guests, and to respond graciously to overtures. Unexpectedly, the duty proved pleasurable. The goodwill he met dispersed the chill that had been with him for so long.

He did not have to seek out the two men he wished to meet. Kao Su and Kee Fong came to him. Without prompting, the enfeebled Kee Fong retold the story of Chao's arrival at Lung Tan Jan and the first meeting with Mei-Mei. Kee Fong's version was insufferably detailed — what he had said to Mei-Mei's father, and what the old man had said to him, and what he had said in response, and what he and the old man had said to Mei-Mei, and what Mei-Mei had said to him. Chao was a minor figure in the tale.

Still, the details differed in no significant way. Kao Su turned out to be eleven or twelve years older than Da. Time had not bent his big shoulders nor lightened their load, but it apparently had loosened his tongue. Kao Su had a theory. Women, he thought, were attracted to standoffish men.

Kao Su's elaboration of the theory was interrupted by Chao's grand entrance. With Mei-Mei trailing behind, Chao came out of the kitchen bearing the roast pig. There were admiring oh's and ah's as he set the heavy platter on the service counter.

"The Lord Pig," said Kao Su.

Da nodded politely.

"The more indifference a man shows," Kao Su said, resuming his discourse, "the more avid the woman becomes."

Impatient, good-humored voices from the service counter diverted Da's attention.

"Let's eat!"

"Starving."

"Let's get started."

Chao stood motionless over the pig. Da discerned that he was gazing with revulsion at the carving knife.

The people crowding the service counter were oblivious.

"Make mine a leg!"

"Cut the head first!"

Chao fought for composure. He poised the knife above the pig.

Mei-Mei, beside him, detected his distress. She tensed.

As the knife came down, Chao gave an involuntary shout. "Go!" In a frenzy, he sawed at the pig's head.

The crowd laughed.

Da hid horror.

Kee Fong, nearby, was disapproving. "Since when has Chao become a clown?"

A bystander said: "You should have seen him last night. Singing. Dancing. Wild."

"Unbecoming."

"Be charitable," the bystander said. "Joy is seldom dignified."

The pig's head rolled aside on the platter. Chao looked down at it with shock.

Da, stricken, felt Mei-Mei's hatred stab at him across the room.

Chao rallied. Averting his eyes from the pig's head, he made a heroic show of cheerfulness as he carved and served.

"Good appetite."

"Have some rice."

"Some head meat?"

Mei-Mei crossed to Da. "Is this how you keep your promise?" Her voice was malignant. "What did you do to him out at the lake today?"

Kao Su intruded. "A wonderful banquet! Never have I seen Chao so happy!"

Leaving the serving counter, Chao hurried outside.

The watchful Mei-Mei started to go after him.

Da touched her arm. "Let me."

She hesitated.

"Please."

After a moment, she nodded.

Da went.

He found his brother by a fountain on the terrace.

"I don't know what came over me," Chao said, shamefaced.

"My fault. I shouldn't have pushed you to remember."

"Nonsense. The least I could do."

Da dipped a handkerchief into the fountain and folded it into a compress.

Chao held the compress to his forehead. "Mei-Mei must be worried. Go in, Da. Tell her I'll be there in a moment."

Mei-Mei was at the counter, serving her guests. Sighting Da, she signaled a servant to replace her and walked over to him.

"He'll be all right," Da said.

"Where is he?"

"He'll be in soon."

"Is it all right for me to go out now to see him?"

"Better not. He needs a minute more."

"What made him do it?"

"I'm sure it won't happen again."

"You stirred up memories."

"Yes. At the lake. Not at any time since. I swear it."

Some of the tightness went out of her lips. "You're tired. Would you like me to get you something to eat? Not the pig. I know you can't possibly touch the pig."

"I'll wait a bit, thanks."

"Some wine, then?"

At Da's nod, Mei-Mei fetched two cups of wine. The two drank.

"Fifteen years ago," Mei-Mei said, "Chao got into some trouble. You made it possible for him to escape."

"In a sense. Yes."

"In a sense. What sense?"

"Let's just say I helped him."

"Because you loved him."

"Yes."

"The memories you stirred up at the lake. Did you stir them up because you loved him?"

"No. Because I loved myself more."

"In what way, exactly?"

"You wouldn't want to know."

"But I would. I do."

"Don't push, Mei-Mei. It may be something you'll regret hearing."

"You tricked Chao into cutting his palm. Why?"

"Who said I tricked him?"

"No one. Did you?"

"Yes."

"What did you hope to gain?"

"I repeat, Mei-Mei: don't push."

"For fifteen years, you didn't laugh. Never were you alone with a woman."

"No woman would have me. They hated me, or feared me, or feared to be seen with me."

"Because you let Chao escape?"

"No."

"Why, then?"

Da did not hesitate. "Because I killed him."

The words vibrated between them, eerie, incomprehensible, incongruous amidst the light-hearted chatter.

"Because you killed him."

"Yes." Da observed Mei-Mei's turmoil with fierce relish. She'd hounded him long enough. She'd asked for it. She'd earned it.

"How can that be?"

"I don't know. I know only that it is." Vainly he tried to hang onto self-righteousness. His satisfaction seeped away. Mei-Mei was pale. She was willing herself not to faint. The effort was visible in her tight mouth, the drawn cheeks. How had she earned such cruelty? By going to bed with her husband?

"What you call your killing. You did it out of hate?"

"No. Out of love."

"There's hope, then."

"Uh."

"You imagine you killed out of love, not hate, and you feel impelled to confess."

"Confess?" Da was bewildered. "I've nothing to confess. I'm proud of what I did!"

"But ashamed, too. That means there's hope you'll come to yourself."

"You don't understand, Mei-Mei. I really did it. Chao was sure to die. I had the chance to help him. As Yung Chang's executioner—"

"No. Please! Why torment yourself? Why torment me?" She swayed but kept herself erect. "You've suffered, Da. No man has suffered more. Because I've never known that kind of suffering doesn't mean I can't feel it. To love someone is to feel his pain." Her voice was deliberate. She had picked up calm now, and

99

control. Color had returned to her cheeks. "A pain so keen it drives you to believe my husband is a ghost. Impossible! Chao cannot be a ghost. For fifteen years, I've shared his life. I can tell when he's afraid or deceitful or when he's lying—"

"I didn't say Chao was lying." Da forced down elation. To love someone is to feel his pain. He would save the words and savor them at his leisure. "If he's a ghost, he doesn't know it."

"If." Her face lighted. "You're not convinced, then. You have doubts. Whatever the ugliness at the lake, you held back your suspicion that Chao is a ghost."

"Yes."

"Thank God! It's not too late, then, for you to accept the truth. You couldn't have killed Chao! He's alive! Strong! A man in every sense!" She floundered. "You understand?"

"This afternoon, you mean."

"This afternoon?"

"When we got back from the lake."

She blushed as she grasped his meaning. "Not only that. His moods. Dreams."

"You needn't be afraid I'll tell Chao. I tried to. Twice. I couldn't."

"Why would you even try? Imagine what it would do to him! Yung Chang is a far land. Let's keep it there."

"Agreed."

"Not just for Chao's sake. For yours. All these imaginings! Somehow, things got mixed up in your mind. If the ugliness spews up again, meet it with the truth. Chao's no ghost! Couldn't be."

"An avalanche," Da said. "Didn't I say 'agreed'? No stopping you."

She drew back. "Uh. I've stopped."

The tension broke. They laughed. It was then they caught sight of Chao standing by the terrace door, and realized how absorbed in each other they had been, and how intimate their attitude must have seemed to him.

Da stirred.

"Not now," Mei-Mei said. "Wait. Give him a chance to get his balance."

"The sooner we straighten out the misunderstanding—"

"Not entirely a misunderstanding. 'To love someone,' I said. You gallantly chose to overlook it."

No mere slip of the tongue, then. She had said it and meant it.

"I've never believed it possible to feel love for two men. Now I don't know what to believe. I keep telling myself it's insane. A man I've known for only a day."

Anxiety kept joy at bay. "It's my anguish you're drawn to, not me."

"Nonsense. If ever I mistook pity for love, I no longer do."

"Or my resemblances to Chao."

"Do not cheapen it, Da. Not the resemblances or the anguish. To pick love apart is futile. By picking apart a fly, do you find out how or why it flies? By splitting seeds, do you find out why some sprout in hours and others take weeks? My love sprouted in a day. A gift. Accept it."

"I cannot."

"That the love is there does not mean it must be fulfilled." Her eyes lowered, and she had to squeeze out the word: "Physically." She lifted her eyes. "To love is one thing. To permit love to hurt my husband is another."

"We must not talk of such things."

"What of thinking them? Is it permissible to think them?" Her gentleness was edged. "It was you who lauded candor."

"Candor used wisely."

"If you weigh the use, it's not candor."

"If you're inept, candor can kill."

"No. No more than love can kill."

Da's hands made a pushing motion, as if to rid the air of talk. Then, bluntly: "Seems to me Chao's so deeply hurt that he can't or won't come to us."

"Let's go to him, then." Without ado, she started toward the terrace door.

Da lagged a step behind. What could he say to his brother? How could he bear Chao's reproaches? He should have insisted on talking to Chao alone. That way, he'd have been able to reason with him. Mei-Mei was arbitrary. She had no right to shun a kindly discretion. Obstinacy was not fitting in a woman. Unseemly.

Mei-Mei clasped her husband's hands.

Chao's head was high, Da saw, and his eyes level. Dignity, a family trait. Why had he ever thought Chao weak?

"I've seldom lied to you, Chao," said Mei-Mei, "and never on important things. What I feel for Da, I feel partly because he's your brother and partly because he is what he is."

Not so obstinate, after all. Feel, not love.

"Love?" Mei-Mei said. "What's love? A closeness? A sharing? Sensitivity to hurt? I hurt when you're hurt, Chao. And I hurt when Da's hurt. Love? Whatever, I'm not ashamed. Quite the contrary. It lifts me."

The avalanche on the move again—tender, lovely. Candor could cleanse as well as hurt.

"I love you too much, Chao, to ever let you have real cause for hurt. Da, too. Da loves you too much." Scorning propriety and the stares of the curious, she kissed her husband. "Please. No more memories, no more sadness. Not tonight, Chao, and not in the tomorrows."

Da waited. His heart sang when Chao slipped one hand free from Mei-Mei's to reach out and draw him close.

Brothers

﹏

To achieve is to live. To chop fast and clean. To sculpt with sure strokes. To swim with grace. To sew a dress or build a chair or cook a stew or shape a pot from clay.

To laze is to live, too, if wonder stays alive. To savor shapes, hues, ideas. To build a sand castle. To skim a stone so it skips on the water's rim. To fish and eat and drink and chat. To meditate.

Happy is the man who loafs or works well.

Happier still is the man who does both. Or thinks he does.

He lives.

﹏

They trudged homeward through the forest's waning light, carrying their poles and the day's catch, listening for the rustlings of night creatures.

"You handled her well today," Da said.

"She bucked a little, I thought. A stiff wind makes her nervous."

"True, but all she needs is a touch."

At the first launch, Mei-Mei had remarked that the skiff they had repaired was too spirited for oars. She had cut and sewn a sail, and they had rigged a pole and sprit. Now the speed of the sleek, low-slung craft put the lake's distant coves within reach.

"Want to play *xiangqi* tonight?"

"Sure."

Ahead, a cow's bellow ripped the tranquil dusk.

The two men emerged into an open area. Near a farm-house, a cow was being slaughtered. She was lying on her side, trussed legs thrashing, head wrenching upward. A farmer hacked at her exposed throat. Gushing blood spattered his clothes. The cow's bawling ravaged the countryside.

Da tried vainly to look away.

"It bothers me," Chao said, "to be beaten by Mei-Mei all the time."

"Uh?"

"By a woman," Chao said.

The frenzied legs were pumping life out onto the soil.

"It shouldn't, I guess."

"No."

"How about you?"

"Me?"

"Yes. Doesn't it bother you?"

"A little."

"Actually," Chao said, "you should be able to beat her. You're as good a strategist as she is, and you've more patience. It's you, not me, who should have been the scholar." He glanced at the cow. "Not a pleasant sight."

"No."

The bawlings were dying now.

"Tomorrow, we can fish the north shore. There's an inlet there we've never tried." Chao smiled. "If we sail in quietly, the fish will think tomorrow is just another day."

"They'll find out," Da said.

The evening was quiet.

Dinner was over, and the customers scattered at the tables were few. They lolled in their chairs, stomachs full, legs sprawling. From time to time, the boy tending the counter fueled their talk with wine.

Da was playing *xiangqi* with Chao near the fire pan. "I'm cornered," he said.

Mei-Mei, serving candied walnuts, studied the board. "No, you're not."

Da looked. He made a move.

"No fair," Chao said. "Now I'm cornered." He grinned at Mei-Mei. "Come over here and help me."

"Hey," Da said to his brother. "You mustn't steal my helper. I need her."

Kao Su, looking on, said slyly: "Let's not fight over her."

Everybody laughed.

"Some day," Mei-Mei said, "I'll learn not to interfere."

"Learn tomorrow," Chao said. "Tonight find a move for me." He scanned the board. Absently, he drank. Wine dribbled from the corner of his mouth.

Inexplicably, Da's vision swam. It seemed to him that Chao's cup transformed itself into a bowl. As Da watched his brother wipe his lips with a handkerchief, Chao changed before his eyes to the Chao who, fifteen years earlier, had swiped at his lips with his sleeve before kneeling at the block.

Shaken, Da willed himself to stop the air from shimmering. The *xiangqi*-playing Chao swam back into focus.

Then a second metamorphosis began: Mei-Mei, who had moved behind Chao's chair, took on the form and features of Jui Hseuh . . . .

After serving wine to Da and the two other men at his table, the barmaid had lingered. "I'm sorry about the verdict."

"Thank you," Da said curtly.

Hurt, Jui Hseuh gave him his change and departed.

Da left the coins on the table. "There's always a chance, I suppose, that Chao can escape."

One of the two men came alert. "Not likely. The jail's foolproof."

"I don't mean from the jail," Da said softly. "Tomorrow, when you escort him to the square."

"If he tried to escape, Da, it would be our duty as court-appointed guards to stop him."

"You might get careless."

"No chance. It would mean our heads."

"Not your heads. Nothing so severe. Especially since Chao has so much public sympathy." Da's hand toyed with the coins. "If Chao should get lucky, you might get lucky, too."

"How do you mean?"

Da stacked the coins. He let them jangle through his fingers. "If you should be unfairly blamed for someone's good luck, you'd deserve to be rewarded."

The second guard became aware. "Say!"

"Generously," Da said.

"What's he hinting?" the second guard asked.

"Nothing," said the first guard.

"Sounds to me like a bribe."

"Nothing like that. Just talk, that's all."

"That's all it better be!"

"Luck, is what we're talking. One man gets lucky and others benefit."

"No one will get lucky tomorrow at dawn. I'll see to that!"

The first guard sighed.

"If you shirk your duty, I'll report you."

The first guard bristled. "Who's shirking duty? Don't get all worked up! Nobody needs to tell me what my duty is!"

Da, defeated, picked up the coins.

An hour before dawn, the sleepless Da was at home, laying out his ceremonial robe. He heard a knock at the door. He ignored it. Jui Hseuh pushed inside.

"Don't go through with it, Da."

"What else can I do?" Da said.

"Let Li Mu do it."

"I can't."

"An insane sense of duty," the barmaid said.

"Duty?" He stared at her. "Who cares for duty?" Flinging the executioner's robe to the floor, he trampled it underfoot. "I spit on duty!

Don't you understand? Only I can save my brother from butchery! Only I can give him hope until the last moment! Only I can make his final moments peaceful!"

"But Chao is your brother!"

For one merciful moment, Da was bewildered. Then he comprehended the revulsion in Jui Hseuh's voice, and he realized the barmaid did not understand and could never understand, and he in his turn felt revulsion —for the girl's glibness, superficiality, and skin-deep compassion. "Get out!" he shouted.

"He's your brother, Da!"

He grabbed her arm and hustled her out the door.

"No heart! A monster!"

Da slammed the door.

From outside, Jui Hseuh cried: "A monster! A beast!"

Her cries continued to assail Da as he picked up the robe and, holding it in his hands, knelt to pray before Buddha. Taking some incense from a drawer, he lit the stick and placed it in the burner.

Having moved his pawn, Chao waited for Da to make the countermove.

Mei-Mei sensed Da's agitation. "Something wrong?"

"What could be wrong?" Da said.

"It's just that you don't seem yourself."

Pouring some fresh wine, Da drank. "If I'm not myself now," he said, "I will be as soon as the bottle is empty."

Everybody laughed except Mei-Mei.

⤝

Da got up early the next morning to chop some wood.

Soon after starting work, he heard the distant bellow of a dying cow. Chilled, he paused.

As he resumed work, the log at his feet took on the configuration of a man. Vainly he tried to shake off the apparition.

Tossing the log aside, he selected a new log—stubby, twisted, in no way resembling a man.

The new log, too, changed into a man as he chopped. He worked on. Imaginings, nothing more. There was no cause for remorse. He had not killed his brother! Chao was alive!

The woodpile became a heap of tangled men, dead and dying. He worked on. Alive! Anyone could see Chao was alive!

Moans assailed Da from the woodpile and the scattered logs. From afar, he heard a bawling cow.

Throwing down the axe, he rushed into the inn.

Chao and Mei-Mei were having breakfast when Da burst in.

"No more!" Da cried. "I cannot take more! I've got to know!"

Mei-Mei flinched.

Chao went to his brother. "What happened, Da? What else do you need to know?"

Da caught sight of Mei-Mei's stricken face. His mouth contorted. He could not speak.

"Whatever you want to know," Chao said. "Whatever you need."

It took all Da's strength to regain control, and to make the decision he now knew had been inescapable. "Chao, I cannot remain here. I must go back."

"To Yung Chang?" Chao said incredulously.

"No!" Mei-Mei cried.

"Why?" Chao said.

"Here, I need to know. I need to be. But to be and to know is to hurt. In Yung Chang, I will be reconciled to not knowing."

"Yung Chang," Mei-Mei said, "is a hell for you. It's unthinkable for you to go back there."

"Another memory lapse, is that it?" said Chao. "Tell me what it is. I'll help you remember."

"No use," Da said. "Yung Chang is where I belong." He turned. "I have to pack."

"Surely not today!" Chao said. "Wait a day or two. Things will be better tomorrow."

"No. Not tomorrow, not ever. Not here. And if I'm going to go, it's better that I go quickly."

"Have some breakfast first," Mei-Mei said.

"No." Then, quickly: "Thank you."

Mei-Mei followed him to his room. "Whatever your imaginings, Da, you're better off here, where you're cherished."

"If I stay here, I'll go mad or I'll drive Chao mad. I've no choice, you must know that. Sooner or later, I would blurt out the truth. What is the truth? That Chao is a ghost? That I'm a ghost? That I'm mad? That Chao's responsible? Intolerable! All!"

"Go to another town, then. Not Yung Chang."

"No. I cannot live with secrets. In Yung Chang, there are no secrets. I know where I stand there. I *am*." Stolidly, he started to pack. "Yung Chang is what fate has decreed for me."

Mei-Mei turned away. In the doorway, she met Chao. "No use," she said, walking past him.

Chao entered. "The *xiangqi* game last night. Is that it, Da? Kao Su, implying we're rival suitors?" He grasped Da's hands to stop him from packing. "You love Mei-Mei. You need her. You need to know she loves you. What you don't appreciate is that in a sense you already have her. She gives you trust, and tenderness, and I do not begrudge it. Truly, I do not. If you will but give your new life a chance, you can be happy. Another month. Another week."

"No."

Chao recognized the finality in his brother's manner. He released Da's hands.

"All right. I'll go with you as far as the marsh."

Minutes later, Da was strapping the saddlebags onto his horse's back.

Mei-Mei handed him a packet. "Some food for your journey."

Da accepted the packet. "Do not grieve, Mei-Mei."

Deliberately, Chao walked out of earshot, giving them privacy.

Da said: "You've got to help Chao recapture his happiness. We've had some sadness, but my visit's not wasted. Our three lives have touched, and from the touching has come love, and love is never a waste."

For the first time, the two embraced. They clung to each other, their bodies tight, and then they knew the moment had come to end it, and they parted.

Chao and Da mounted their horses. They rode off toward the distant mountain. When Da looked back, Mei-Mei still was standing there.

They rode steadily on. They passed their favorite fishing spot. Some time after leaving the lake, they reached the foothills. As they started to climb the mountain, Da brooded.

At the mountain crest, the sky darkened. The mists closed in. They started down through the dark and tangled wood. Soon, the steepness of the slope forced them to dismount.

Da said: "We may as well say goodbye here."

"I'll go with you as far as the marsh."

"Why prolong it? Mei-Mei will be worried. You'd best start back."

"Under one condition. You should have a stronger horse. Take mine. I'll take yours."

Da hesitated. Then he shifted his saddlebags from his horse to Chao's.

Wordlessly, he gave his brother a parting embrace.

"Remember me," Chao said.

"Always."

Leading Chao's horse, Da headed down the slope.

Overhead, interlaced branches dripped. Halting, Da looked up at the oaks.

Chao hurried down the slope to Da's side. "Change your mind? Want me with you as far as the marsh?"

Da did not have the heart to refuse him.

The two men resumed the downhill trek.

It was dusk when the two reached the marsh. They halted at the hollow where Da once had tried to build a fire. To one side of the log, Da saw the rotting carcass of the discarded hare. "Well, Chao," he said. "This has to be it."

"I'm afraid I've not been very good company."

"Neither of us is good company. But there are many good days to remember. Cherish."

"Yes." Chao fumbled with his reins. "One last drink together."

Da nodded. The two men tied their horses to a tree. Da got a flagon of wine from his saddlebags. They drank.

"Da—"

Da looked up.

"If you love Mei-Mei, and she loves you, I've no right to hold on to her."

"Don't!" Da said, appalled. "Don't open it up again! Pointless. Love can't be measured, but Mei-Mei's love for you is no way diminished by her love for me. You must believe that!"

"You do love her, then. You want her."

"Yes, I want her. But I'm not a boy, Chao, with a boy's insatiable cravings. What I feel for Mei-Mei, and what she feels for me, can be expressed in other ways—has been expressed in other ways. What we feel for each other had no bearing on my decision to leave."

"Why, then, do you leave? Is it something I've done?"

"No! Believe me, Chao. No!"

"All our lives, we've been close. In the years we were separated, my love for you never weakened. Yet somehow I'm to blame for your leaving." Dropping to his knees, Chao clung to Da's legs. "In some way, my love is killing you."

"We've been through that, Chao. Be sensible. Love can't kill."

"Then why hold back the truth? Confess! Get the ugliness out! I'm driving you away! To Yung Chang! In some way, I am your executioner!"

111

"You must not use that word!" From the distance, Da heard dripping water, faint axe blows. He started. "You must not blame yourself! I cannot bear it! You're in no way to blame!" Da looked down at Chao, kneeling at his feet. It seemed to him that his brother's neck shimmered in bloody light. Water thundered in his ears. Axe blows rang. The sounds had echoes: a bellowing cow, the groans of dying men.

Da screamed. "Go!" Then, haltingly, in a kind of delirium, the words at last found release. "Our memories differ slightly. The details matter . . . "

Dawn.

The town square.

Escorted by two guards, Chao Tsung reached the execution block. After glancing at the knife at Da's belt, he calmly drank from the bowl. The wine dribbled from the corner of his mouth. He wiped his lips with his sleeve. Before kneeling, he exchanged a long, loving look with his brother. As Da Tsung stepped forward, the crowd shouted its abhorrence.

"Shame!"

"Shame!"

"Shame!"

The drums sounded. The crowd grew still. Da raised the axe. The hush was deeper than silence. Da delivered the downward stroke. The axe sliced cleanly through Chao's neck. Chao's head dropped into the basket.

Da held back tears. Head high and proud, he stepped down from the platform. The crowd opened before him. All eyes were hostile. Everywhere, he encountered hatred and revulsion.

He walked steadily on.

Da's head was bowed, his eyes tear-filled. "So it was," he whispered, "that I did what I had to do."

Da opened his eyes. To his astonishment, Chao was nowhere in sight.

He whirled. The horses still were tied to the tree. No sign of Chao.

He heard a flutter of wings. Through the swirling mists, a crane arose from the marsh. Waves rippled to the shore, causing the reeds to sway.

He turned back. His eyes caught the base of the log—the spot where Chao had knelt at his feet. He recoiled in horror and disbelief.

At the spot where Chao had knelt, there was a pool of blood.

Da stood gaping. Truth could kill.

Love could kill, too. It had. Twice.

Pulling himself together, he mounted his horse.

Leading the other horse by the halter, he started back up the hill in the direction of Lung Tan Jan.

He halted. Groggy, he considered. His shoulders slumped.

Wheeling, he rode past the hollow and started across the marsh in the direction of Yung Chang.

Reflections
on an
Extraordinary Crime Stopper

How to Be a San Francisco Shamus
James N. Frey

Rule *numero uno* in this business is never take on a client that you know in your gut is loony tunes.

Okay, so here's how it happened: She comes hip-swaying into my office one Tuesday morning dressed in a slinky blue shimmering dress with a slit up to where it ought to be illegal and says: Look, I need a snooper and from what I hear on the street, Joe Smigelski knows his way around this hamlet. I tell her she heard right. I'm anxious to please her, catch, on account of business is as usual stinko.

She's wearing dark glasses with lenses the size of dinner plates and has this white thing that looks like a turban pulled down to her ears so I can't even eyeball the color of her hair, real mysterious-like. She has too much orange-red lipstick on otherwise okay lips and a small, rather cutesy, upturned nose, which don't go with the slinky type. I figure she's someplace between thirty and forty, right in there.

She says: I know all about you, Mr. Smigelski. You're divorced, no kids, you play golf often and badly. You can't afford a secretary and you drink martinis without the olive and not much vermouth—have I got this right? Mostly you make a buck by serving subpoenas and being a security guard at ball games.

Your biggest case last year involved tracking down forty-one owners of defective water heaters.

Forty-two, I says. Then I says: So you been talkin' to Henry, the blind guy at the newsstand downstairs, who's got a mouth big enough to swallow Oakland. What vice brings you to my digs—and don't tell me you want to write my biography because it wouldn't be all that fascinating to anyone but my mother.

I need a shamus and I need him now. What do you say?

I says: What's the action?

She fiddles with her sunglasses and looks over the office, which is never going to make the cover of *Office Beautiful* on account of the cracked plaster, the brown water stains under the window, the threadbare green rug that don't go with the brown drapes, the desks and chairs I got from a St. Vincent de Paul close-out sale. Then she says somebody's trying to kill her.

I inform her that such practices are truly against the law, so why didn't she call a cop?

She has her reasons, she says with this sort of faint, mysterious smile on her orange lips, and if I don't help her she won't have nowhere else to turn. I asks her what her name is and she says it's Wonder Hopp, which even as she says it sounds phony, and I think to myself, who the hell does she think she's dealing with, a cretin? I haven't time to play with yo-yos so I leans back in my swivel chair and says: I get two bills a day plus expenses, figuring she ain't about to push a load that heavy. This fazes her not in the least. She puts a crisp new five-slam bill on the desk in front of me. The picture of McKinley looks up at me like he wants to be friends and I remember rule *numero uno*—that you don't accept a loony tunes client—and think, should I or shouldn't I?

There's more where that came from, she says, giving me the once-over with rather large brown peepers over the top of her shades.

You got yourself a shamus, I tell her.

Have you a rod? she asks. Real cool now. She means do I have a gun. I tell her sure, but I don't keep it here in the office because in San Francisco you can't get a ticket to pack one, even if you were Saint Francis himself, catch. She stands up and says in a hush-hush voice that I'll need it. She'll meet me, she says, at Bush and Mason at ten o'clock tonight. Be on time, she says. Worry not, I says. Then I says: You want to tell me just a tweak of what's going down here?

She tells me she's trying to locate a certain object that a certain fat man—whose identity she can't divulge—also wants, and there's a guy name of Thurston Floyd who wants to kill her because he wants this certain object for himself. He followed her to Frisco, she says, from Taipei. The rest, she says, I'll find out when she knows me better.

I tell her don't say "Frisco," 'cause it incites the natives to mayhem, and if she's in danger, maybe I'd better go along with her. She says danger is her business. No kidding, says it straight out just like on *Miami Vice* or something like that. But underneath all the slink and tough talk I got a feeling she's scared as a cockroach in a Raid factory.

Okay, so I watch out the window when she leaves the building. The fleabag office I rent for two slam a month is on the fourth floor facing Fifth Street and I can see her okay when she gets out onto the street. I fish my 40-power binos out of the desk and watch her cross the street to the hack stand and get into a Yellow Cab that has the number 4485 on the side. I calls the Yellow Cab dispatcher and tell her I'm Sgt. Wilbur Munez of the San Francisco Police Department and this is a police emergency. I give her a phony badge number—I know they're too damn lazy to check—and tell her I want to know the destination of the fare that was just picked up by 4485. She makes me wait for ten lousy minutes, then comes back on the line and says 4485 is en route to the St. Mark Hotel.

I break the five-slam bill at the newsstand where Henry the blind guy takes bets on the horses and so he's always got a pile. I tell him he finks on me again and I'm gonna punch his lights out, which I realize now was a cretin thing to say to a blind guy, but I was a little hot at the time. Next, I chow down a couple of Jumbo Jacks at Jack in the Box on Market, then stop at Macy's toy department and plunk down fourteen bucks for this Jr. Crimestopper stub nose .38 that honest to God looks as much like the real thing as the San Francisco Giants look like a real baseball team, but ain't. Then I head up Powell to the St. Mark, where out-of-town tourist dinks pay a hundred and eight-five a night for a single. This pencil-neck clerk in a red blazer looks at a little index and chirps that they have no such person as Wonder Hopp staying there. So, having no other choice, I check with J.T. Morrow, widely known as the crookedest hotel dick in San Francisco. He hears the description of my client, then says, oh yeah, he's seen her around, she's going by the moniker Honey O'Hara, and for a slam and a half he'll check her out. I know from past dealings there's no negotiating with this bandit, so I lay out the bread, but promise him if he don't come up with something I'm going to throw up in his lap.

Rule *numero two-o* in this business is always think twice before making an ass out of yourself.

The fog is thick as coffin padding when she shows up twenty minutes late at Bush and Mason and says I should follow her. She's dressed in black now: black coat, ankle-length black dress, black broad-brimmed hat pulled down over her face. Real secretive, she asks me where's my rod. I jerk my Jr. Crimestopper .38 out of my trench coat pocket and she stares at it, bug-eyed. Teflon bullets, I tell her, hot-load 185-grain slugs. I grin an evil grin and she buys the whole package.

Okay, so we stop half a block up from Stockton at Burritt Alley and she shows me this bronze plaque that says:

ON APPROXIMATELY THIS SPOT

MILES ARCHER,

PARTNER OF SAM SPADE,

WAS DONE IN BY

BRIGID O'SHAUGHNESSY

Well? she says. Well what? I says. She wants to know what I know about that plaque and what it's doing there.

I tell her I don't know what it's doing there but that as everybody on this planet knows, Sam Spade was this make-believe detective and he had a partner who in the book, *The Maltese Falcon*, got himself killed here, but it never really happened.

It happened, she says. Just like that. Matter-of-fact. I feel a shiver go up my back because I know now for sure I'm dealing with somebody who probably belongs in the monkey house. But so what, I tell myself, some of my best friends monkey out on me every now and then. She squeezes my arm now, like she was making orange juice out of it, and whispers into my ear that she can prove it.

Okay, I tell her, that's well and good, but why bother? Whoever did it would be a hundred years old by now, maybe. She looks at me like I'm a cretin and says: You're forgetting about the bird.

The bird?

Let's get off the street, she says—the fat man's on to me, and Floyd Thurston might have picked up my trail again. I asks: Why do you think so? But she only gives me her mysterious smile and won't say nothing. Next thing I know I'm sitting in a booth with her at Herbert's Grill on Bush, where a lot of business dinks hang out after work and drink until they're blind. Here's what she says: This guy Dashiell Hammett who wrote *The Maltese Falcon*

121

came to San Francisco in 1921 and became a Pink—an operative for the Pinkerton Detective Agency—working out of the Flood Building. She says this Hammett guy works on a lot of cases, including one that involved this ship, the *Sonoma*, which came in from Sydney, Australia, with 400 pounds of English gold sovereigns missing. That was $125,000 worth then, but worth forty times that much today.

She sits back and munches on a filet of sole while I drink a martini and try to multiply it in my peanut. Comes to $5 million, somewhere around there. Okay, I says, so what happened to it? Dashiell Hammett, she says, recovered it and returned it to the rightful owners.

So where's the mystery? I asks.

I'm getting to that, she says. You see, she says in a secretive whisper, there was something on that ship worth far more than gold. She clams up while the waiter fills her water glass. Okay, she says, listen: In 1530 an order of knights made a deal with Emperor Charles V of Spain to rent the island of Malta. The payment was to be one golden falcon per year, okay? The one for 1537 was special. Nobody knows why, but they do know this falcon was jeweled and worth . . . who knows. Millions and millions and millions. She blinks her big brown peepers at me and says: The bird made its way from country to country, stolen so many times nobody could keep track, ending up being war booty in the Franco-Prussian War in 1870—you should be taking notes—and was smuggled out of France to England just before World War I. From England it went to Constantinople, where it was bought by a Russian army officer named Kemidov, who had no idea it was worth so much. He found it missing the night of September 3, 1921. The next place it turned up was Australia, and that's how it got on the *Sonoma*, and that's how it came to San Francisco, and that's how Dashiell Hammett found out about it.

How do you know all this? I asks. She says she can't tell me, but it's true. I asks her why she can't tell me and she says she can't, that's all.

Tell me more, I says, playing along. Hammett, she says, gave the kiss-off to the Pinks right after the *Sonoma* incident and it wasn't long after—get this—he went to work for a jeweler! Samuels, right up there on Market. Get the connection? Samuels? Samuel Spade? Her eyes are flashing now. Add it all up, she says, along with the fact that Brigid O'Shaughnessy in the book is told to hock her jewels at the hock shop at Fifth and Mission, when it was really one block west at Fifth and Market—I checked—are you following all this, Mr. Smigelski?

Lady, why don't you stop all this yabber and tell me who you are and what you want? Her eyes get dark and sullen all of a sudden, like a kid finding out her trip to the circus has been cancelled and she has to go to the dentist. You telling or not? I says.

She sits there with her eyes lowered for a minute, then looks at me all innocent and hurt and says the real Brigid O'Shaughnessy's name was Rosie O'Wiggins. Okay, good, now how do you fit in? I says. She stares at me. Tears in her eyes. Then she says, okay, she'll confess, but first she's got to use a hankie and clear her sinuses.

I'm beginning to feel sorry for her—which in my profession is a definite no-no—I have to resist such feelings with all my strength of character.

Sinuses cleared, she takes a deep breath and blurts out that Rosie O'Wiggins was her grandmother on her mother's side. Then she just sits there and waits for me to digest this pablum and see if it gives me gas. Okay, I says, give me some proof. Proof? she says. She bites her lip and says: Can't you just take my word? Hey, I says, I'm a P.I. We deal in facts, facts, facts, facts. She says: Puhleeeeeze believe me, Mr. Smigelski. No, no, no, I says. I'm looking real close at her, trying to decide if the tears in her eyes are real or a put-on, when she suddenly grabs my arm and her eyes explode with what looks like righteous terror. She stammers: That man there, at the window, that's him! That's Thurston Floyd, the man who wants to kill me!

I turn and see this burly, bearded giant hurrying away from the window. He's wearing this big-brimmed hat and a pair of gold-rimmed specs on his beak. Be careful, he's armed to the teeth! she calls after me, loud enough for every dink in the place to hear.

Okay, maybe now I'm gonna find out what all this marmalade is about, I figure. The guy is half a block away by the time I get out the door, but I catch him easy and tell him if he don't stop bothering the lady he's gonna get some terrible holes blown in his overcoat. The dink blabbers something about not having any money, he's a poor family man, and the like. I take my Jr. Crimestopper .38 out of my pocket so he can see I'm kidding him not. The guy's hand zips into his coat and I think, oh, oh, his cannon might be Smith and Wesson, but what he comes out with is a wallet. He flips it at me, then bolts down the hill and vanishes in the fog yammering for a cop. I circle around the block and duck into a Chinese restaurant and ask to use the bathroom, where I take a peek inside the wallet and find there's a driver's license in the name of Rabbi Irving C. Brockman, credit cards, pictures of a round little woman and four curly-headed kids. Six bucks cash.

So now I think, either Thurston Floyd has got a pretty good disguise here, or this is one very cunning, cool, murderous rabbi who's been posing as Thurston Floyd. Or then again maybe I've been fibbed at right to my face by my own client, catch? That would make me angry, and when I get angry, like about a ten-megaton bomb, I make a lot of rubble.

So I head back to Herbert's to confront her with the facts and—yeah, you guessed it—she's gone like the morning fog on a hot afternoon.

Rule *numero three-o* in this business is never let a dink client get away with nothing.

J.T. Morrow calls me first thing next day and tells me her name is Gloria Fritz and she lives in Danbury, Iowa. He found her MasterCard taped to the inside of the toilet tank in her room. You got a bankcard number, you got everything. Twenty minutes later, I know where she works (Henderson Feed and Drygoods Company), how much she made last year ($21,512.78), what she owns, owes, and every friend or relative she ever named as a reference on a credit application. Thing I still don't know is what the hell she's doing in San Francisco. Okay, so I get out my directory of private eyes and call this soda cracker in Fisher City, Iowa, the closest P.I. to Danbury, and after I tell him what I want, he says he'll bomb over in his pickup and look into the matter. He won't give no professional discount and he has me wire him a hundred for a retainer, so I tell him make it quick or I'll stick pins in a voodoo doll and give him hemorrhoids.

Most of the morning I spend reading this cornball book, *The Maltese Falcon*. This guy Sam Spade takes guns away from two different guys in this fairy tale. Hey, some dink points his iron at me, I give him the whole cookie jar and so would anybody that's got a brain in their peanut. Anyway, it's clear this Hammett guy knows not what of he speaks. But I see where my dink client got Thurston Floyd, 'cause the guy who's killed in the beginning is Floyd Thursby, so I know by not too much deduction that the rabbi is who he claimed to be. I send him his wallet via U.S. mail and keep the six bucks, for expenses.

Just before lunch my fellow shamus calls me from Iowa and says he's asked around a bit and knows what Gloria Fritz is doing in San Francisco. Seems she belongs to the Danbury Lady Adventurers' Club and every year the club sends one of their members to some exotic place where they have an adventure based on some book so they can talk about it all winter. Iowa, he says, has long, cold, boring winters. Okay, I tell him, he won't be needing Preparation H. I hang up the phone with one thought bouncing around inside my melon:

Revenge.

I don't have to wait too long to get it either. She phones me just before lunch calling herself Mary O'Brady—which she swears is her real name—and says she's so sorry that she put me onto the wrong guy and I tell her that's okay, no harm done. I even chuckle, let her know what a good sport Joe Smigelski is. She says she's on her way over to the office and I says okey-dokey. I leave a note scribbled on my notepad that says St. Mark Hotel and her room number, which she'll be sure to see, then I head out, leaving my door unlocked. I always leave it unlocked because the lock hasn't worked since maybe before the '06 quake.

After you're in this business two weeks you find out you should always use the right tool for the right job, so I stop at the store and get a king-size bottle of Hunt's catsup, a tennis ball, and some baby powder. Heinz is good for hamburgers, but it's too slow coming out of the bottle for what I got in mind. For fifty bucks, which wipes out most of the profit on this job, J.T. Morrow lets me into her room. I smear the baby powder on my face and rub it in real good so it gives my skin this nice grey pallor. Then I smear the Hunts all over the front of my shirt and sit in the chair and wait for her, with the tennis ball under my arm. I know for sure when she sees that note on my desk she'll be flying on up here. I only have to wait ten minutes, tops. When I hear the door unlock I lean back like I'm dead, holding my Jr. Crimestopper .38 in my hand.

Now comes the good part.

What I get is this muffled scream and I know I got her, the dumb dink. She stands over me bawling and sniffling and moaning, oh, me, oh my, oh me, oh my! I squeeze down on the tennis ball, which shuts off the circulation in my arm so there's no pulse at all when she takes hold of my wrist. She whines and I figure she's gonna faint, which makes little champagne bubbles of joy in the interior of my cranium. But she don't faint; she gets right to work. I hear some quick shifting around—suitcases opening and closing and the like—then she exits, and I spend the next ten minutes sitting on the floor laughing until I feel like I might get a hernia.

Rule *numero four-o* in this business is never look back, and if you do you're a dink yourself.

Okay, so I get back to the office and even Henry the blind guy can see my regular self I'm not. He says maybe I ought to get an appointment with a urologist because I'm almost that age. It's got nothing to do with my spigot, I tell him.

So I go up to my office, get cleaned up, and sit in my big swivel chair, looking out the window at the commuter dinks pouring out of their office buildings and heading home to their swimming pools, cable TVs, and headachy wives.

I keep chuckling over my little scam and then I get to wondering what would happen if she ever saw me again and maybe just seeing the look on her face would be worth a big laugh, so I head for the airport. It isn't too hard to find her; there aren't that many flights to Sioux City. I find her sitting in the lounge waiting for a stand-by seat. She looks plenty different with no eye shadow, no big hat, no shades, no nothing, just her. She's all Iowa and she looks it now, with her big brown peepers full of being scared, and freckles on her nose. Her hair is straw yellow and kind of mussed up. I come up to her real slow, watching her eyes.

When she sees me she covers her mouth and gives a little yelp. She stands up and it looks like she's going to run, but all of a sudden her body starts shaking all over and her knees buckle and so she sits back down, never once taking her big brown peepers off me. I looks down at her and smiles and says, ain't it funny how we keep bumping into each other. She tries to speak, but all that comes out of her mouth is a squeaking sound, and for some stupid reason I start to feel sorry for her even though she's a dink—which is against the P.I.'s creed but I can't help myself—so I get her a drink of water and let her get used to the idea that I'm not a ghost.

She swallows the water in big gulps, then she like straightens out some invisible wrinkles in her skirt and she looks up at me all soft and trembling and says, okay she had it coming for playing games with me and she was sorry about that. She got into the whirlwind, she says, and even when she knew it was getting out of hand she didn't want to spoil the fun. She said she knew it was dumb and stupid, but she operated a feed store fifty weeks a year, sixty hours a week, and this crazy ninny she knew named Ethel Muller who teaches school got this totally zany idea of an adventurers' club after she saw Indiana Jones. She swore she'd never have nothing to do with Ethel Muller again if only I wouldn't have her arrested. She'd get on the plane and go back to Iowa and never come back to Frisco—San Francisco—again.

Shaddap, I says.

She looks at me for a long minute and I give her my iciest stare that's been known to shrivel the dorsal fin of a shark. Then I asks what makes her think I'm cretin enough to buy this doggie piddle? I show her the picture of the bird I pulled off the cover of the book. I says: You think I'd forget this trinket that easy? If you run a feed store in Iowa, I'm Ronald Reagan's wigmaker. Look, I says: The fat man came to call this afternoon and I had to fake getting iced so he'd put his attentions elsewhere. Sorry you had to get mixed up in this goulash. I traced the bird last night from Samuels Jewelers to the Chinatown Wax Museum— which by the way has been turned into a McDonalds. What's that tell you? McDonalds in Chinatown! Something's stinko, catch? By the way, I figured out who you really are, Ms. Wonder Hopp-O'Hara-O'Shaughnessy-O'Brady, so you can stop the yarn spinning.

Oh, she says, and who am I?

You're a Kemidov, granddaughter of the old Russian general in Constantinople, and the rightful heir and now the legal owner of the bird.

Her yap clamps shut. A giggle escapes her lips.

I says we better lay low for a while, then check out the dancing tonight at the Sir Francis Drake and see who follows us, how's that? Maybe we have a little dinner at that Chinatown McDonalds. I tell her that twisted rabbi she put me on to might be a lead. Then later, I says, we might head down by the wharf. They got another wax museum down there and we maybe ought to give a look-see, huh? So I says: Well, what do you say—Kitty Kemidov?

She puts her arm around me on the way back to the city in the cab and gives me a little kiss on the cheek, which proves what? Nothing truly, except maybe that if you're gonna be a San Francisco shamus you can't always go by the rules, and you're a dumb dink if you try.

Reflections on Evil

A Letter from a Far Place
Lester Gorn

Poland: October 1944

Maintaining the proper interval, the troops trudged through the gently rolling hills in two files along the shoulders of the paved road. The murky light blurred their movements. Lead elements of the strung-out column were lost to view beyond the crest of a long, steep grade.

Striding down the center of the road between the two files, *Kapitan* Kurt Haekel scanned the faces of the men. The column had been on the move for two days, but neither fatigue nor the slanting rain had disheartened them. With the rain had come surcease from cold and respite from battle. The proximity of the road to the railroad tracks might attract planes, but poor visibility made a strafing attack unlikely. Nor did the countryside pose a threat. Polish partisans rarely operated in daylight, and the Russians were too far away to worry about. Artillery fire to the south and east could scarcely be heard. Reconnaissance planes had reported no significant enemy movement.

Kurt's SS Division—once at full strength with over 500 tanks—now could field only 150. The regiment had been ordered to pull back, turn over their remaining tanks to Division, and then move north to take up reserve positions in the Wolgard sector. Some replacement tanks in reasonably good condition would be waiting for them at Wolgard. Newly formed crews would test the weapons, check out equipment, fuse into teams. The men would be able to bathe, shave, eat hot meals, wash their rancid clothes, and sleep snug and dry in requisitioned houses. Only after they were rested would they be called on to load ammunition, fuel, rations and water for the battle ahead. Officers and crewmen without tanks would be utilized as infantry, and they would be readily available as replacements when casualties occurred.

The troops started up the grade. Their faces were drawn, their eyelids heavy. The harsh light prompted them to squint when they looked into the distance. The river, Kurt knew, lay beyond the crest. Word had come down the line that the railroad bridge over the river had been knocked out by partisans during the night, and that a northbound train was stranded there until the bridge could be repaired. Possibly, the train was carrying perishable food. If so, the troops might be able to load up their rucksacks. The extra weight would only have to be carried for a few hours. Wolgard was seven kilometers beyond the bridge.

They arrived at the crest, and the valley came into view. On the downward slope, the road curved through the dead brown grass toward the railroad tracks, then veered to run north alongside the tracks through the valley, flanked on the east by a bleak, mist-shrouded forest.

A kilometer ahead, the parallel routes—road and rail—crossed the river, which flowed from east to west across the valley floor. Both the railroad bridge and the two-lane bridge serving the road had been sabotaged. Explosives had turned the two-lane bridge into a mass of shattered concrete and twisted steel. The railroad bridge had sustained relatively minor damage. Although one end had collapsed, engineers would be able to elevate it within three or four days.

Downstream from the sabotaged spans, a pontoon bridge had been thrown across the river. Advance elements of the column already were crossing over it.

The locomotive had been hauling a first-class passenger car and a string of boxcars. Now the boxcar doors were open. About a thousand civilians had been offloaded and put to work digging tank traps on the river's south bank. Train guards had set up machine gun posts atop the cars and on knolls overlooking the work site.

Catching up with Kurt, *Obersturmführer* Ludwig Francke fell into step beside him. He nodded toward the train guards. "SS-*Totenkopfverbande*," he said. "Swine. Their war is with civilians. Deportees."

"Jews?

"Probably. Or politicals or homosexuals or Gypsies." Ludwig's voice took on a sardonic edge. "Or intellectuals—clergy, teachers, writers."

"Careful, Ludwig," Kurt said. "Such talk is not—prudent."

"And let's not forget the deformed and retarded. Eaters who toil not, neither do they spin."

Kurt scowled. Over the past year, he'd repeatedly warned Ludwig that his freewheeling talk was dangerous. Granted, there might be some truth in his grumbling, but it was a truth distorted by ugly rumors and exaggeration—even tales about "death camps" where people were gassed and burned in ovens. No government could be expected to put up with sedition, especially in wartime.

How Ludwig had passed muster at SS Cadet School was a mystery. An unsightly facial scar had won him soldierly admiration until the day he'd proudly explained he'd sustained it "honorably"—in an auto accident, he said, rather than in a duel. He lacked command bearing. No amount of practice shouting could confer resonance on that squeaky voice. An architect in civilian life, he reportedly had been discharged by a renowned architectural firm after it became apparent his vision was at odds with the massive edifices of the New Germany. No wonder other officers shied from contact with him.

As Kurt and Ludwig reached the midpoint of the downward slope, the work site along the river came into clear perspective. Even in the gray light, it could be seen that many of the civilians were women and children.

"We all must work for the greater glory of the Reich," Ludwig said, *sotto voce*. "We cannot—must not—countenance idle hands."

Kurt groped for some innocuous words—any words at all—to cover his foreboding. He said evenly: "Why tank traps here, so far south?"

Ludwig shrugged. "A mystery."

They fell silent.

The silence lasted until they neared the first boxcar. A sanitation detail had just started its task. Guards kept their dogs under leash as they supervised the removal of the dead—four or five bodies in each car. Workers—women as well as men—tugged the corpses to the open doors, then lowered them to the ground. Both the workers and the dead wore the yellow Star of David patch.

Some bodies were swollen, others emaciated. Bloat had stretched fabrics, displaced buttons. Flesh had turned color: gray, blue, mauve. The queasy-sweet smell licked at Kurt's throat. He could taste it.

"Stand-up casualties, from the looks of them." Ludwig wiped rainwater from his neck. "Overloaded. Delays along the route. Suffocation."

Two workers started to ease a girl's body to the ground. Apparently, their journey had weakened them. Although the body was slight, it slipped from their grasp and tumbled into the muck. An arm flopped onto the shoulder of a male corpse nearby. Decorously, one worker pulled down the girl's soggy skirt to cover the lower thigh.

"Also," Ludwig said, "malnutrition, strokes, miscarriages."

As the soldiers plodded past the first boxcar, the reek of excrement assailed them. Slop buckets in the cars had over-flowed. The floors were slippery with blood, urine, feces, vomit.

The soldiers shook their heads in disgust as they moved down the line. The corpses were piling up. Some of the workers were handling the bodies roughly, as if to disavow sentiment. Their faces were coarse, their movements furtive. They paused only to scratch at crotches or open sores or matted hair. They avoided eye contact.

To keep his voice steady, Kurt concentrated on the pragmatic. "Where did they get all the entrenching tools, I wonder?"

"A quartermaster depot, probably."

"Out here in the middle of nowhere?"

An angry voice rang out. In the field across the road, an unusually tall SS officer—patently the train commander—was badgering *Standartenführer* Kaspar Friedrich Eigen. He edged so close that the regimental commander was forced to take a backward step.

"What's going on?" Kurt asked Ludwig.

"Let's find out."

Dropping out of the column, they joined the aides clustered around the two senior officers.

The train commander, *Standartenführer* Wolfgang Dietrich, shook a manicured finger at Colonel Eigen. "May I remind you that my mission has priority over routine troop movements." Despite the drizzle, Dietrich's dress uniform—rarely worn in the field—seemed to retain its creases and the belt its shine. The three plaited threads on his shoulder tabs and the oak leaf on each collar shed silver, runic light on his sleek black uniform. His black cap bore the silvery death's head. A trim moustache and a high-domed forehead gave distinction to his face. "It will take three days to repair the bridge. My Jews cannot wait. They are scheduled for special treatment no later than noon tomorrow. To upset the schedule is to impose a strain on camp facilities."

Kurt tensed. No. No. It could not be true. Special treatment did not mean what the rumormongers distorted it to mean. It had to do with processing—showers, delousing, fresh clothing, housing, work assignments. It could not be a euphemism for systematic slaughter.

Somewhere, a baby cried. Kurt peered into the gathering mist. The site resounded with the chink of shovels and the rumbling of wheelbarrows. Already, the excavations ran deep. People working inside the pits were lost to view, but Kurt could see the rise and fall of their picks. At ground level, children and the elderly—the less able-bodied—were hauling dirt in buckets to a rampart on the river line.

Nearby, one of the workers—a gnarled, pockmarked man wearing an incongruous double-breasted, pinstriped suit—dropped to his hands and knees to lap up water from a puddle.

As Kurt watched, a guard—pleasant face, stalwart bearing—opened his fly and urinated an amber stream that landed half a meter from the worker's face. Startled, the worker raised his head. Quickly, he wrenched his mouth into a grin, as if to demonstrate gratitude for the opportunity to provide an amusing distraction.

It was at that moment that Kurt's longtime oblivion—rotten at its core—fell apart. Shock brought cold sweat to his brow as he acknowledged that rumors of gas chambers almost certainly were true—and, moreover, that he'd known they probably were true for at least two years.

"The camp is forty kilometers north," the train commander said. "A full day's march. A thousand Jews can be a security problem, especially at night. Some of them are Poles. They know the country and its language. I need help. Surely you can provide thirty men for escort duty."

"My men can't be spared, *Standartenführer* Dietrich."

"Twenty, then. They can be trucked back by 0100 tomorrow afternoon. I'll lay on transport for them."

The scarred, leathery Eigen flicked dry mud from his field uniform. "No."

"Be reasonable, Colonel! Deportees have to be processed in orderly fashion. The quotas must be met! It is the *Führer's* wish."

"My orders are to proceed to Wolgard—a two-hour march— and reorganize the regiment with all possible speed."

Dietrich fell back on sweet reason. "Look at it as a *quid pro quo*. I build tank traps for you. You lend escorts to me."

Col. Eigen ran out of patience. "The battle, *Standartenführer*, will be decided on the plain northeast of Wolgard. I suggest you wrap up your antediluvian tank traps and carry them there."

Dietrich looked down his long, slender nose. His eyes were pale and opaque. "When I report your attitude to my good friend, *Reichsführer* Himmler, he will not be pleased."

The angle of Eigen's stubbled jaw did not alter. He nodded toward the aluminum chevron on his right sleeve. "That chevron, Herr *Standartenführer*, is awarded to old fighters only. My party number is 8414. Do you know where that puts me? In the vanguard! When you were home sipping schnapps, I was out in the streets handing out leaflets, begging for donations, enduring insults and police harassment!"

"Apparently you do not understand the situation, Colonel. Berlin is determined to end the *Vaterland's* lingering pestilence. It now grants rail transport of deportees its highest priority."

A shout interrupted his pitch.

Kurt looked toward the siding. A guard lashed out with his whip at a swarthy worker who was raising a canteen to his lips. Even as the whip struck, the worker drank greedily. Water trickled from his cracked lips and down his chin. As Kurt ran forward, the whip whistled down again. The worker cowered. The canteen fell from his hands.

Kurt pushed past the soldiers gathered around the guard. "What's going on?"

The guard snapped to attention. "A thief, sir."

An indignant soldier spoke up. "The Jew stole my canteen, sir. I was walking by and he grabbed it out of my hand."

Kurt looked at the worker. His eyes were black pebbles. He stank. Reaching, Kurt unfastened his own canteen and held it out. The worker gaped. Then, reassured, he seized it. With shaking hands, he unscrewed the cap. His raw fingers resembled claws. He drank avidly, deeply.

A hand snatched the canteen from the worker's lips. Water splashed over the rim to the ground. "*Verboten,*" Dietrich said to Kurt. "Nothing may be given the prisoners without my express consent."

"*Jawohl!*" Fearing abhorrence would show in his eyes, Kurt avoided looking directly at Dietrich. "I hereby request your consent."

"Denied," Dietrich said.

Col. Eigen appeared at his elbow. "What's the problem?"

Gunfire from the excavation site aborted Dietrich's reply. About thirty deportees—mostly young—were bolting for the nearby woods. As Kurt watched, clattering machine guns brought down half of them. Police dogs caught up with three others—one snarling leap and the quarry fell. Fangs tore hunks of flesh. The survivors disappeared in the forest.

"After them!" Col. Dietrich cried.

Kurt looked at his regimental commander. Col. Eigen nodded.

Kurt drew his Luger. He and Sgt. Multcher, followed by a dozen men, sprinted across the field into the woods.

"Spread out," Sgt. Multcher called.

The men scattered. Sgt. Multcher vanished into the underbrush.

Alone, unobserved, Kurt slowed to a walk. To some extent, the trees had protected the forest floor from the rain. Dead leaves yielded to Kurt's boots. He was lulled by the spongy ground, the tangled foliage, the hazy sky patching the spaces separating the dripping oaks and pines. To become one with the forest and its gray mists was to palliate the revulsion and grief raging in his heart, and to shroud the periodic shots that signaled a capture or a summary execution, and to give remoteness to the train and its commander and its cargo.

From behind him, he heard the sound of twigs snapping underfoot. He whirled in time to glimpse a hulking figure closing in on him with an upraised club.

Instinctively, Kurt fired. The shot echoed in the moist, gray air. The assailant fell.

Kurt stood over him. The club—a fallen branch—was about three inches thick. The man he had taken to be a giant actually was slight and middle-aged. He lay in a hollow at the base of a stump. His pale hands were blistered, his nails broken. His eyes were closed. The bullet had mangled his stomach.

Alerted by the shot, two soldiers came crashing through the underbrush. Kurt gestured that no help was needed. With a glance at the dying Jew, they went off to resume their search.

Kurt raised his Luger to administer the *coup de grace*.

"Anna," the man murmured.

His tender tone gave Kurt pause. He looked at the man's face. The graying beard was flecked with mud, the sallow skin torn by thorns. The mouth seeped blood and spit. Yet the face— particularly the nose and lips—had a delicacy that could not be ascribed solely to the fall of light or the onset of death.

The man's eyes opened. His lashes were long and glossy. He looked up at Kurt with loathing. The lips moved. The words were slurred, unintelligible.

Kurt holstered the Luger. Dropping to one knee, he took off his helmet.

No fear appeared in the red-veined eyes. "You look human," the dying man said in German. "A man like other men."

Gathering his strength, he sucked air into his lungs. "If you exist," he said, shaping each word, "God does not." The effort drained him of remaining life. He sagged.

Kurt listened to the stillness. He set down his helmet. Then his hand went to the worn envelope in the man's jacket pocket. The envelope bore American stamps. It was postmarked "Chapel Hill, N.C." and dated August 2, 1939, a month before the invasion of Poland. Carefully, Kurt drew out a three-page, ink-smeared letter addressed to Prof. Joachim Horner at the University of Warsaw. Constant handling had caused one crease to come apart. The letter had been written by the Professor's niece, Serena. Although Kurt had studied English at the gymnasium, he was far from fluent, and it took him ten minutes or more to complete the translation:

> *We're worried more and more about the prospect of war. Is there news of relatives in Russia? I'm afraid to write to them. I don't want to get them in trouble. But it's you who worries me the most. It's been twelve years — twelve years! — since you visited here, yet I can still hear your laugh. Amazing, the impression an uncle can make on a ten-year-old girl.*
>
> *I cannot bear the thought that you may be caught in Warsaw by the Nazis. Why must you persist in regarding yourself as a German in exile? I beg you, Uncle Joachim, to stop dreaming about a return to what you call the Fatherland.*
>
> *Along with copies of our financial statement and our 1938 income tax report, I enclose a notarized affidavit assuming responsibility for the livelihood of your family. By this time, the Warsaw Embassy should have received the letter from the University of North Carolina. The earlier your visa is approved, I'm told, the higher your priority number.*
>
> *Father has sent similar documents to Uncle Peter in*

Prague and Uncle Alfred in Vienna. I understand your reluctance to accept a part-time position, but many scholars in the humanities share your plight. After a year or two, you may well win a full time post—at Harvard or elsewhere—in keeping with your eminence in the field.

It would be an exaggeration to say we are prosperous, but there is time for books and music, tennis and picnics. And Ricky, Laura's son, gives us much joy. Although Laura's husband is in the army and seldom home on leave, Ricky— now 3—is the happiest boy on earth. Nothing fazes him. He has no fear of the steep slide at the playground or the up-and-down horses on the merry-go-round. He takes delight in a flower, a pebble, a crawling ant. It would be wonderful if he were to acquire an uncle, an aunt and cousins he never has seen.

We pray for you, Uncle Joachim, and for your dear wife and children.

Serena

Kurt gazed for a while at a sparrow perched on the branch of a huge oak. The ground sloped down and away from the oak, as if burdened by its weight. Kurt straightened. Unhooking his pick-mattock, he set about digging a grave. Under the moist topsoil, the pick encountered tangled root systems that had to be severed. When *Oberscharführer* Multcher ran across Kurt, the grave was less than a meter deep. So intent was Kurt on his task that he did not sense the sergeant's presence.

"Sir?" the sergeant said.

"Yes?"

"Are you, uh, all right?"

He kept digging.

"We tracked down most of them, sir." Sgt. Multcher's eyes held perplexity and concern. "It's time to get back to the column now."

"I'm all right, Sergeant." Kurt gestured with the entrenching tool. "Reasons of hygiene."

"*Jawohl.*" He drew a necklace from his jacket pocket and dangled it from his fingers. "Picked up a souvenir, sir."

"Very nice," Kurt said.

"Real pearls, I think. Magda will love it. My Jew had it hidden in his jacket lining." He hesitated. "If you wish, sir, I'll finish the digging for you."

"No. Go on back, Sergeant. I'll be along shortly."

The sergeant left.

Kurt was tamping down the earth of the grave when he heard heavy machine gun fire.

He ran back through the woods toward the clearing.

Emerging from the woods near the riverbank, he stopped short. Train guards had stripped the Jews of their valuables—watches, money, jewelry, dolls, toys—and piled them by the tracks. Now they were being annihilated. Since every fifth round was a tracer, the lethal streams were visible. Machine guns hosed down one group, then traversed to hose down the next. When one gun misfired or became overheated, another picked up the tempo. As one belt was expended, a new one was locked in with scarcely a pause.

Half the Jews already had been cut down. The work site reverberated with shouts and screams. Those who could reach the tank traps had taken shelter there, out of reach of flat trajectory fire. Some were burrowing among the corpses. Others had fled through the slanting rain to the river.

The fire zones constantly shifted. A bloc of people frantically pushing north toward the river came up against a bloc of people pushing south toward the excavations. Stalemate. Panic. A woman stumbled and was trampled underfoot. Children wailed. An old man at the edge of the crowd knelt to pray. The crowd surged over him.

Disregarding the danger from stray bullets, some soldiers at the pontoon bridge lighted their cigarettes and watched the show and took pot shots at Jews attempting to swim across the river. Bullets kicked the surface and found bobbing heads, streaking the water red. Swimmers dove under water to elude the fire. Snipers bet cigarettes on where they would reappear. One swimmer—a girl—showed exceptional strength and endurance. Diving deep in midstream, she stayed hidden from view for nearly two minutes. She broke the rain-pelted surface within ten feet of the northern bank. Seconds later, her head disintegrated into a pulp of tissue, bone and hair.

Kurt felt a hand touch his elbow.

"You'd better get down, sir." Sgt. Multcher spoke loudly so he could be heard above the din. "Poor fire control. Ricochets, too."

Kurt came aware of the bullets thwacking into nearby stumps and tree trunks.

Looking across the field, Kurt saw Col. Eigen accost the train commander. From Eigen's forceful gestures, it was clear that he was making a protest, and that he was overriding Col. Dietrich's every objection.

As Kurt started across the field toward the two senior officers, the gunfire momentarily lifted. Guards sporting whips moved among the survivors. Singling out the younger, stronger Jews, the guards ordered them to dump the dead into designated tank traps. Those who refused or hesitated were summarily shot. Most readily obeyed.

Forcibly separating the wedged-together bodies, the youths carried or dragged them to the excavations. There were glimpses of heads without faces, faces without eyes. As bodies toppled over the parapets, some still showed life—a moan, a tremor, a lifted hand.

Guards cradling submachine guns moved in from the perimeter to tidy up. Standing at the edges of the pits, their feet slightly apart, their forearms braced, the guards inclined their weapons at a diagonal from the hip and triggered their lethal bursts, silencing the cries.

Then, for no apparent reason: a lull.

A strange calm set in among those who thus far had survived. Some were dazed or numbed by terror, cold and rain. Others seemed resigned. Most simply waited. They neither wept nor pleaded nor complained. A mother crouched to rock and hug a shivering four-year-old girl as her husband, fighting tears, looked on. An elderly couple, holding hands, quietly talked. A young woman stroked a baby as she sang to it. The baby gurgled. A teenage girl clung to a teenage boy. He maneuvered to block her view of the youths manhandling the bodies, and used his free hand to point to a moving cloud. She looked up and nodded.

The two senior officers still were arguing heatedly. Ludwig, looking on, nodded to Kurt as he arrived.

The train commander said: "First, Col. Eigen, you refuse to provide escorts, forcing me to resort to a distasteful alternative. Now you presume to interfere with my operation."

Eigen said: "Do you expect me to sit by and let your incompetence endanger my men?"

It took a few seconds for Kurt to understand the import of Col. Eigen's question. He had assumed the regimental commander objected to the liquidation on moral grounds. The actual reason, he now realized, was faulty fire control. Stunned, he glanced at Ludwig Francke. The lieutenant was staring at the two senior officers with loathing.

Eigen said: "Either you'll reposition your guns, Col. Dietrich, or I'll do it myself!"

Ludwig had the temerity to intervene. "If you wish, sir," he told Col. Eigen, "I'll find twenty volunteers to escort the prisoners to the camp."

Dietrich said quickly: "Very good of you, Lieutenant."

"Out of the question," Eigen said.

Kurt took a step forward. He gazed directly into the regimental commander's level eyes. "Sir," he said. "I respectfully request you to reconsider."

Col. Eigen returned his gaze. "Indeed? Why?"

"If you consent to provide escorts, sir, the massacre will end."

"What difference, Capt. Haeckel, whether the massacre—as you call it—occurs here or at the camps?" Eigen's voice was icy. "Is the liquidation more acceptable if it occurs out of your sight?"

Kurt stared at him. Then, turning, he walked blindly toward the tree line.

As he neared the sheltering forest, the machine guns resumed firing. The teenage boy and girl went down in the first burst.

Fleeing the sound of the guns, Kurt plunged into the labyrinth. He ran wildly, blindly. Low-hanging branches tore at him, inflicting cuts and scratches. He splashed through streams, scrambled over logs. He bumped into trees and tripped over roots. He ran until he could run no more. He sat down on a stump. Now the gunfire behind him was sporadic. Col. Dietrich's operation was all but complete. The mop-up should not take long.

Blue lightning forked through the sky. From somewhere nearby, Kurt heard a wailing sound. He scanned the trees.

It took him some time to realize the sound was his own.

🙰

He still was sitting on the stump an hour later, when Sgt. Multcher bulldozed through the brush into the clearing.

"We're moving out, sir," the sergeant said.

147

Kurt, hunched forward, did not respond. His eyes were intent on the insect life at his feet.

"Col. Eigen was asking about you," the sergeant said.

Kurt's head slowly lifted. "Col. Eigen?"

"Yes, sir." The sergeant pulled a flask from his jacket pocket. "I have some schnapps, *Herr Kapitan*, if that would help."

Accepting the flask, Kurt drank.

"Finish it off, sir, if you like."

"No." Kurt capped the flask and returned it. "Thank you, Sergeant."

"I am honored, *Herr Kapitan* Haeckel."

Kurt stared at him. "Honored," he said.

"*Jawohl, Herr Kapitan.*"

"Because I shared your schnapps."

"*Ja.* And because of who and what you are."

" —who and what I am."

"*Ja.*"

"*Wunderbar.*" Kurt considered. "If I inspire honor, I must exist."

"Sir?"

"No matter." Rising heavily to his feet, Kurt set off in the direction of the bridge. Sgt. Multcher fell in behind him.

"I exist," Kurt said fiercely.

"*Jawohl, Herr Kapitan,*" said Sgt. Multcher.

"Positively," Kurt said. "Inerrantly. Even if God does not."

"*Jawohl, Herr Kapitan,*" said Sgt. Multcher.

Where True Love Can Take You
James N. Frey

My name is Debby Jax, the one you been hearing so much about on the news. It's my full intention to tell the whole truth and nothing but the truth, so help me, God. Somebody's got to know my side of it. The newspapers and them TV shows have been telling so damn many lies, including photos showing me on the Riviera. I am definitely not on no Riviera. I'm about a million miles away from the Riviera.

Okay, it started a long time ago when I fell in love with the wrong guy and he's the one turned me on to the bad stuff and I want you to know exactly how that happened.

I met Charles King—that's what he called himself—at the Lazy S, a bar down on State Route 42. I was sitting there with my best friend, Cindy Lou, nursing a cold draft. The door was open, and you could see the sun just going down over the western hills, the sky turning that deep purple it does at sundown, which many people like, but to me, it always looked sort of ugly. A warm breeze was blowing in, warm and dry, the kind that makes your skin itch.

Anyways, I was looking out the door thinking how I'd love to find out what in hell was on the other side of them hills some day when I seen Charles King come in and, bam! I started turning all gushy inside.

He was dressed clean and neat, a cotton plaid cowboy shirt and jeans, his wavy, to-die-for blond hair like shimmering in the strobe lights. He had an easy way about him, moving slow and graceful. He came over to our table and asked polite if he could sit and Cindy Lou said sure, even though he wasn't looking at Cindy Lou like most of the men did. Cindy Lou had a lot up front, and she wore low-cut blouses to show off what she had. Me, as you probably seen on TV, I'm a little on the skinny side and a little flat. Cindy Lou weren't no prettier than me, though— I mean in the face. I got a nice face, heart-shaped, and most everybody tells me I got nice eyes. They're robin's-egg blue.

Charles had a square, handsome face and nice, even, white teeth. My ma said once that a man that cares for his teeth will care for you. He tipped his new-looking, brown cowboy hat on the back of his head and said he was from Arkansas, new to the desert west, and liked it just fine.

He had soft hands, no calluses at all. Not used to hard work, I figured. Probably worked with his head. He looked smart. He kept staring at me, like he knew me or something. Knew me, or wanted me, and I felt this little tingle of excitement. I knew right then I wanted him, even though he was a little older. I always went for older guys.

I wanted him even though I knew there was something that scared me about him, something I couldn't quite explain even to myself. But that only made me tingle all the more. I was sick to death of sitting around on my ass in Jackson, Nevada, while my life just melted away like an ice cube in a stale drink.

Charles drank only a certain kind of bottled beer—Sierra Nevada Lager—and he drank it slow, with a look of concentration and pleasure on his face.

Cindy Lou, leaning over and showing off her nice cleavage, asked him what he was doing around Jackson. Charles hardly looked at her, saying something about finding a little land to buy, not taking his eyes off me, I swear. And then he added that he was always looking for some excitement and he had a feeling I was too.

It was the way he said it, like he meant it. Like he could read my mind. Me, I was nineteen with a runny-nose kid and a fuck-off husband that took off with a lady Greyhound bus driver. My life was about as un-exciting as you could get. Doing office work for a goddamn exterminator. Killer Rodale, he called himself— he was on the news too, saying what a low-life I was, as you know. What you don't know is Killer Rodale loved to pat me on the ass with his fat little hands every chance he got. It was like being in prison in that stinky office all day and I was busting at the seams for some excitement.

That first night, the way Charles went on about life being meant to be thrilling to those who took hold of it sent my goddamn heart to pounding. He talked about how he once went all the way to Africa on a freighter. And how another time he drove a race car on a real, paved track. He said he even met Prince Charles in person at a casino in Monte Carlo. He said a lot of things that got me pumped.

Then, while Cindy Lou was dancing with some cowhand, he reached over and took my hand, looking at it like he was reading all about me in the palm. I could see then he was older than I first thought.

He was maybe thirty, maybe even thirty-five, but that was okay with me; the young jerks I knew did their thinking with their cocks. Their idea of excitement was doing it in the bed of a pick-up truck.

Charles looked real serious all of a sudden, still studying my hand hard, and asked me if I believed in Satan. I said I never gave it much thought, but I didn't think so.

I must have looked a little scared, him talking like that, because suddenly he smiled and said that his last girlfriend believed in Satan and that's all she could talk about. How Satan was tempting him and how he needed Jesus in his life. He said he just wanted to make sure I didn't have the same hang-up.

I told him I didn't go to church. Not that I thought it was a bad thing. I just never went. He said he was glad of that.

Later that night me and Charles danced close and he smelled real good, real manly. Dancing, he was easy to follow. We glided around the floor like we'd been practicing a year. Under his shirt, I could feel his muscles; his body was lean and hard. When the music stopped, he kissed me on the lips, just a little one, but it made me sort of woozy inside and I knew right then I was really going to fall hard for him, even though there was a little voice somewhere telling me to go slow.

After a while Cindy Lou left with a foreman from the water company, a married guy she fooled around with once in a while. He pleasured her good, she told me; that's why she went out with him. He knew what she liked.

Me and Charles left about eleven, neither of us drunk, and drove out into the desert and looked at the stars. I told him about how fucked up my family was, my mom being a compulsive hand washer, my dad loving cough medicine. Stuff I never talked to nobody about, but Charles just had a way of getting me to talk about the serious stuff, how my old man's half-brother, a retard who lived with us, used to come into my room sometimes and jerk off, but he never touched me. And how my first boy friend—I was about twelve—ripped me when he went in the first time I did it with anybody. Hurt like hell, got blood all over his mother's nice, new couch. I never told nobody about that before. Charles didn't laugh or nothing. He said he understood how scared I must have been, being understanding.

All Charles said about himself was that his old man took off when he was a kid and he grew up with nothing and now he figured life was short and you had to cram all the living you had into a few years. He talked about how society put you in a little box of boredom and you had to make your break for freedom on your own. I just kept saying how right he was. Goddamn right.

We smoked a joint, really good Maui-wowie, then he got a sleeping bag out of the trunk and put it on the ground under the stars and he went down on me for what felt like at least an hour before he went in me. I came and came and came, like it was never going to stop. No man had ever pleasured me like that before.

I got home at dawn. My ma was pissed as hell because she was babysitting and I'd told her I'd be back at midnight. She ragged on me for an hour before I finally told her to stuff it, I was going to bed.

Charles didn't come around the next day like he said he was going to, and at first I was worried he might have skated on me. Then when he didn't come the next day or the next, I started to get pissed. He came on Thursday night after my kid was asleep, bringing me a single white rose. He said he'd been called away on business. I was so happy to see him, I forgot about being pissed and started quivering all over. He was barely in the house when we ripped off our clothes and started doing it on the living room floor like we'd been prisoners in a monastery for ten years.

After, we laid on the bed and just talked and had a few beers, him making little circles with his fingers around my nipples. I asked him about his tattoo, a jagged star he said he got in prison. A preacher in the joint said if he wore that on his chest, he'd one day see the devil and Charles said he was looking forward to it.

We laughed about that.

The next day he called and said he'd rented a place and I should come on Saturday. I had to work in the morning, but I told him I'd be there maybe about two. It was hell getting a sitter.

My kid had the miseries, but finally I got my ma to do it by promising to get the kid into some fucking head-start bullshit program she wanted him in.

Okay, so I went with Charles to his place. It was a ten-mile drive on a rutted dirt road, out past the stone quarry. The road used to go to the salt company that's been closed up for fifty years. He had a trailer parked there all by itself, a big wide one, in a cottonwood grove by a little, dried-up creek.

He made some margaritas and we drank them sitting outside. We did a few lines of coke, the kind that makes you light as air, and after we stripped naked and laid on a big flat rock down by the creek and I felt like I was up in the sky flying with the birds. He told me that it felt like we'd known each other in another life and we'd recognized each other right off. I never believed in that stuff before, but when he said it, I felt it was true because I'd felt something strong between us that first night in the Lazy S. I felt something, too, when he made love to me; it was like we really went into some weird zone. It was magical.

Going home after that weekend to a sickly, whiny kid and a stupid job was about as hard a thing as I'd ever done. Charles called me a few times over the next week or so, said he was busy with business, but he'd see me again as soon as he could. I never asked him what his business was. I didn't care nothing about it. I just wanted to be with him.

It was the first Saturday night in June that things got strange. We went to a couple of bars and were drinking heavy, both of us. He seemed edgy, like he was on something. In the Shamrock, a used-car salesman named Tucker was being too loud telling dirty jokes and Charles told him to shut up or he'd rip his throat out. The man turned red. He knew Charles meant it. Charles had that intensity about him. Inside, like a hate he could squeeze down into a terrible force.

Later, Charles bought a bottle of tequila and some limes and we drove around for a while, then stopped in the old cemetery just north of town, parked, and walked through the busted iron gate, me holding Charles' hand like it was a rope and I was hanging from a cliff. I told him I wanted to get the hell out of there, but he said it was important: he had to teach me something. We sat on a tomb from the pioneer days. I was feeling creepy, but he said you couldn't be free until you faced your worst fears and stood up to them. Then he took hold of my shoulders and said I just had to face up to the fact that I was going to die some day. To be really free, he said, you got to realize that. Once you face it, once you say, okay, if I die, I die, but I'm going to live free until I die, then you can be really free.

That's when he said he wanted us to die together. He said it almost in a whisper and I felt a chill come over me, and then he laid me back down on the cool marble and he laid beside me, holding my hand, and said we should imagine being dead, but being together through all eternity. He loved me that much.

I was feeling real, real creepy, but then he kissed me, and said we didn't have to be scared of death no more because death is what separates people from each other and we're never going to be separated. Then he started undoing my jeans and he fucked me right there, bare-assed, on that cold marble. He did it slow and easy, like it was some kind of a pagan ritual, and the chill I was feeling seemed to fold over me, like death itself had put its bony arms around me. It was strange, but I felt suddenly close to death and it didn't scare me no more, and the chill just flowed out of me and I said I'd love him forever and I wanted to die with him and be with him through all eternity. This made him smile and laugh and then he came and I did too.

We left the cemetery singing a silly song about walking in the graveyard we more or less made up. I knew then that I'd changed, that I was no longer the same woman I'd been, that I'd passed some sort of test and from now on life was going to be totally different.

It was the next day, with my kid whining in the back seat, that he let me drive his old 300 ZX up in the mountains. On them curvy two-lane county roads. He kept putting his foot on top of mine, making me go faster and faster. When the tires squealed and the car started sliding around the curves, I started screaming, but Charles, he was laughing and saying that to live you had to cross over into the place where fear can't get you and, damn, if after a while I started feeling high, my heart racing as I nosed into the curves, the tires screeching like a rock band as we sailed along the sharp cliffs. Better than any coke. Better than sex. Better than anything.

When we came down from the lake near Carson a cop got us. He lectured me on driving like that with the kid in the car, but I didn't give a shit. The kid was in the back seat strapped in real good and seemed to be liking it.

The ticket didn't mean nothing. I'd write my old man up in Idaho and he'd pay the ticket to keep me out of jail.

After we got out of sight of the cop, down on the straight stretch through the flats heading back to Reno, I was hitting a hundred and thirty and even Charles seemed a little tight, but he laughed a forced laugh, which made me feel good. Hell, my kid went to sleep. I unzipped my pants and had Charles put his hand in there to pleasure me as we went flying across the flats, the speedometer needle buried, the desert flying by in a blur. My skin felt on fire. I was tingling all over and it felt like the top of my head was gonna blow right off like a mountain going volcanic.

I left the kid at home and told the neighbor to check on him.

When we got back to his place, me and Charles fucked for a couple of hours until we were both sweaty and exhausted and fell asleep in each other's arms on his bed.

When I got home the next day my ma was waiting with a welfare lady who had a legal paper saying I was an unfit mother and my ma could take my kid and if I wanted him back I had to go to a hearing. That was it, they took the kid. The kid never even looked back when they put him the car.

At first I was pissed, but then I thought, hell, I had a lot of living to do and maybe being free of the kid wasn't such a bad thing. What the hell, my ma wanted him, let her have the little shit. My ma said I'd have visiting rights and see him once in a while, which was about all I could stand of him anyway.

That night me and Charles drove over to Reno and had supper at one of those fancy casino restaurants that serve roast beef you don't hardly have to chew. Then we went over to East Reno where they built this big shopping center and right on the corner is this big supermarket called Nevada Shopper. We parked outside. He smiled at me and asked me to open the glove box. Inside was this huge gun. My old man was a gun nut, and I used to go shooting and liked guns. But I didn't think Charles was going to go shooting with this and I was suddenly scared of what he might have in mind.

That's when he said he was going to take the supermarket down. Rob it, in other words. He said that being free was a matter of taking life by the balls. He said taking this supermarket down was going to be easy. They had a sack of money that an armored car picked up every night. He said before the truck came the manager was in his office loading the sack, counting the cash. Charles said this manager didn't trust nobody so he was always alone.

When the manager heard the truck pull up and beep its horn, he came down the back stairs. He always locked the door when he came to work at eight. It was super easy, Charles said, to jimmy that door and lay in wait for the manager to leave his office and go to the back door. Bing, bang, boom, it's over. We drive away and be in clover for the rest of our lives.

I had this hollow, scared feeling in my body. I told him I didn't like none of it. By Jesus, it sounded bad to me. He said he'd planned it perfect. He was going to tape the manager's mouth, tie him up good. Nobody'd get hurt.

I screamed I wanted to get the fuck out of there. He said okay and we drove away.

He took me home. The trip was over an hour. We said not one damn thing to each other until he dropped me off. Then just as I was about to get out in front of my house, he said there'd be a hundred and thirty thousand in that sack and that would buy us a hell of a lot of freedom.

I slammed the door on him.

The next day, he didn't call or come by. Not a word. A week, then two went by, and I started missing him something terrible. Killer Rodale's office felt like being trapped in a goddamn sewer. I couldn't breathe.

I wasn't sleeping good. It was weird. I couldn't get it out of my head that we could grab that bag full of money. And then there was the idea of walking in with a gun and taking it. The boldness of it made me tingle.

I hated Charles King for thinking of it. The bastard. It was causing me to have terrible sick headaches, me wanting so much to be free and scared at the same time.

Cindy Lou came over one night and we watched a video and drank some beer. It'd been the first real hot day of summer, and the beer tasted so good. She'd found a new boyfriend, a pit boss at the New Fountainhead Casino who was dealing a little coke on the side and so he had plenty of money to spend on her. After we knocked down about a six-pack each I told her she had to swear an oath never to say nothing about what I was going to tell her. She swore, and so I gave her the whole thing I'd been going through with Charles. Driving fast, fucking in the cemetery, everything. Including the idea of robbing the Nevada Shopper.

When I was finished telling her, she looked at me with a lot of fright in her eyes and said if I did something like that, I wouldn't be me any more. I'd be a criminal and there wouldn't be no turning back. I said that was something to think about, but I was sure that I could do just this one thing once, just to see what it was like, then me and Charles would take off and disappear. Maybe go to Europe or someplace, get out of this fucking desert. Get away from Killer Rodale's stinking office.

She laughed and said I'd been saying I was gonna get out of the desert since I was six years old and I was still here, and probably would still be here when they buried me.

I had to drive her home because her car was in the shop and on the way, she said I was just kidding, wasn't I, and I said sure, I wasn't no robber. But I reminded her she'd sworn not to say nothing.

Two days later I was still puzzling about it, being not able to make up my mind. Then about ten o'clock in the morning Killer Rodale put his hand on my ass as I was bending over a file cabinet. I didn't say nothing. I went into the little kitchen area we had there and boiled some water, then I went over to his office and asked if I could speak to him for a moment. He said, sure, come right in little lady, some crap like that.

I went over by his desk, keeping the pot of hot water behind my back. I stood next to him. He asked me what I had behind my back. I said it was something that was going to excite him a lot.

I reached down and ran my hand along his thigh. He said some shit like I was waking up his Elmer. That's when I asked him if he'd really like to get hot and he said he sure would.

That's when I dumped the pot of scalding water in the bastard's lap. He started out of his chair, lunging for me, then he sort of turned to the side, folded up, and flopped on the floor, screaming his head off. I jumped up and down, giggling my head off, not believing how good feeling free really was, how high being bold could make you.

That night I drove out to Charles' place and told him I'd do what he wanted me to, help him rob whatever he wanted to rob.

Two days later, me and Charles made a dry run on the supermarket so I'd know exactly what to do. It was easy. All I had to do was sit in the car with the motor running and wait for him to come out and pick him up. Charles said he'd done these things fifty times and it was all in the planning, and this was planned down to the smallest detail. All I had to do was drive and keep a clear head. I said I knew I could do it.

Charles swiped this new Buick for the job. Took it out of the parking lot at the airport so nobody'd miss it maybe for a week or two. It was a four-door Regal, gray and shiny and new-smelling. I liked driving it. Charles had switched its plates. Just being careful.

Charles seemed different now that we were actually doing it. Not scared, exactly. But cautious. Not like you'd think he'd be. Me, I was on a high. Getting a rush. It was like I'd found out what I was meant for.

We pulled into the parking lot about a quarter to ten. I was supposed to sit in the car and wait for the armored truck to pull up in back, then I was supposed to drive around to the far side and keep the passenger door open and wait for Charles, who'd be along in two minutes with the bag of money.

Then we were going to head for the freeway, driving nice and easy and natural like a housewife in her Buick done with her grocery shopping. We had a hole dug in the desert near his place; Charles told the guy with the backhoe it was for a septic tank. We were going to bury the Buick and maybe they'd find it again in a million years. God damn, but he had it all worked out neat as hell.

Charles kissed me, asking me if I was okay. I told him hell yes, even though I was excited, but scared. The first time is always scary.

He put on his ski mask, then rolled it up so it looked like a knit hat. He had a big patch on his nose and had shaved his eyebrows, which made him look weird and impossible to recognize. He said he'd learned a lot of tricks while in the joint; he really knew what he was doing. He was a real pro, he said, and I shouldn't worry.

I said I wasn't worried, I knew he'd planned it good and had the nerve, and so did I.

Charles got out of the car and went into the front of the store.

I watched the green-lighted clock on the dash and when two minutes was up I drove around the back, my heart pounding like a son-of-a-bitch. Out back, right on time, there was the armored car waiting, one of the armored car guys standing by the door, his hand on the grip of his gun. He looked bored. I drove on past to the other side of the building and parked by the employees' entrance and opened the passenger's door. I listened to some Johnny Cash on the radio, fingering the dash, trying to stay cool. Charles was late by half a minute. That's when I heard what sounded like firecrackers going off inside.

I felt a wave of panic come over me, and for a second I was gonna floor it and get the fuck out of there. I started sweating. More firecrackers that I knew were gunshots. More seconds running off the clock. Then I heard this alarm go off, loud as hell, like the whistle on a train, and the door flew open and Charles came flying out, pushing this woman in front of him. He shoved her in the back seat and got in with her and I took off a little fast with a screech of rubber. In the mirror, I could see nobody was coming after us.

161

Pissed, I asked what the fuck he'd brought the woman for. A hostage, he said. Seems the manager had a gun and wanted to shoot it out. Fucking maniac, Charles said. He thought he hit him once in the arm. I asked him if he got the money and he said hell yes.

At least he got that part right.

We headed down Virginia Street. I stayed right with the traffic, just as we'd rehearsed. I was so clearheaded, it amazed me. Real, real cool. Everything was as sharp as crystal, like I was looking at the world with new eyes.

The woman hostage was crammed up against the door looking like she was trying to make herself part of the upholstery. She was even skinnier than me, but older. Maybe forty, forty-five, wearing a sweatshirt with a duck on it. She had her arms wrapped around herself and was trembling. I drove onto the interstate. The hostage sniffled. I told her it was okay, we weren't killers, she had nothing to worry about.

But inside, I was thinking that she'd seen me. A police artist could make a sketch and my face would be on the news.

I felt this big lump forming in my throat. A vision of a cold damp cell passed in front of me. Even Killer Rodale's office ain't as bad as the Nevada State Women's Prison.

Charles kept looking back, nervous as a cat. I played the radio, K-SKY, a country and western station. They interrupted once to report the robbery, saying the robbers got away in a gray car, but nobody knew the make and they didn't get the license number. Then they played the voice of a cop who made a plea to release the hostage. They said we were armed and dangerous.

More like armed and stupid, in Charles' case. I thought the guy had such force. Man, taking this woman, that was about as stupid a thing as you could do. Some pro.

After a few minutes the hostage stopped sniffling and said she had to go to the bathroom. I told her to hold it.

I got off the freeway past Mustang and drove out into the desert on the road to Morgan. I stopped the car where a gravel pit had gone out of business. We let the hostage out to take a piss behind a bush. There was no reason for her to run, nothing around but desert and we could follow her footsteps in the sand with a flashlight real easy.

As soon as she got out of earshot, I said he'd have to kill her. She'd seen my face, it was the only way.

I could see her checking out the bushes, finding her spot. She looked back over her shoulder once in a while, thinking, probably, about running. Thinking, though, it was a dumb thing to do, because it would just get us riled and there was no place to go.

Charles was still wearing that ridiculous mask. I could smell the fear on him. He said he never killed nobody, especially no woman. There had to be some other way.

I took the gun away from him. He said they'd burn us bad if we went down for killing, that we might even get the gas chamber. I said I didn't want to go to prison and that was that. You want to be free, you got to do what you got to do.

Getting out of the car, I felt regret. Maybe a little fear too, fear and feeling sorry that circumstances had come on me like this. She'd just found her spot behind a bush, and I guess she thought I was coming to hurry her up. As I walked up to her I could hear the piss hitting the ground. I aimed. Suddenly it was like everything stopped and I could smell the clean desert and her warm piss, and I could take in all the stars that glittered across the sky. I didn't feel like I was taking a life; I felt like I was taking hold of mine. Like I'd gotten into this, and I had to get myself out of it and this was the only way. I jerked the trigger and the gun jumped in my hand and made a sharp cracking sound and spit a flame into the night. The woman on the other side of the bush just went down flat.

I went around the bush and stepped over her puddle of piss. She was twitching and making a gurgling sound, but then she stopped. I pulled up her panties, then went to get Charles. He was like a zombie, mumbling how he couldn't believe this was happening, how he had it figured so good. We managed to get her into the trunk of the car, then drove on over to his place. We got rid of the Buick and spent half the damn night shoveling sand on top of it, Charles all the time making low noises in his throat, but we finally got the job done.

~

For the next couple of days Charles stayed drunk. He didn't even help me count the money, which only came to $26,485. Nothing like what he said it would be, but then, as I was finding out, Charles was long on bullshit.

I spent my time mostly watching TV. They had a lot about the kidnapping of Jane Cravins—that was her name—and a lot of tearful appeals from her family not to hurt her. Charles couldn't hardly look at it, but me, I found it sort of funny, her fat, bald husband bawling on the TV, saying how much he loved her, that he only wanted her back—when all the time she was already worm food inside a Buick that was under all that sand.

But then a couple of days later they announced a reward of five thousand dollars for any information leading to the arrest and conviction of the perpetrators of this heinous crime. I felt like I'd been hit with a ball bat; it rocked me right back on my heels. Five thousand dollars was a fucking fortune to Cindy Lou. For five thousand dollars she'd fuck every member of the United States Marines.

I went into the bedroom where Charles was laying down with a washrag over his head. He hadn't had nothing to drink yet that day but looked like crap. I done a terrible thing, I said. He sat up to listen to me. I told him how I'd gotten drunk and talked to Cindy Lou before, when I didn't think I was gonna do it, and now, sure as hell, as soon as she heard about the reward and gave it a little time to work on her, we were gonna be in deep doo-doo.

He stared at me, leaning on his knees, looking almost green, like he was going to throw up. I said we didn't have no choice, we had to do what we had to do. He knew I was right. I told him I'd do it, but that I'd appreciate it if he'd go with me, help me get rid of the remains.

How could I do it, he wanted to know. Cindy Lou being my very best friend. I said I wasn't going to go to jail, that's all there was to it. The bitch would sell me out sure as hell. She'd talk herself into it in a day or two and we had to get to her first.

He said this had to be the end of it. And I said sure, this would be the end of it. After Cindy Lou we were home free.

But already I was thinking he wasn't the man I thought he was. And one day, he was sure to fold on me. Make a deal to save his ass, some bullshit like that. That's when I got it in my head that maybe he'd be better off to spend eternity with Cindy Lou than with me. It just came to me, right there in a flash.

⤖

We had to wait all day until it was dark. I was getting antsy. I mean, the longer we waited, the more that five thousand dollars would eat away at her mind.

We parked around the corner from her house. I told Charles to give me ten minutes. Then I went down to Cindy Lou's and knocked on the door. She didn't want to open it, even when I told her it was me. But then I said I needed a friend and she was the best friend I had in the world and I wanted her to help me give myself up so I wouldn't be shot. Besides, I said, I wanted her to get the $5000 reward. That sold her.

She let me in, and right away she saw I wasn't there to give myself up and she started crying like a baby, saying she didn't want to die. I asked her if she'd told them yet, and she swore she'd never tell, that if she had, wouldn't my face be all over the TV by now? She swore she'd never tell, that we were best friends. I told her how sorry I was that I couldn't take that chance and I pulled the gun on her. I made her lie down on the floor and put a pillow over her face, then shot into it to smother the sound and all the time she kept whining and crying that she was my best friend and all. I said how sorry I was. And honest, I was sorry, too.

When I pulled the trigger the gun made a little poof sound, and feathers went all over the room, like a snowstorm.

Me and Charles borrowed a shovel from Cindy Lou's garage and put her in the trunk of Charles' car and drove out into the desert way beyond Sparks. We picked a spot for her on this little hill covered with manzanita bushes that bloom in the spring. She always liked it when the desert bloomed; she'd always said it was the reason she stayed in Nevada.

Charles dug the hole while I watched. He hadn't said nothing since I'd done Cindy Lou and I could tell he was doing some hard thinking. Thinking of dumping me, no doubt. He could talk the talk, but he couldn't walk the walk.

When he was finished digging, he looked up. There was a big old moon out that night and it was near bright as day and he could see I had the gun pointed at him. He didn't seem surprised.

"That preacher in prison said I'd meet the devil and, sure enough, here you are."

"Trust counts most in a relationship," I said. "And you just can't be trusted."

He flung the shovel at me and hit me on the shoulder, then he lunged for me as I fired, hitting him in the face and exploding the back of his head. I was real sorry it ended that way, him trying to kill me. I'd been a good woman to him. It wasn't my fault. He'd gotten himself into something and really wasn't man enough to handle it. Deep down, I think he knew it, too.

So the cops figured they were looking for Charles and Cindy Lou and I was in the clear, at least for a while.

⚓

I was sticky and sweaty as hell after filling in that hole and was really looking forward to a shower at Charles' trailer. And it sure would have been good for my sore shoulder. But when I drove up the back way I could see a mess of police cars there, red lights flashing. I never did know how they got onto Charles. Maybe my own mother told the cops on him and me.

A wave of panic came over me. I killed the headlights, my heart racing. I watched them cops going in and out of the trailer, getting stuff out of their cars, checking the back yard.

A weird thing happened. Suddenly my head cleared like I was in another zone. I felt a real rush.

Here they was not a mile away and they had no idea where I was. I had them running circles. It was like a game and I was way up on points. All I had to do was keep my wits about me.

I had the money in the trunk and so all I had to do was to ditch the car and get another one at the airport, just like Charles taught me. Once over the hump into California, all it would take would be a bottle of hair dye, a hair cut, a pair of glasses, some new clothes, and I'd just disappear among all them millions of sun-loving Californians.

I figured what the hell, I hadn't really settled the score with Killer Rodale for good and so I stopped by his house down on County Road 4 on my way out of town. The bastard had company, so I left him alone. Shit. I'd have loved to have popped him.

I went out to Boomtown where a lot of truckers get gas and bummed a ride to Sacramento. I left the car there, parked down by the RV lot, figuring it would take them a year to find it and connect it to me. I wiped it clean of prints.

So I guess I'll never see my ma or kid again, but at least I'm free of the damn desert at last.

⤶

I met a guy in L.A. a week after I got there—built like a Greek hero, Ajax or one of those—and I might have married him if he kept asking. Name's Brad Dudley. He had his own auto body shop business—Dudley's Do-Right Autobody—and was doing real good. For excitement, we traveled a lot, did some skydiving and river rafting. It wasn't as exciting as taking down a supermarket and dropping the hammer on somebody who's got it coming, but it kept me feeling alive.

You see, Brad had a hot tub and everything, and in the warm California evenings we'd sink into that redwood hot tub, all warm and swirling and sip smooth California wine, and then we'd go inside and make love slow and easy on this super-soft, round bed with mirrors on the ceiling. I mean, we had it real good. And Brad knew how to pleasure a woman—I mean, really pleasure a woman about as good as any man could. He'd been to some seminar in Hollywood to learn it. How pain could make you really pop if it was done right, and he done it right.

I got a new name—Dominique Graceland—and colored my hair red and lost a few pounds. Things was going so great I felt I'd been blessed by God. After a couple of years I practically forgot the cops was hunting for me. Except one day I seen an old blurry high school picture of me in the post office. I was number four on the FBI's Ten Most Wanted list. It gave me a shudder, knowing they hadn't forgotten about me, and it kept me up nights for a while. But then I figured hey, nobody was going to recognize me from that old photo. They were spinning their wheels. I'd gotten a new social security number and everything, and a real California driver's license. Hell, they were never going to get Debby Jax; she'd disappeared into thin air, too smart for those jerks.

The only problem now was that Brad had this bitch ex-wife who kept bugging him about alimony payments. She don't square up I might have to deal with her, I started thinking.

Clarice, her name was. A fourteen-carat bitch if ever there was one.

She'd come over to Brad's condo all the time, leaning on him for more money, accusing Brad of being late on his payments, always wanting to get the lawyer after him, drag him back into court. The kid needs braces, she'd say one week. Then next week, the kid needs psychotherapy. Next week, the kid needs liposuction. I mean it—that was the neediest fucking kid you ever seen.

Stacy, that was the kid. Freckles, bad nose job, sticking her tongue out at you if you tried to straighten her out. I'd have kicked the shit out of her, if it was up to me.

But I kept completely out of it. I mean, completely. All I ever said to Brad was Stacy was a cute kid, things like that. Brad liked the kid, so I had to pretend to like her, too.

Clarice was a yoga instructor. She always wore this white turban and white robe like she was a priestess or some damn thing and had a funny herb-tea breath and smelled of chemicals that Brad said was anti-bacterial soap she liked to use. She had this terrible fear of bacteria that nobody could really explain.

Anyway, Brad sold his classic Porsche Super 356 with red Imron enamel paint to get the bitch off his back. I really liked that car. I mean the leather was cracked and it always smelled of oil and rode hard, but it looked sporty as hell and when we drove around in it, people always looked at us and it made me feel special, and I think Brad did too, and that bitch made him sell it.

But that didn't make me decide to do her—I mean I was cool about everything—but then the bitch crossed the line.

It was when we—me and Brad—was going to go to Hawaii with the auto body association. Brad was running for president and it was real important for him to go and that bitch froze his bank account the day we was supposed to pay for the tickets. She got some judge to listen to her whiny story about being behind in the alimony so she gave Brad's bank a court order from this dumb-ass judge and there was nothing the bank could do.

I still had some money stashed from the supermarket, but I couldn't say nothing about it because Brad would have wanted to know where I got it and there was no way to explain having all that cash.

I was boiling mad. I really wanted to go to Hawaii, but I didn't let on to Brad how I felt. I said, Oh well, we'll go some other time. But I said to myself I was going to do her real smart, so that not even Brad would suspect it was me. He didn't know about my past, of course, and I'd already made up my mind to never tell him or nobody else, except maybe my kids, if I ever had any more, and then only after I was maybe ninety. My mama didn't raise no fools.

So I had this idea to do her and make it look like a street crime. I mean, there was a lot of street crime in L.A.; you saw it all the time on *Action News*.

Clarice lived off Sepulveda Boulevard almost to Holly-wood in a modern, low-slung, tract house that Brad was paying for. Had a bunch of dumb Chinese lanterns outside. Me and Brad picked the kid up there sometimes, so I knew exactly where it was.

Using some of the supermarket money, I bought this old van for a couple of grand and used it to watch her, learn her habits. I could sit in the van and watch her come and go through a little peephole I'd drilled in the side and, believe me, the bitch had a schedule and she kept to it.

Okay, so here was my plan, and it was a good one. I thought nothing could go wrong. I'd wait in the van at the corner late at night. There were lots of trees there and she went out late, usually at eleven forty-five, to take her little frickin' white poodle for a walk so it could do its business in this little grove of trees on her neighbor's yard and she didn't have to clean it. The bitch, I guess, never heard of a pooper-scooper. Anyway, that's when I was going to do her.

There was nobody ever on the street at that time. I figured I'd jump out of the van and grab her and slit her throat with one quick stroke. I bought a knife as sharp as a surgeon's scalpel at a cutlery store on Rodeo Drive in Beverly Hills way away from where I lived. The one where O.J. supposedly bought his. The clerk said they see movie stars all the time. Cher was in there once, she said.

Brad went to Frisco on business on a Friday night and I figured I'd do it then. I was a little out of practice, so I was nervous. And I didn't have no gun. I wanted to do this with a knife. It seemed right. In my mind, I could see her feeling her own throat, seeing the blood and knowing in that moment that I had done it and she was gonna be dead in about two seconds. I wanted that moment bad, her knowing she was dead and knowing it was me that done it.

Sitting in that van in the darkness I felt real strange. Like time stretched thin around me. Like there was nothing left in the world but me and the bitch and time—and for her, time was about to stop. It made me feel like a god, almost. Like I could do anything I wanted and nobody or nothing could stop me.

Eleven forty-five finally came and right on schedule she strutted around the corner with her teeny white poodle on a gold leash. The poodle was getting all excited, yapping. I had my door open a little and I was scrunched down so Clarice wouldn't see me. I could smell jasmine and pine and could hear the faint sounds of the freeway a block away. My heart felt like a balloon expanding in my chest, pushing out in all directions. I held that knife tight as a mountain climber holds onto his rope.

Suddenly she was past me and I swung the door open and jumped, reaching out to grab her head with my left hand and give her one quick clean stroke with the other, but suddenly she dropped. I mean, she went down like a giant invisible hand had pushed her and I found myself flying, hitting the pavement hard on my hands, and as I fell she pushed my legs so I did a somersault. She let out this god-awful yell and the next thing I know she's got a foot at my throat and she's got my wrist all twisted up, hurting like hell, and the knife flies from my hand.

I told her she was hurting me, but the bitch wouldn't let up. I told her I wasn't really going to hurt her, I was just gonna scare her so she'd lay off Brad, but the bitch didn't buy it. I said if she let me go I'd be out of town in two hours and she'd never see me again.

She said, no such luck, *doll-face*, she was turning me over to the law.

Doll-face is what Brad always called me. That really hurt.

So that's how I got here on the row. Me, Deborah Irene Jax, the first woman condemned in Nevada since 1890, when they hung Elizabeth Potts and her husband on the same gallows at the same time in Elko for the crime of killing and mutilating a guy named Miles Faucett.

Using a knife, that was my big mistake. I should have gotten a double barrel sawed-off and blown the bitch away in a gazillion pieces. When you got a job to do, use the right tool.

The neighbors heard Clarice screaming and the cops came, handcuffed me, took me to their station house, finger-printed me and, as a matter of routine, sent the prints to the FBI and that's how they found out I was not Miss Dominique Marilyn Graceland but was, in fact, the infamous Debby Jax, fugitive from justice, number four on the FBI's Ten Most Wanted list.

Clarice said they shouldn't hold me for attempted murder, let Nevada have me. Big of her, huh?

The stupid trial in Reno lasted eleven months. Eighty-two witnesses, mostly prosecution witnesses, pretty much proved I was the one involved in what the papers called a horrific killing spree. I'd have pled guilty if they'd have given me life, but no, the hatchet-nosed prosecutor had something personal against me and insisted I get the needle.

So we had to have this big long boring trial where the evidence was so overwhelming I'd have voted me guilty myself. Forensic evidence, they call it. Members of the jury, ten women, two men, kept looking at me like I was Charles Manson.

My lawyer got this moon-faced lady shrink to say I was crazy, which I'm most certainly not, but even she had to semi-admit when the dumb-ass prosecutor kept hammering on her that I knew right from wrong, which is what the law goes by.

The judge, when he sentenced me, said I was a depraved killer without remorse. I smiled and blew the old fart a kiss.

My old daddy who ran off when I was just a sapling used to tell me, Girl, any lame-ass can quit, but a winner, hell, a winner never quits. He told me that ten thousand times, I guess, on account of everybody thought of him as a loser, but by him saying he hadn't quit yet, I guess he was making himself into a potential winner.

But that always stuck with me. And even after the judge said I was going to die for my crimes, I kept telling myself that a winner never quits.

So right from the first day in custody, I figured some way, some how, I'd be free.

First, I thought maybe I could work something out with my lawyer, get him to fall for me, then I'd see if maybe I could get him to smuggle me in a gun. Turned out the guy was a Mormon with eighty kids and the one time I put my hand on his leg he practically chopped it off.

In the jail there was a preacher that came to visit the prisoners. He was fifty, maybe, and had a strange odor like he didn't bathe regular and when we met and I tried to cozy up to him and purr a little, he said something like Satan be gone! and screamed for a guard. Made me laugh.

After I was sentenced and all, they sent me up to the row to await the inevitable. Nobody ever broke out of the row.

My winner-never-quits determination was fading fast. I was left in a room about the size of a horse stall with a Bible, a writing table, and some blank pages and a pen. At night, I'd have this dream about space aliens coming to put a needle in my arm. I kept dreaming about Cindy Lou and Charles and that weenie-whiny hostage I shot while she was peeing in the bushes. They looked like they were rotting, but they were moving and laughing at me. I'd wake up in a sweat.

Death row was torture. The worst part was my lawyers kept saying they'd keep the appeals up for maybe twenty years. Twenty fucking years in hell.

The second month on the row I met Marshall Stephenson. He was a guard and right away I could feel the chemistry was right and I was suddenly bursting with hope.

Whenever he seen me, I could sense him getting short of breath. He was tall and gray and a little fat and he had his twenty-five-year badge sewn on his sleeve. Twenty-five years of being a guard would fry anyone's brain—not that Marshall Stephenson had all that much brain to begin with.

On the row, you ain't never alone with a guard hardly. If they open the door to your cell there's at least two of them, and usually three. Sometimes, like when they pass the food trays through, you can talk to them individually, and they can see you through the peep hole, but you can't see them. It ain't too private, though, because the other inmates can hear everything and the other guards can too if they happen to be passing by. Because I'm a woman, they let me cover the peep hole when I use the facilities. But I never did figure out how to use that to my advantage.

The only chance I had to speak to a guard alone was when they let me outside into the exercise yard. Some yard. It was actually just a cement enclosure with no roof about ten feet square with bars above and a guard looking down on you. But it's the one time when you can speak to a guard with nobody else hearing.

Now the people who run the prison ain't total idiots. They know it's dangerous to have inmates and guards fraternizing—that's what they call it—so they made it a rule that guards ain't never supposed to speak to inmates except to tell them to get into a cell or they have a visitor, something like that. Official business, they call it.

So even when you're outside and it's just you and the guard standing on the platform above you and you say, hey, it's a nice day—something like that—they don't even answer you. And if you get pissed and put them down for it and call them a donkey or something, they don't get mad and yell at you, they just cite you Rule 47—the non-fraternization rule. It's spooky, they're so well trained. Like dogs in a circus.

Anyway, the guards rotate jobs and Marshall Stephenson wasn't the guard in the yard box for about two months. I was getting anxious, thinking maybe he wasn't coming back. Then one day he appeared.

I was wearing the usual prison stuff, which the men also wear: denim shirts that button up the front. Only I made sure a few top buttons didn't button that day and I could see his eyes fixed on my front, but he didn't say nothing and neither did I. I only kept giving him this look—no smile, nothing like that. Just this cool look—not unfriendly, but not exactly friendly either.

He told me to correct my uniform, to button up.

I said he should come down and make me, being sassy. I could see his face flush. Then I smiled and buttoned up to show how cooperative I was. He seemed pleased.

He didn't have box duty for two more weeks. This time I buttoned up all the way to the top. I asked him if he preferred it that way. He didn't answer me.

I could sense his relief that I wasn't pushing things. That just let me know I had his attention.

He was back again the next day. My buttons didn't make it to the top. He didn't say a thing. He kept staring off in the distance, not keeping a close watch on me.

Meanwhile, I figured I needed to know a little more about Marshall Stephenson. For that, I'd need somebody on the outside to help me.

Brad never came to visit me, except once, right after I was arrested. He said he was shocked the way I'd lied to him and all and he thought it best if we never saw each other again. This hurt something awful, considering the big favor I tried to do for him that got me into this mess.

My family didn't come to see me either. My mama died while I was on the run and my kid was still a little kid. I told his foster parents it was best if he didn't know about me. A few cousins came; I think it was only to gawk.

Though reporters were always wanting to visit and get my story, I was pissed at the way they portrayed me as a serial killer—which I definitely am not—so I never had much to do with them. But then I had this brainstorm, and I wrote to a few that I'd like to talk about the possibility of doing a book about me.

That's how I met Jenny Gilroy, who wrote for the tabloids. She was trying to break into book writing. They let me talk to her in one of the private visiting rooms, just us two. She was this dumpy, dishwater blonde, with sharp, cold eyes set deep in her head. She wore a baggy, gray pantsuit and her tongue kept darting out from between her lips. I had a good feeling about her. She reminded me of my cousin Sally, who was a twenty-dollar whore in Vegas.

We chatted for a while about the food they served, what I thought of my lawyers' attempts to prove me insane and all that bull, and I asked her about how she felt writing for the tabloids and she gave me a big shrug and said it was a living, but I sensed she was looking for the big score and my life story was it.

Then I told her that she was the one I picked to tell my life story—under one condition. That after I . . . died, the proceeds from the book coming to me would go to Marshall Stephenson.

She asked who he was and I said he was this wonderful guard who worked on the row. I just wanted to know if he was really worthy of getting all that money and wasn't just scamming me.

She shifted her weight in her chair, her cold black eyes suspicious as hell.

She shook her head and said she wasn't stupid.

I told her if she was stupid I would not want to make a deal with her. Then she said she'd done enough checking on me to know I was not to be trusted.

I told her she could have ninety percent of the royalties; ten percent was enough for Marshall. She had greedy eyes, just like my twenty-dollar-whore cousin. She stared at me, her little lizard tongue slicing out between her lips. Then she asked what exactly did I want to know about him.

Nothing real special, I told her. His family, what he does in his spare time. His habits, his friends.

She got up and went to the door and I thought maybe she was leaving. Maybe she was going to report me. But then she turned and said she wanted it all, no ten percent to anybody else.

"Agreed," I said. I told her she resembled my dear cousin Sally and from the first moment I knew we were going to be great friends.

She said she knew Sally was a whore. I said I guess she'd been checking me out pretty good and she said yeah, down to the natural color of my pubic hair.

⁂

So she found out everything I wanted to know about Marshall Stephenson, and all of it was really interesting.

First, he hadn't ever been married. He lived with his mama, who was sort of sickly and kind of a shut-in. She suffered from sick headaches, asthma, a whole bunch of stuff. Hands gnarled with arthritis. Marshall took real good care of her, the neighbors all said. Took her to church every Sunday. They was Baptist. My mama was a Baptist, too, before she met my daddy and become a big nothing. I told Jenny to keep up the good work and I laid all my secrets on her, didn't leave nothing out—except what I was planning to do with the information she was digging up for me. I'm sure she had her suspicions; she weren't no idiot.

She found out Marshall was in a chess club and used to have a dog until his mama made him get rid of it 'cause she was allergic. A golden retriever. He had a girlfriend once back in high school and for a few years after, but she married a sailor and took off for the east coast.

I kept telling Jenny I needed more. She kept saying that she had to be discrete. That she couldn't give me more than she already had. I told her then I'd given her all she was going to get and I just stopped talking to her.

Three days later she comes back and tells me that twice a month Marshall and his mother go to séances and speak to his dead daddy.

That's when I knew I wasn't going to be on the row much longer.

≫

Over the next couple of weeks Marshall Stephenson was in the box almost every day. He had to be switching assignments somehow to get that duty so he could spend some time alone with me.

I worked him slow, telling him how bad I felt about me getting mixed up with Charles King and later about that business with Clarice and how none of it was my fault. At first he kept saying Rule 47, but after a while he stopped that. He was listening. His big eyes were softening just a tad. He kept staring like he was hungry for me. I had him hooked good.

I started telling him about how bad it was being caged like a rabbit. Having six by ten feet of hard floor under you and bars on the window and only an hour of fresh air a day. How it felt being called names in the press and people gawking at you like you were a freak. How it felt to be waiting for the day when they drag you down to the green room and stick a needle in your arm.

He just kept staring at me as I talked, and I knew he was falling for me hard. I was unbuttoning all my buttons now when I was outside, even when it was cold, and I'd left my bra in my cell. I wanted him to be sure to get a glimpse of the goods.

But then, just as I thought I really had him, he suddenly told me to button up, and every time I started talking he told me to be silent. My guess was I was scaring him, and I sure as hell didn't want to do that.

A couple of weeks later, on a overcast morning in May when he was getting back on box duty after a few days off, I told him I had had a dream.

He told me to be silent, and he quoted Rule 47, but I didn't shut up. I told him a man came to me in a dream. A man named Vernon, and he said the strangest thing.

"Vernon?" he said. I knew from Jenny his daddy's name was Vernon. "Vernon who?"

"He didn't say . . . You know, all my life I've had strange dreams that nobody can explain," I said. "Sometimes I dream things that later come true. Usually about people dying. It's the strangest thing."

"What did this Vernon look like?" He said it low, like he was afraid of the answer.

"He was a large man, with big, heavy glasses. Bushy eyebrows. A mean-looking man."

I knew this is just how his daddy looked when he was alive.

"W-what did he say?" He was shook up now.

"He said I was to help out his son. Isn't that just the strangest thing?"

"Help his son do what?" he asked quickly.

"He didn't say."

It was then the buzzer sounded and it was time to return to my cell. I went back a happy woman.

Now that I had him, I had to make sure not to lose him. Jenny Gilroy managed to find out from a neighbor lady that Marshall's old man must have buried some money and that's why they was always going to séances—they was trying to find it.

Over the next few weeks Marshall had box duty a dozen times. He didn't ask me anything—in fact he never said much at all, but I could tell he was thinking real hard.

"This Vernon," I said, "tells me strange things, things I don't understand. Like he was a traveling man, and he made a lot of money he never did tell nobody about."

Marshall just kept staring straight ahead. I had his attention, though; I was positive.

"What I don't understand is," I said, "why is he bothering with a woman caught up in my circumstance? Ain't I got enough on my mind? Sure is a puzzlement, isn't it, Officer Stephenson?"

"Nobody understands the spirits."

The next day he was escorting me to my session with Jenny Gilroy with this other guard, and the other guard stops to have a few words with one of the other inmates. That gave me a minute with Marshall alone. I whispered: "My friend that visits me in the night, this Vernon guy—he says I'm going to get out of here. I'm going to be a free woman again."

Marshall didn't say nothing—we just keep on walking—but I sense he's a deeply troubled man.

"This Vernon says that he's going to show me where some money is and I'm to have a reward of my freedom for giving it to his son."

I sensed him really being eaten up inside, but he still said not one thing. He let me into the interview room and walked away.

After that, the only time I seen him was when he was walking down the row on bed check or passing out the food trays, but he didn't talk to me or come near me.

Then, in the middle of this god-awful heat wave in August, Jenny Gilroy came on a Wednesday afternoon. The interview room had all the windows open and a fan going, but the air didn't seem to be moving. I asked her right off what was going on with Marshall Stephenson.

She told me he'd put in for retirement. I nearly collapsed. I could see the bitch was amused. I called the guard and told him our session was over.

Back in my cell, I was burning with rage. If I could have gotten my hands on that dickhead Marshall Stephenson at that moment, I'd have crammed him down a garbage disposal a tiny piece at a time.

For the next several days I never saw him, not once. I figured he was either on leave or he was working the grill gate at the employees' entrance.

I spent my time stretched out on my cot, barely lifting my head. I'd been working on him for almost a year and it was all going to be for nothing.

Then on a Tuesday evening, the night before they were going to inject this black radical that done a couple of cops over in King City, the meal cart rolls by and as the tray comes through the slot, I hear Marshall's voice say, "Be sure to eat your soup."

He then whispers how soup is so good for me. Like he was so concerned about my health. That's one thing you definitely don't give a hoot about on death row—diet and exercise—and you can go right ahead and smoke all you want.

Then he moved on. I lay back down on my cot. I didn't feel like eating. But then I got to thinking, why would he bother to tell me to eat my soup?

So I dipped my spoon into the soup and hidiho, what you know, I found this little plastic bag with a note inside: *When you see Justice wearing a hat, better go to the bathroom. Stall number three and no other.*

I flushed the note down the toilet and didn't eat no soup. I couldn't sleep that night, trying like mad to figure out what that note meant. It had to be some kind of code, but when I worked around the words and letters I couldn't make no sense of it at all.

The next day Marshall Stephenson was gone. Retired for good.

And I got real, real depressed.

Okay, so over the next few weeks my lawyers were busting it trying to get me a new trial by proving my first lawyer, the

Mormon guy, was an idiot and didn't give me a good defense. I went along with it because I'd have done anything by that time to get out of that damn cell even for an hour.

Old cons will tell you your mind starts doing weird things when you're locked up a long time. As the years roll by, you start thinking you deserve it because you been bad. Every-body says you're evil; well, it must be so. Me, I kept telling myself I was a human being and wouldn't let my mind turn on me. I was a victim of Charles King, plain and simple, and I did not deserve to be put in this damn box for twenty years and then given the damn needle.

On the third of July my number-one lawyer (I had three by then) comes by and tells me that I'm having a hearing in a week to see if the court will give me another psychiatric exam.

"You mean we got to dance that dance again?"

"Afraid so," he says. He was a young guy with a blond ponytail down to his ass, full of optimism and high moral prin-ciples. He was against the death penalty and all that. He was Harvard Law School graduated and loved telling you that he was.

I told him the last several shrinks thought I was a sociopath—whatever that is. I said it must mean I'm nuts, but not nuts enough to bag a trip to the funny farm.

Then he explained that him and his colleagues got a new theory of law they were going to try. That even though I know right from wrong, the *paradigm* of truth and falsity is different with me. In other words, he explained, right and wrong with me are different than they are with most people, that I had my own definition. So I could not be held to the knowing-right-from-wrong standard.

Sounded like bullshit, but what the hell.

"Think the judge will buy it?"

"If we can blow enough smoke his way."

The following day, right after breakfast, a woman guard brought a couple of dull, pukey dresses for me to try on. I picked a beige one. Real conservative, the way my lawyer wanted me dressed. Like a Republican, he said.

They put me in leg irons and handcuffs and me and two male guards and the female guard go down through the front sally port and out to a gray van in the parking lot. There they put a chain around my waist, like I'm on a leash. With a guy, they put a ring around his balls, too, and attach the ring to the leash. They ain't taking no chances.

They turn me over to two sheriff's deputies, one a moose-faced woman, the other this young guy who looks a little scared of me. Outside, it's hot and dry and smelling of dust and asphalt and it's wonderful. I turn to the sun to feel it shine on my face for about ten seconds before they shut me up in the van.

Inside, the van is blissfully air-conditioned.

Mooseface gets in the back with me. All along the way she reads this paperback romance with a pirate lady on the cover showing a mile of cleavage and slinging a huge sword over her head.

It takes about ten minutes to get to the courthouse. We park in back and go in through a security checkpoint. A couple of TV reporters zoom in on me, trying to ask me questions. I tell them I hear the voice of God talking to me in Latin. This creates a stir and gets more of them to swarm around me, which is sort of fun.

Finally we go through this other checkpoint and up the back stairs, where they don't allow no reporters. We start down the hall, and that's when I see a big statue of Justice holding scales and, hey, it's wearing a cowboy hat.

Like in the note in the soup. Then I see the ladies' room and suddenly I get it. I feel so excited I want to let out a whoop, but

184

I'm careful not to let it show. I turn to Mooseface and tell her I got to pee.

She says the hearing is about to start, but I tell her I gotta go real, real bad and she don't want me wetting on my Republican dress, so she says okay.

She has me stand with these two sheriff's deputies—big huskers they are—while she goes in and checks out the ladies' room. She comes back out and says it's all clear and they let me in. Mooseface comes along. While I go into stall number three, Mooseface primps herself in the mirror. In the stall there's this ventilator and damn if it ain't pulled away from the wall and I hear this voice out of the blackness telling me to hurry. It's Marshall Stephenson, God bless him.

Careful and quiet as hell, I pull the grating away from the wall and crawl into the darkness. A light shines through down the way. I creep along, quick as I can, scraping the hell out of my shins. Inside the ventilator it's tight and musty, and the dust is thick as a carpet, but I manage to worm my way toward the light, my heart going like a machine gun with the trigger stuck.

Suddenly I'm at the light and I feel hands pulling me through into this little closet full of mops and buckets. It's Marshall Stephenson, wearing a fake beard, looking funny.

"Marshall, thank you!" I whisper.

He says I can thank him later and he takes off my chains, leg irons and handcuffs. Then he gives me some overalls and boots and a big army jacket and a knit cap and tells me to go out the front and down the elevator and cross the street and get in an old red Chevy pickup.

So out I go, back into the hall I was just in not two minutes ago, pushing this pail and mop, the knit cap pulled right down over my head. I pass right by the two guards waiting for me and Mooseface to come out of the john. My heart's flipping out, but I don't hurry. I keep moving slow and easy, a sorry janitor getting paid by the hour.

I get on the elevator and go on down to the main floor and right out the door. A moment later, Marshall joins me and we're heading out of town toward the mountains in the distance glimmering in the sun.

I take hold of his arm and tell him I plan to be real good to him tonight. Real, real good.

He looks over at me and grins like an old letch, and I think, man, I'm going to have to dump this clown quick. Probably have to do him to get away clean. I feel sorry about that in a way, him doing me the biggest favor anybody ever done for me.

We were heading up into the foothills and he suddenly turns off onto this narrow dirt road barely wide enough for the truck. He tells me they'll be having roadblocks, so we got to be careful. He's got a hideout for us where they'll never look.

I tell him how smart he was, thinking of everything. I roll down the window, sucking in that wonderful, free air. I feel like bursting open I'm so happy. We go through a gate with warning signs about nuclear danger.

"I put them up to keep everybody out."

"Pretty sharp, Marshall, I mean it. You got a great criminal mind."

He don't seem amused.

We go through a dirt canyon and he parks the pickup under this sort of overhanging rock so it can't be seen from the sky. I follow him through a scrub pine grove; it smells so sweet. There's a hot wind blowing up from the valley, but it don't bother me none. In fact, I kinda like it.

We come to this sort of cement blockhouse.

"Built it myself," Marshall said.

"Looks real sturdy."

We go inside and it's kinda dank and gloomy, but cool. He lights a lantern. That's when I see this big iron cage.

"What's that for?" I ask. And when I turn around I see he's got this big old shotgun pointed at me.

"Your new home," he said.

He shoves me in and slams the door and locks it with a padlock the size of a toaster.

"Wait till I tell your father," I say.

He just laughs. "My mama believes all that dither. I don't."

"Then why'd you do this?"

He smiles and sits down on an old straight-back chair. "I just like looking at your pretty face," he says. "I couldn't let them give you the needle, it would have been a tragedy. Now we got all the time in the world," he says.

ᴥ

That was six, maybe seven, eight years ago, I ain't sure. Time sort of drags in here. I'm growing old pacing up and down in this damn cage.

Marshall comes every day to feed me and empty the chamber pot. Once I pretended to be passed out and when he came in I whacked him with the chamber pot. It staggered him, but he didn't go down. I whacked him again and he hit me across the nose with his stick. My nose bled all over the place for three days.

Every day he sits on the chair and spends several hours looking at me, just looking with this dull expression on his face, looking with those big, sad, stupid brown eyes of his and not doing nothing. It's creepy. I tried turning him on—once I even stripped naked—but he turned away. He said he wasn't the kind of man to take advantage.

He loves buying me new underwear, and a pretty dress every once in a while. He wants me to color my hair to cover the gray that's coming in, but I won't.

Once he left me for a week, said he had to have an operation. He left plenty of Kentucky fried chicken and two gallons of water, but it got me thinking: What if something happened to him? I'd starve to death in this goddamn cage. I'd never get out.

When I told him that, he just grinned and said if you can't stand the punishment, don't do the crime.

One more thing that would be Charles King's fault, may he rot in hell.

I get to take a cold shower once a week out back in a tin shed with a gravel floor. Marshall keeps me chained by the ankle in the shower. He lets me read books, Christian books like *The Purpose Driven Life* that is total bunk crap, about how you can only be happy if you fulfill God's plan for you, like, oh yeah, God just whispers in your ear telling you what you gotta do and you do it.

Marshall lets me write my journal, and every night he makes me say the Lord's Prayer ten times or I don't get no food. I chew on the bars sometimes.

Sometimes I see Cindy Lou sitting on the floor outside the bars with her legs crossed, sipping a brew, just smiling at me, like she's really enjoying seeing me in this damn cage. I've started talking to her knowing she ain't real, but what the hell. Like when I was a kid, I had an imaginary friend, Fred, a talking mouse, and I knew he wasn't real. Cindy Lou hates my guts for killing her, but she's company. She keeps calling me stupid. Last week she told me that the only way I was gonna get out of there was to kill myself. She said I could tear my veins open on my wrist with my teeth. She keeps saying *do it, do it, do it.* She won't shut the hell up.

I'm leaving these pages stuck in the walls, hoping somebody'll find them some day. We're moving way up in the hills soon, he says, because of some new shopping center. A Nevada Shopper—no shit. I can hear the bulldozers in the distance. When Marshall's not around, I scream myself hoarse, but nobody hears me.

Marshall brought a tabloid article about me this morning. It said I was spotted on a beach on the Riviera getting a great tan. Marshall had himself a big laugh over that, and damn, if I didn't start laughing too, laughing so hard I cried.

Spanish Lesson
Lester Gorn

Fall 1945

The jeep sped down the solitary dirt road, trailed by the van. Dust churned into the orange groves. The springs bounced and squealed as the jeep hit a pothole.

Wrestling the wheel, the sergeant succeeded in taming it. He flashed a gold-toothed grin at Erich Schmidt, in the passenger seat. "*Bueno*, General," he said, patting the wheel.

Erich said nothing. During his three months in Latin America, Erich had disdained to learn Spanish. The language was soft, flowery, effeminate. Virtually all of his friends in Asuncito were *kameraden* and the city's ruling class was able to speak German or English. He could make the sergeant understand simple instructions. That sufficed.

He squinted toward the horizon. The vast orchard shimmered in heat and glare. His shirt, stinking of sweat, clung to his back. What was he doing here? How had he been inveigled into traveling this rutted rural road under the sweltering sun with a driver who could not drive and a van full of soldiers who could not soldier? He grimaced. Inveigled? More like extorted.

Stunning, this reversal of fortune. Until last week, luck had worked in tandem with good planning. The *kameraden* had shielded him from persecution and shepherded him through

189

Austria to the Vatican. Help had been unstinting: false identification papers, travel documents, safe houses. After arriving in South America, it had been a routine matter to cross borders. Truly responsible people declined to regard honorably defeated soldiers as war criminals.

The welcome in Asuncito had been no less heartening. A party honoring the *kameraden* had been held in the palace and hosted by the president. There, under the massive chandeliers in the glittering ballroom, Erich had danced with the president's lady and basked in her warmth. The other ladies at the party were sympatico, too. Erich had been charmed by their beauty, their gowns and the variety of their lures. Demure. Wicked. Playful.

Erich had purchased a house in the hills overlooking the harbor and settled in to await a change in the political climate at home. The change would not be long in coming, he was certain. The bloodlust of the barbarians might well be satiated by the so-called war crimes trials, conducted under new laws retroactively applied. Already, the military attaché at the U.S. Embassy in Asuncito was chatting with Erich about the Russian threat, the reliability of certain Berliners, and security problems in the Americas. When he'd first arrived, the attaché had stared right through him.

Although Erich missed his wife, life was not unpleasant: music, books, cafes, walks through the countryside. Ample funds had been banked in Zurich, and Henrietta had meticulously followed the investment instructions he'd sent her. His mind was at ease.

Then, last week, misfortune had struck. Erich had been invited to dinner by *el presidente*. To his surprise, he had turned out to be the sole guest. He did not know whether the president was wearing his sash of office because he intended to discuss business or because he simply felt uncomfortable without it.

After dinner in a zebra-striped room said to resemble the interior of the El Morocco, a nightclub in New York, the president's lady withdrew with a headache. Erich and the president strolled into the study for brandy and a cigar. The oak paneled study was dominated by an oil portrait of the president in his general's uniform, which bore many decorations. Standing under the portrait, the president hooked his thumb over his cummerbund—rather like thumbing a trigger guard—and humbly requested Erich's counsel. He was quick to add that Erich should not feel in any way obligated to repay the country for its hospitality or its tax concessions. Naturally, Erich expressed pleasure at the opportunity to be of service.

It seemed the president had a security problem. Lately, the communists had been more troublesome than usual. Not content with high wages, they now were demanding that large estates be broken up and the land redistributed, and they were spreading false rumors that the armed forces were responsible for *los desaparecidos*—the "disappeareds." Their agitation disturbed even the *norteamericanos*. If the benefactors were to withdraw from his country, the economy would collapse. It was essential to restore stability, and the army lacked proper training for the task. Erich was an expert in security. The democratic republic would be eternally grateful if he would take a few soldiers under his wing for a month or two. The *norteamericanos* would be grateful, too. To have the gratitude of the *norteamericanos* was no small thing.

Erich turned on his most sincere voice. He explained that his wartime experience had been limited to transportation. Other SS officers in Asuncito were better qualified.

"You're too modest, General," the president said. "Transportation has its security aspects, I'm told. When a crisis arose at Schoenberg, you acted decisively. I have confidence in your judgment and abilities."

Schoenberg. Erich almost had forgotten. In 1941, twenty deportees had made an escape from a slow-moving train before it reached Berlin's city limit. Erich had been notified at 2:03 a.m. He had driven to the Schoenberg area to personally direct the manhunt. Houses and gardens had been systematically searched. Train guards augmented by dogs and a detachment of the *Sicherheitsdienst* had succeeded in flushing out eighteen of the twenty escapees. At Erich's order, the eight hundred deportees were disembarked from their freight cars to witness the eighteen hangings. Some light standards had served as gallows.

What Erich did not tell the president was that he had been hard put to keep from vomiting. The guards stupidly had neglected to bind the hands of the condemned. The eighteen Jews had struggled frantically to slip free from the nooses. Some had voided themselves.

In the months and years ahead, Erich had resisted the temptation to avoid field trips. To do so would sully his honor. Fortunately, pressing duties and appointments had kept him in Berlin most of the time, and he had never been called upon to personally pull a trigger or a rope. Rank had its privileges.

Yet now he found himself in a jeep, jouncing through potholes in the sweltering heat, on his way to personally lead the first mission of the newly organized Freedom Task Force.

Sourly, Erich gazed at a lone chicken scrabbling in the dirt before a one-room shack on an eroded hillside. He could not understand why so many shacks had tin roofs and walls. Without trees for shade, the shacks were even hotter than the noontime heat outside. Where did these people keep their brains? Erich watched an old woman in a ragged dress tending an earthen oven. Thin smoke wafted from the vent. Beans, probably. Why do your baking in the midday sun? The woman's flaccid breast poked through a hole in the fabric. Why didn't she patch the dress? All it took was a needle and thread. How could people live this way?

A grinding sound made Erich wince. It was produced by the fat sergeant as he shifted gears. The idiot! With such treatment, the gears would be stripped within a month.

Erich turned his attention to the open map in his lap, then checked the mileage gauge on the dashboard. The crossroads should be less than a kilometer ahead. The sun was directly overhead. Excellent timing. Emilio Lopez, the sergeant's cousin, had informed him that the workers—ordinarily scattered over the fields—could be found between noon and one o'clock at the packing shed, having lunch together. One worker—Emilio— would be absent today. Perfect.

Erich touched the sergeant's sleeve. The jeep pulled off the road and stopped in the shelter of the grove. The van followed and parked behind it.

Climbing out of the jeep, Erich beat the dust from his fatigues. The soldiers slouched toward him. Their grimy uniforms hung on them like motley. Scanning the eager, inquiring faces, Erich hid impatience. One would never believe they already had been told what they were to do and had repeated back their instructions.

"One last briefing," Erich said to the sergeant.

The sergeant nodded. After giving instructions to the two drivers designated to stay behind with the vehicles, he gathered the other men around him. Kneeling, he used a stick to draw a rough map in the dirt: their present location and the location of the shed in the clearing north of the crossroads. To assure surprise, the men would open fire from concealed positions at the edge of the orchard. Although the positions were quite far from the shed, the soldiers could be sure that they'd have a clear field of fire and that the communists would be well within range of their M-1 Garand rifles.

Squatting, their Garands dragging in the dirt, the ragtag soldiers listened intently. Now and then one of them said *Por que?* but most of the time they all nodded and said *Bueno.*

The sergeant turned to Erich. "Is good, my General," he said. *"Muy bueno."*

"They clearly understand?"

"Have not fear," the sergeant said.

Erich and the sergeant coordinated their watches. Then the unit split into two details—one led by Erich, the other by the sergeant—and set off through the grove.

The soldiers shambled through the trees as if on a church outing. Not one walked erect. They held their rifles like picnic baskets.

Pocketing his compass, Erich trudged down the lane. Incredible, for an SS general to be leading five scarecrows through a Latin American orchard! He breathed deeply, and the orange fragrance soothed him. It made him think of his wife. None of the ladies he had met in Asuncito could measure up to her. Wanton? Henrietta could be wanton and shy at the same time, just as her touch could be both feathery and demanding.

A humid wind stirred the trees. Erich could feel dust in his nostrils and sweat trickling down his sides. He reverted to thoughts of Henrietta. Her mockery never ceased to infuriate and tantalize him, in the bedroom and outside it.

Erich heard voices in the distance. Halting, he raised his right hand. The soldiers unlimbered their rifles. Erich went forward to the orchard's edge and dropped to the dirt. His view was obscured by a horse and wagon near the shed. The skeletal horse was eating from a feedbag. The wagon sagged under the weight of five or six full-to-the-brim garbage cans.

Erich crawled to a position affording an unobstructed view. About forty *campesinos* were gathered in the shade of the packing shed. They were seated on crates or on the ground with their backs braced against the wall. Most of them had finished eating lunch. They were talking, gesturing, smoking, drinking. A wineskin passed from hand to hand. A youth played a guitar.

An old man dozed with his *paja* straw hat tilted over his eyes. Two women chatted.

Shade and distance obscured faces. So much the better—it would be easier for his soldiers to subdue qualms.

Twisting from the waist, Erich signaled the soldiers to come forward. Clumsily, they moved in a crouch to positions on his left and right. Now their eagerness faded. They were jittery. They did not take to the prospect of firing on unarmed *campesinos*. Erich did not blame them. It would have been better if the communists were armed with a few weapons—the soldiers then would feel more like soldiers.

Erich glanced at his watch. One more minute. Thus far, the operation had gone better than he had dared to hope. He waited. Birds twittered overhead. An unwelcome thought crowded into his mind. If his son could see him now, all hope of reconciliation would be extinguished.

Rising to one knee, he flipped the safety switch of his Browning automatic rifle. A glance to his left and right confirmed that the others were ready.

The BAR jumped in his hand as he fired the first burst. Birds took fluttering wing. Blood splashed the shed. Bodies toppled. Cries and screams despoiled the sunlight. To his surprise, Erich did not feel queasiness. He was a soldier, doing a soldier's job. He held the gun steady and squeezed off a fresh burst. This time the barrel did not jump. As the soldiers to his left and right opened fire, the din buffeted his eardrums. Bullets raked the shed, splintering the siding and then moving on to living targets. The horse, whinnying, toppled over in its traces, overturning the wagon. Garbage cans bounced onto the dirt, spewing putrescence.

Reaching for a fresh magazine, Erich felt a kind of exultation. Five years after Schoenberg, he was learning that his lapse there had been transitory, and that pulling the trigger was no more difficult than ordering others to do so. With cool detachment, he watched a clutch of communists run crazily in all directions. One by one they went down.

Fire broke out from the flank. As anticipated, the sergeant and his men now augmented Erich's frontal fire with enfilade. Erich watched waist-high tracers traversing the length of the shed. The *campesinos* clustered together, clinging to each other as if to seek solace or offer protection. They fell like tenpins. The last one standing was a woman. Her long black hair shone in the sunlight as she knelt over a body. Bullets spun her backwards.

Erich stepped into the clearing so he could be seen by the sergeant. He raised his arm. "Cease fire!"

Gradually, the firing stopped.

The echoes died.

Erich strode forward to inspect the bodies. Off to his left, he saw the sergeant emerge from the orchard and walk forward to join him.

The clearing hushed: no bird calls, no cries or moans.

Erich scanned the countryside. In the distance, he saw two men armed with scythes running toward the shed—peons, probably, alarmed by the gunfire and stupidly intent on helping their comrades. He fired a burst into the distance. The peons turned and fled.

Slinging the BAR at his shoulder, Erich pulled out his Luger and walked among the fallen, their doughy-dead faces contorted by fear, horror, panic. Erich walked carefully to avoid blood puddles and grotesquely twisted limbs. He detected movement only in an old man whose fingers still clutched a wineskin. Placing the muzzle against the nape of the man's neck, he pulled the trigger.

Turning away, he saw a soldier pluck a hand-carved guitar from the ground. "No," he said sharply. "No looting."

The soldier tensed. He hugged the guitar close, as if protecting it. With surprise, Erich discerned that he was a mere boy—thirteen, perhaps, or fourteen, and so starved that his cheekbones stretched the veined, transparent skin. In his hollow eyes, and in the eyes of the others, Erich detected a crippling grief and remorse.

"Looting is unsoldierly," Erich explained. "*Comprende?*"

The boy shook his head. "Dishonorable," Erich said.

The sergeant reached Erich's side in time to translate. "*Deshonroso.*"

"Ah." Comprehension made the boy's eyes light up. "*Deshonroso.*"

Other soldiers echoed him. "*Deshonroso,*" they murmured.

Startled, Erich scanned the faces. Apparently, the soldiers were famished for reassurance, and he had stumbled on the right rations. Dishonor restored faith that honor still counted. Soldierly killings were sanctioned by the soldier's code.

The boy set the guitar gently on the ground.

A moment later, the two dirt-crusted vehicles arrived. Lurching into the clearing, they skidded to a stop. The soldiers piled into the van. Erich climbed into the passenger seat of the jeep. Replacing the driver at the wheel, the sergeant headed south with the customary clashing of gears.

It did not take long for Erich to discern that the sergeant was troubled: his mouth surly, his hands tight on the wheel. Perhaps he needed an extra dose of *deshonroso.*

The sergeant wiped his eyes. "Emilio," he said somberly.

"What?"

"Emilio. Emilio Lopez."

"Our informant? What about him?"

"Among the bodies at the shed," the sergeant said. "*Muerto.*"

"You saying he was there? That we killed him?"

"*Si*, General."

"How could that have happened? He was supposed to stay away."

The sergeant squirmed.

Erich stared at him. "Wasn't he notified?"

"I asked of my sister," the sergeant said slowly, "to tell Emilio's brother the day and time." The jeep reached an inter-section and turned onto a paved road. "She is young. All the day she dreams."

The sergeant stomped on the accelerator. The jeep shot forward. The breeze, though warm, was preferable to the stillness. The sergeant's head lifted. "But we did good, my General, as I promised. Did we not do good?"

"*Bueno,*" Erich said heartily. "*Muy bueno.*"

Further Reflections
on an
Extraordinary Crime Stopper

Murder Is My Specialty
James N. Frey

The truth of it, being a dick ain't a breeze like that Magnum guy on TV makes it look, catch? Him living in this mansion on the beach and driving a red Ferrari and all that crappola. Me, I live in my nine-by-twelve office with a worn rug and pasty walls still showing cracks from the '06 quake. You want to be a dick, you got to sacrifice, catch? And you got to be creative. A dink like Magnum living fat, he don't make it two days in the business for real.

Take the Robards case. That one took all the creativity I could create, catch?

It begins when this Tracy Robards dink calls me on the horn on a Saturday morning. I'm laying on my army cot which is crammed between my desk and the window overlooking Fifth Street in downtown San Francisco. I'm nursing a stinger hangover, watching a *Magnum* rerun on my nice black and white. I grab the horn on the second ring and announce they got Smigelski Investigation, Joe Smigelski himself speaking. There's been a murder, a female voice on the other end of the line squawks. So call the police, I says. She tells me she already called the police and a hundred other private eyes but they all think she's cuckoo. I asks her if she can handle a five-hundred-dollar retainer, cash, and she says no problem, so I tell her it's her lucky day—murder is my specialty.

I get her address and I head on out there as soon as I see how Magnum bags the perp. That's P.I. talk for *perpetrator*. You want to be a dick, that's the way you got to talk.

Anyway, this Tracy Robards dink lives in a flashy condo out on 47th Avenue by the beach. She comes to the door dressed like a business type: gray skirt, gray sweater, little gold necklace. A real neat dresser. She's maybe thirty-five, with a plain face, auburn hair combed straight down the sides, bangs in front. No ugh-o, but no raving beauty either. Her eyes are puffy and pink from doing a lot of crying. She has a firm handshake and invites me into the living room, which is full of brass and plants, real modern-like, smelling of leather cleaner. Floors as shiny as a showroom Lexus.

Me, she gives a long look-over and I guess she thinks maybe my shoes are too scuffed and my old brown suit's a little wrinkled, but hey, she hired a dick, not a dink to pose for a cover of *Gentleman's Quarterly*. So where's the corpse? I says. She doesn't know, she says. So who's the victim? I says, and she says she thinks his name is Sam, but she isn't too sure of that, and she thinks he lives in North Beach, but she's really not too sure of that either. Mysteries, it seems, are bouncing around the living room like somebody dumped a bag of ping-pong balls.

So I asks her if she's sure there's been a murder. Yes, she says. Of that, she's certain. She says I should follow her, which I do, and we go up these thick-carpeted stairs to a bedroom and inside there's a silvery computer and printer, all that modern dink stuff. Click, click, she flashes some writing on her huge blue screen. There, she says, showing me this thing that looks like a poem, and it's full of all this crap about sunsets and sunrises and how the universe has stood still since meeting fair Tracy. I near puke.

So what's this? I asks.

This, she says, is the kind of thing Sam the Lionhearted had been sending her by e-mail. E which? I says. She explains that it's like writing letters on the computer and so I says, yeah, and so what, so where's the stiff? She shows me this other letter and it's signed by a guy named Abner Doubleday, and it says that an emergency came up and Sam the Lionhearted had to leave the country and was never coming back.

A single tear, about the size of a grape, rolls down the dink's face. She says she was desperately in love with him and now that he's been murdered she wants the guilty party put away for life—but not executed—she's against the death penalty. Dead against it.

Okay, I says, so the guy had to leave the country. Let me ask again, where's the body? Then she says she doesn't know, but for sure he was murdered because he'd never leave her, them two being so much in love. So I says, okay, good, let me have a description of Sam the Lionhearted, and this is when the dink lays on me that even though they've been sending this gooey love poetry to each other for two years over the computer they have never actually met like two flesh-and-blood lovers usually do, at least in circles I been traveling in.

Which proves, I think, that no matter how long you're in this business, a dink can surprise you.

If he wasn't dead, he could access the net anywhere, she says. Sob, sob. The net? I says. That's right, the net—the Internet—the information superhighway, she says, which I remember vaguely from some election campaign, but I thought it was part of the Interstate System and so I voted for the guy because I like freeways. Sam could, she says, send her e-mail at her e-mail address TracyR@Telenet.com. And I says, oh yeah, sure. So I ask her for the five hundred retainer and she says okay, and she gets her purse and counts out five slam and I say if there's a corpse, I'll smell it out. She says I should maybe start with his e-mail address, which, she says, is Lionhearted@World.On.Line.com. I tell her I'll be in touch. She says that World On-Line will not give out any information on their members, absolutely, and hacking your way in just wouldn't be possible.

It's best not to let on you don't have no idea what the hell a dink client's talking about, so I tell her that for Joe Smigelski the impossible is as easy as making a peanut butter and jelly sandwich.

From this Robards dink's place I go to my sister's apartment in Oakland. She's got a smart-ass twelve-year-old kid named Edgar, "The King of the Hackers," as he calls himself, who for a slam goes bingo-bango with his Macintosh computer and spits me out a name: Samuel Lionel Molner and an address in The City (which is what San Franciscans call San Francisco and never "Frisco") over on Filbert. I says to the kid I think he's stiffing me, a hundred bucks for what don't take ten minutes. The smart ass says I'm lucky I'm his uncle, otherwise he wouldn't waste his time—he gets ten times that from the FBI.

So I have some supper at this Mexican joint called The Bean and Me that has a hot sauce the City of Oakland requires be served with a fire extinguisher. I have the *Supremo Grande* dinner. Then I head back to San Francisco. I find the address on Filbert and go directly to the manager's apartment. Turns out he's a bald cretin, maybe fifty, chomping on a cigar—wants half a slam to talk and we negotiate down to a quarter slam. I ask him about this Molner dink and he says he's never seen him—he sticks to his room and ain't been out in the daylight since he lived there. But sometimes, late at night, he hears his car going out. So how's he make a living? I ask, and he says he's maybe a vampire. Chuckle, chuckle. I says I heard he may be a murder victim, and the cretin just laughs and says I watch too much TV. I ask him if he knows this Abner Doubleday and he says sure, he invented baseball. Now we're getting someplace, I says, catch?

Funny, but every time I go over to Oakland and visit Edgar, I get a lot of gas. I pop a few Rolaids and go up to Apartment 3 and knock on the door. Nobody answers, so I bang my fist and yell that I'm the cockroach inspector and if he don't open up I'll have the cops on his ass for harboring cockroaches. This is what it means to be creative.

The door opens a crack on a thick chain and a sleepy voice says like he don't got no cockroaches and where's my ID. It's dark inside. I ask him if he's Molner and he says who's asking. So I asks him about this Doubleday dink and he shouts that Sam the Lionhearted is gone forever and she should forget him.

And he slams the door in my face, and the truth of it is, I don't know from Montana what the hell's going on. So I figure to hang around and see what the dink does next, now that I've stirred up the soup a little, catch?

So here I am. It's three in the morning and I'm across the street sitting in my cozy old VW bus, sipping coffee and munching chocolate donuts—the dick's diet, one of the best things about being a dick—when I sees a Toyota coming out of the dink's garage and so I tail him without turning my headlights on which is dangerous as hell, but us dicks, we feed on danger. I follow the Toyota out Bay Street all the way to the end, where he turns and goes over to Geary and out Geary to Land's End, where he goes up over a curb and gets on this sort of path leading down to the cliff above the ocean.

Here, I follow on foot, taking with me this flashlight that cost me $25.95 at Radio Shack and is about a million candlepower. The sea is pounding away, and it's windy and cold and foggy and smells of dead fish. I find the Toyota with the trunk open and hear some grunting and I head down toward the cliff and I see the guy lugging this huge chest. The dink's getting rid of the stiff, I figure. I get all excited, thinking I'm gonna get my mug on TV, drum up a little business, which has in fact been a little stinko of late.

He drags the chest over some rocks to the edge of the cliff and I know if he gives it a push, it's good-bye Charley. I hit the light and yell freeze, and the dink, he jumps about four feet in the air with his hands up. Don't shoot! he screams.

That's when I see the dink's wearing a ski mask, real mysterious.

I tell him to open the chest. He fumbles with the lock and opens it, then stands back for me to see.

I shine the light inside. No corpse, catch? It's full of computer stuff. I put the light back on the perp. He's still got his hands up.

So what's this? I says. Illegal dumping, he says, and I got him dead to rights and he wants to confess and hope they lock him up and throw away the key and nobody ever hears from him again. Then he says how he had to get this damn computer and modem out of his life, how if he had it around it would mock him. Mock his life.

What the hell is he talking about, I ask. Tracy, he says. He fell in love with her, he says, his voice squeaking when he says her name. I tell him I don't get it. He says it's all too horrible, too tangled, too grotesque. His life is a shambles because of the damn computer, he says, so he wants to feed it to the fishes.

Then the dink sits down on a rock and starts bawling through his ski mask. This guy, I think, needs a weed whacker for his brain. I sit down next to him and tell him I ain't a cop, that I work for Tracy Robards and he says he knew it as soon as I asked for Sam the Lionhearted. He says he found out where she lived from a kid in Oakland called The King of the Hackers and he went over to her beach condo and watched her leave for work one morning, and that's when he saw what a knockout she was.

I tell him it's all about as clear as soap.

So he explains how they started writing each other on this network, and she started reading his poetry and how she even got a poetry magazine to buy a few, and how he won an award, and how it was only her that inspired the poems, and how he fell in love with her and told her he was six-foot tall and he's really five-eight, but worst of all, he told her he was average-looking, when in fact he had a hideous, disfigured face that no woman could ever love. He said he knew a chick that looked that great wouldn't give him the time of day. He says compared to him, Herman Munster was Cary Grant.

I says I got it now.

So I help the dink toss the chest off the cliff into the ocean and when we're on the way back to the car I'm figuring how to be creative about this. A dink like Magnum, he'd be lost. I says to this Molner dink that I'll report back to my client that he's really dead, on one condition—that he pay me two thousand bucks. He looks at me through the eyeholes in the ski mask and calls me a blank blank blackmailer. Hey, I says, business ain't been so good. You want me to do you a favor, you got to pony up—I got to make a living too.

He'll pay, he says.

So I know this cretin named Benny the Toad who runs a girlie joint down in the Tenderloin called Satin and Silk, and I tell this Molner dink to meet me down there to give me the bread Monday 'cause on Monday the Satin and Silk ain't open. Time: 11:00 hours. That's dick talk for eleven in the morning. I figure to give him time to get the two bang out of the bank.

Monday comes and I got everything ready. I get Tracy Robards to come with me and sit in Toad's office. Here there's a two-way mirror and you can see into the girls' dressing room. In this office me and Toad have spent many a pleasant evening. Then I go into the girls' dressing room and wait for Molner. At about two minutes after eleven Benny lets the dink in. He's wearing a coat with the collar up and a knit hat down over his head, and huge dark glasses so I can't see his face. First thing the dink says is he wants some proof that this is the only payment and I tells him that Joe Smigelski is the straightest dick in San Francisco and when he says he's only gonna tap you once, that's it. I tell him I ain't about to lose my rep for nothing. He buys it, taking out the money and counting out twenty one-hundred bills, crisp and new smelling, fresh as cut grass.

He starts to leave and I tell him to wait a minute—I want to see what he looks like on account of I'm real curious. He spits out some nasty words about my mother's sex life and starts for the door, but I block his way, reaching into my pocket where I got a hero sandwich for lunch but I make him think I got a heater and tell him to take off his hat and glasses and let me see or I'm going to open a portal to his liver. He steps back—the dumb dink thinks I'm gonna do it, catch—and he rips off his hat and glasses and damn if he ain't an ugh-o. His eyes are as close together as the barrels of a shotgun and he's got a nose as flat as a dance-hall floor. See what a geek he is, he says, sob, sob.

Man, I think, did I make a whopper of a mistake. Better to think he's dead than to think she was getting love poems from the Creature from the Black Lagoon.

But that's when I hear Tracy on the other side of the two-way mirror, yelling that he's beautiful, catch? Then a second later she's running in and hugging this Molner dink and kissing him and he's hugging and kissing her, and the Toad comes in and he starts bawling, and a bunch of the girls who was hanging around rehearsing come in bawling, and maybe I got to use a Kleenex, too, but only because I got something in my eye. Real dicks never get mushy.

So two days later Tracy Robards and Samuel Lionel Molner go to Reno and commit matrimony and about nine months and two days later she has a baby that they name Edgar after The King of the Hackers. Okay? See what I mean about a real dick being creative?

You probably want to know what happened to the two bang left on the table, which vanished like a puff of smoke in all the excitement and kissing and bawling. It was never found. Hey, unlike that dink Magnum, in the real dick world some mysteries ain't never solved.

Reflections on Fate

The Good-bye Room
James N. Frey

Early on this Friday morning, Danny McCall paces in his cell on death row in the dim light filtering through the bars from the gun tower outside. Danny's gaunt and drawn, dragging his feet as he marches off the length of the cell in four strides. At each end, he puts his toe behind his heel, turns, and marches back again. As he paces he hears the other condemned men snoring, coughing, moaning, talking in their sleep. They give off a strange odor at night, pungent as ammonia. Fear, he'd been told. Fear made them smell like that. They were scared even in their sleep.

Danny knows about fear. His name is next on the dance card. He feels his flesh smoldering as he struggles to keep the image of the green death chamber out of his mind. The green death chamber where soon they plan to strap him to a wooden chair and put a black hood over his face. Then they'll shut the massive steel door and seal him in alone where the last thing he'll hear is the hiss of the gas.

In just a little while now he'll be taken to the holding cell right next to the death chamber. The cell the guys on the row call the "good-bye room."

There a doctor will examine him. There he'll have his last visit from relatives—if any of the sorry bastards come. In the good-bye room he'll have his last meal just before noon: blood-red steak and French fries, and a couple of cans of malt liquor. A week ago when he put in his order his mouth watered, and he looked forward to the malt liquor most of all, to that sweet taste of the cold liquid sliding over his tongue and down his throat. But now his mouth is parched and the thought of eating anything turns his stomach. The malt liquor would be like drinking piss.

For the past few nights he's refused to sleep no matter how much his eyes burn. To sleep is to lose hours of consciousness. To sleep is to turn out the light that will soon be forever dark.

Mike Phelps, Danny's young lawyer, had stopped by about midnight. As usual, he was wearing a gray, pinstriped suit with a vest, looking like a teenager playing dress up. The appeals court had rejected their latest appeal, Mike Phelps told him. Mike Phelps' associate was still in Washington appealing to a Supreme Court Justice for a stay, he said, but it didn't look good. Danny had already had three stays. Each time an appeal had been heard, a judgment rendered, a new execution date fixed. This time Mike Phelps and his associate were asking for a stay based on the argument that Danny didn't have good representation at his trial, that there was something wrong with the judge's instructions to the jury, that Danny should have had a psychiatric evaluation done by his original defense team. Mike Phelps left saying they had a good shot at it, that Danny shouldn't lose hope.

Danny only vaguely understood these legal proceedings. All he knew for sure was his life was hanging by a thread. If the Supremes turned him down, all that was left was the possibility the governor might grant clemency on a so-called "personal appeal." The guys on the row all said the wimpy bastard was squeamish about gassing human beings. It was the Last Chance Cafe.

In his personal letter Danny had laid it on thick about the gas choking you, breaking blood vessels in the lung, making you feel like your head was about to explode. Gruesome stuff. And he wrote a lot about how much he'd changed in prison, how he was in counseling with a psychologist. How he was sorry for everything he'd done wrong in his life. Everything the law had him for, and everything else he'd done wrong, too. Like not staying in school. Like nicking his sister once with a knife. Like killing squirrels with a BB gun for fun. He figured he had a good shot with the governor.

It was the waiting to hear that was the torture. These endless stays and appeals were eating his guts. He picks up the tempo as he paces, his mind feverish—not just about what was gonna happen, but how he'd gotten where he was. He'd even been talking to a pinched-faced lady psychologist about how he came to be here. There had to be a reason for him turning evil. There had to be a reason the madness came to him sometimes and made him do bad things. Some kind of logical explanation.

In the first years after his arrest and conviction, he'd never given it a thought, but lately, as the clock ran down, he found himself becoming obsessed with knowing himself. The "why" of himself. Could he have been born bad? Have an evil nature? Somehow, it didn't seem possible. Before his mother died when he was six, he wasn't evil. Everybody said he was a sweet child. Everybody. Aunt Agnes told *Time Magazine* he was as huggable as a Paddington teddy bear. And the neighbors who knew him then, they said he loved to lick the center out of the Oreos that his mother gave him for being good, and he always said please and thank you, real respectful.

And then one morning he found his mother lying in her own puke, her skin as gray as fish scales, mouth agape, staring up at nothing through frosted-glass eyes. Until that day he was a good boy with no evil in him, he was certain of that.

That means the evil had to have started with Margo.

He remembers the night he met her when he was six years old. His father bought him new shoes for the occasion. Brown and white saddle shoes. Shiny and new-smelling. And his Aunt

Agnes dressed him up in a blue sport jacket and bow tie. Quite the little man, Aunt Agnes had said, all dressed up to meet his new mom.

He remembers the way Margo smelled that first time. Oily and perfumy, sickly sweet. She had on a new dress with little white flowers, flashing a big smile. She'd bought some Good & Plenty for Danny, trying to buy his affection, he thinks now.

He still remembers his father secretly holding her hand in the theater that night. Hiding their hands under a pink coat. How angry it made Danny feel. His real mom had only been dead a few months. Sure, she had been sick a long time, but she had been in the ground only a little while and Danny still hurt real bad.

Sweet-pretending Margo, always wanting him to hug her, and he would, too, at first. Before she turned mean on him. Like when she started making him buy Kotex for her. He had no idea what Kotex was, but there was something not too nice about it. The clerks would always shove the box in the bag quickly.

And then sometimes it would be snowing and cold and she'd send him to the store for cinnamon or something. Just to get him out of the house. She never wanted him around. Especially after Angela was born. Ah, yes, little Angela, always dressed in pink, pink bows in her hair. Cute little Angela. Darling little Angela, who could do no wrong. Did he hate the mother or the daughter more? It is hard to know. When dealing with megatons of hatred, exact measurement is difficult.

And then there was Margo's bitching at his father: When you going to fix the porch? Why haven't you gotten the car washed? How come you never take me to dinner? Most every night he'd take it for a while, then he'd slink off to Morgantown Tavern. How many nights had Danny laid in bed and listened to her harangue his father in the next room? A thousand? Ten thousand? Day by day, week by week, month by month, the old man seemed to get physically smaller. He had been a large man, a former Marine. Danny watched him shrink down inside himself. Turn from a man into a bar rag. Then finally dying of a stroke while sitting on the can with his pants down around his ankles. Fifty-six was all he was.

Even before the old man's stroke, Danny remembers how he, Danny, spent many happy hours dreaming of the exquisite pleasure of putting his hands around Margo's throat and squeezing the life out of her like he'd squeeze the juice from an orange. What rapture it would be!

But he remembers his dad saying over and over, "I love that woman. Please, Danny, be patient. For me. Be real nice to her. If you don't, she'll take it out on me."

And he remembers how he tried to be nice to Margo, how he tried to make her like him, but by then, it seemed, she no longer wanted to like him and there was a wall of meanness between them.

Danny remembers how the bitch would sit around with her robe half open, showing off her boobs and looking at him with that hungry way of hers. Him at thirteen, maybe, when he didn't know what it was all about, but feeling the burning inside, the burning that a woman can bring on a man.

And he remembers the first time he got into trouble, when he'd pulled down the panties of the Jenson girl up the street, just playing, really, horsing around, wanting to see her box, and then her screaming rape and Margo talking about it for months afterward, telling her friends on the phone how they were keeping him around the house, keeping an eye on him. Like there was something freakish about him.

Then there was the pink couch. How Margo loved pink. How Danny was told he couldn't sit on it. His own house, and he couldn't sit on the damn living-room couch. Even when he was a teenager, having friends over. The damn pink couch sitting there like a shrine.

And she'd make peanut butter cookies and hide them, keep them for herself and Angela. The selfish bitch. He feels the old rage rise within him. It wasn't the cookies, it was the feeling of being outside the family. Like he was dog shit.

He kicks the bunk.

The guard at the desk down the hall says: "Cool it there, McCall."

Danny sits on the bunk and rubs his cold hands together. The hands that had got him here. Soon they'd be dead, just like the rest of him. They'd be bluish and waxy-looking and they'd start to rot.

Bile rises in his throat, gagging him for a moment, his mouth suddenly watering like he might vomit, but he fights it down.

He leans back and lights a cigarette, the match illuminating the little cell, showing the huge mural he'd scratched into the wall with the tip of a ballpoint pen. It shows girls playing softball. He'd seen a bunch of girls playing softball once on a hot July day. It seemed real strange, them playing ball in all that heat. The sweat on them had excited him, but he hadn't done anything to any of them. That day he'd only looked and he was glad of that, they were all so pretty and young and fresh.

But there were others he had done bad things to and he still didn't know why. He didn't have anything against them. He didn't even know them. It was the madness that took him over.

The pinched-faced psychologist had asked him to think of the bad times he'd had. The things that made him mad. Every time he thought of what made him mad he thought of Margo. How she wouldn't let him take the car even after he got his license because she might have to take Angela someplace. How she wouldn't let him bring his bike in the entry hall and how it got stolen out of the driveway. How she wouldn't let him join the Little League because after school he had to watch Angela so Margo could go to the beauty parlor or visit her dumb friends.

Could that have done it? Like the Chinese water torture, where they drip water on a man's forehead until he goes mad. Could it be that he'd been driven mad by a million little hurts at the hands of a master torturer?

Suddenly all the lights on the row go on and a buzzer sounds. The six a.m. breakfast call. The men on the row stop snoring and start bitching. Charley Knox crowing like a rooster. Sid Brennen, in his deep baritone, sings a blues song. Willie-the-Toad Granger starts praying, asking the Lord for a permanent stay.

Suddenly the metal slot in the door opens and a tray slides through with his breakfast, his next-to-last meal: oatmeal, milk, juice, coffee.

Looking at it makes him want to vomit again.

He goes back to pacing, thinking of Margo and those peanut butter cookies he never got to eat, knowing it wouldn't have meant anything to anybody else, but to him it was like one more drop in the Chinese water torture. He feels the anger all over again, yet . . . yet simultaneously he feels strangely elated because he was finally getting an understanding of this thing. This evil. This madness.

Then he hears a key in the thick iron lock on his door. News of his stay? He sits back on the bed, hands behind his head. He tells himself not to let them see him scared.

His cell door opens and Mike Phelps, his well-dressed kid attorney paid for by the ACLU, steps in. He says, "Sorry, man, really," hanging his head. "The Supreme Court Justice didn't buy the argument." He adds brightly: "But there's still the governor."

Danny says, "You did your best, I sure do appreciate it, Mr. Phelps."

Now the assistant warden comes in. Brown, baggy suit. Gray, sad eyes. "It's time to move you, Danny. I hope you're not going to give us any trouble about it."

"No, sir, I'm on my best behavior today."

Noticing his kid lawyer fighting back a tear, Danny thinks he doesn't have the balls for this kind of work. Maybe if he'd had more balls, he would have gotten the stay.

Two guards come in and put the cuffs and leg irons on Danny. A matter of form, they tell him. Rules. Procedures. It's all been regularized, bureaucratized. Danny notices the assistant warden's shoes are scuffed. He finds this strangely offensive. Like the man did not give proper weight to the proceedings.

"You want to take along any of your books?" the assistant warden asks.

"Won't be needin' them, sir. No time for reading today."

"How about pen and paper?"

"I've about written myself out, you want to know the truth of it."

"Okay, then. Let's go."

Out into the corridor now, feeling the eyes of the other row inmates on him. Danny holds himself erect, showing no fear. Being a man about it.

"There's still the governor," his lawyer says again, like there's really a good shot here.

"Yeah," Danny says, turning to the assistant warden. "Hey, if he does come through, do I still get my steak and fries and two stout malts?"

"We'll have to see about that," the assistant warden says.

At the end of the corridor Danny stops and turns to the other inmates. "Okay, you guys, been a pleasure knowing all you scum, and if the governor don't come through, I guess I'll be in hell waiting for you."

They give him a round of applause, him going out with aplomb. Abel Tanner gives him a rebel yell, "Yahoooooo," that echoes into the exercise yard outside.

"Suck it quick!" Willie-the-Toad calls out.

Now through the steel door and up the stairs, slowly, one step at a time on account of the leg irons. The guard opens the door. Now through it and down a hallway. Opaque windows admit yellow, ghostly light. Through another door to the good-bye room, a cell about four times the size of the one he'd been living in on death row for eight years. There's a table and bench secured to the floor, and a cot. Flickering fluorescent lights. And it smells of the grave, like it'd been closed up for a hundred years. Here he can taste the fear that hangs suspended in the air.

His lawyer says he's going to check on the governor. He'll let Danny know, he says, soon as he hears one way or the other.

As he goes out, a priest comes in. He's Father Darcy, a large man with a round, drinker's face. Danny already told him he wasn't a Catholic any more but he kept stopping by every once in a while to ask if he could do anything. Get him stamps, writing paper, books to read, things like that.

"You mind me being here, Danny?"

"Naw." Danny thinks the priest is brainwashed and full of bullshit, but otherwise an okay guy.

The guards take off Danny's cuffs and leg irons. One of the guards gives him a pat on the shoulder, as if to thank him for not creating a stir. The guards want to do their killing in an orderly way, by the book, Danny thinks. That's all that matters with them. It ain't personal. They leave and close the door so he can be alone with the priest.

"How much time I got?" Danny asks the priest.

"Five hours, almost. They do it at noon. They'll bring you your meal at eleven-fifteen."

"Feels hot in here, don't it?"

"Perhaps a little. Is there anything I can do for you, Danny? Do you want to pray? Let's kneel and pray together."

"It's a little too late for me to do any praying."

"Don't put any limits on God, Danny. He loves you, you know."

"Me and God, we went our separate ways a long time ago."

Danny asks him why it was when Adam and Eve fell, that the animals suffered too, and the priest launches into a rambling discourse on God's will, God's plan for suffering humanity, and the redemptive power of Christ that Danny can't quite follow, but he finds it comforting and so he sits there and listens as the priest drones on and on.

An hour passes; time has become a thick syrup. A knock at the door. The priest opens it. A white-haired man comes in, the assistant warden at his elbow.

"This here is Doctor Mills," the assistant warden says.

The priest says he'll be back in a few minutes, he'll see if there are any visitors. He leaves.

"What's the doctor here for?" Danny asks the assistant warden.

"He wants to listen to your heart, won't take but a minute."

The doctor, an old man with a gray pallor, puts his stethoscope to his ears. "Open your shirt, please, Mr. McCall."

"What the hell you want to listen to my heart for?"

"It's required."

"Hey, that's the answer for everything around here. What if I say no?"

"You really don't want to make it hard on yourself, do you Danny?" the assistant warden says. "The time is short. You don't want to be shackled."

"Hey, I was just asking. A guy's about to be done in, he's got a right to ask things, don't he?"

"I suppose," the assistant warden says.

The doctor listens to his chest for a second or two, then shines a light in his eyes. "Not sleeping, eh? That's common."

The doctor asks Danny to hold still, whispering, "You want me to give you something later, make it easy? It's allowed, but it's up to you."

"Naw, I want my wits about me."

"Okay, son, but if you change your mind, just tell one of the guards."

"Okay."

The doctor shuffles out of the room. The assistant warden and the guards follow him. They close the door; Danny hears the key in the lock.

He's alone again, alone with his thoughts. He starts thinking of Margo and the Chinese water torture, thinking of what she did at his father's funeral in the back of the Cadillac on the way to the cemetery. It was just the three of them—Danny, Margo, and Angela, who was maybe eleven at the time. Margo was crying, but Danny thought she was faking it. Her saying, "I know one is not supposed to say this, but it's the truth and somebody's got to say it. It was you that killed your father, Danny. Him worrying about you all the time, that's what done him in. Especially what you done to that girl."

Meaning the one he'd taken to the high school dance, Mary Ellen Lubcheck, the cock teaser who'd come on to him in the back of the car after the dance and then wouldn't give out, so he slapped her around a little and the bitch had him arrested. Then that hotshot assistant DA wanting to call it felony attempted rape, and his dumb lawyer pleading him out so he only got eighteen months. Some deal.

And then in the limo at the funeral little twit Angela nodding and saying how awful it was having a jailbird for a brother.

Now in the good-bye room Danny feels his stomach burning. He should have killed them both right then and there. Just grabbed them both by the throat and not let go and when they got to the cemetery they could have just dumped their stinking corpses into the ground.

A knock at the door. Everybody nice and polite, Danny thinks. They kill you nice and polite.

"Come in," he says.

It's the priest. "I've got some good news, Danny. You have a visitor. They're bringing her up now."

"My Aunt Agnes?"

"She wanted to come, Danny, but she's way up there in years now. It's your mother."

"Won't that be something of a miracle? My mother's been dead for thirty years."

"Sorry. I meant your stepmother."

Danny feels his stomach tighten. He hasn't seen her since the trial and still his stomach gets tight at the word "step-mother." Tight as a tourniquet.

"Think I'll pass, Father. Don't think I want to see the bitch—excuse my French."

"It won't look good, Danny, not seeing her. All the news people are outside the cell block—TV cameras—you don't want it getting back to the governor that you wouldn't see your mother."

"Okay," he says, "bring the bitch in."

While the priest goes to get her, Danny paces, feeling weird in his gut, hollow and full of fear.

After a few minutes the door opens and there she is in the doorway wearing a soft pink dress, her face fleshier than when he'd seen her at the trial eight years ago, her hair now streaked with white. He notices how her breasts heave when she gulps in air and he thinks about seeing her one time in a towel when she was coming out of the shower all wet and sweet smelling, and her giving him that sly smile and that hungry look, but him not doing anything except looking.

She comes in with the priest, the assistant warden, and two guards, who go and stand on either side of Danny, but not touching him. Giving him a little respect, a little dignity, this being his last day on earth maybe.

Danny can't take his eyes off Margo and the way her breasts heave up and down like that, like she was always in heat.

"Can't I be alone with my boy?" Margo says to the assistant warden, in what Danny knows is her sweetest, most sugary voice. "You searched everything, you know I don't have nothing on me to pass to him."

"Sorry ma'am, regulations," the assistant warden says.

"If I can't, I can't," Margo says, giving up too easy, Danny thinks.

"Hello, Danny," she says. "Good to see you."

Danny stares and says nothing.

She purses her lips. "I know you never accepted me as your mother, though the good Lord knows I tried to be a mother to you. . . ."

He watches Margo's mouth move, but for a moment her voice fades and he thinks how sweet it would be to plunge a knife into the soft flesh showing over the top of her pink dress and watch the blood make splotches all over it. And what music her screams would be, he thinks, what ecstasy to hear her death rattle, to slit her open and smell her guts.

Now hearing her say, "I came today because it was my duty to come and try to comfort you. I always did my duty to you, Danny, I'm hoping that you might acknowledge that."

In the light of the flickering overhead fluorescent lights, the pink of her dress seems almost to glow.

"That shade of pink, that have a name?" he asks, his voice sounding to him like it's coming through a hollow pipe.

"Lover's pink," she says. "My favorite shade. Your father loved me in the color, it brings out the tones in my skin."

He can't keep his eyes off the glowing pink dress. He remembers now the first one he did for real. She wore a pink scarf, the same shade of pink as that dress. He chased her down as she was jogging along a trail by a lake and took her into the weeds where he did her quick, breaking her neck in his hands.

Margo now saying, "I didn't come here to talk about me, I came here to comfort you." She pats her face with a handkerchief, mopping a film of sweat.

He thinks it is the same shade of pink for certain. Yes! The very same. He remembers the jogger coming down the trail, the scarf flopping behind her like a flag. It was the first time the madness came over him so he couldn't control it. Like a devil had him in its jaws and wouldn't let him go.

Margo prattling on, Danny catching: "Your father, it would have been awful," she says. "In a way, it's good that he didn't live to see this. I think of you and your father often, Danny, and wish things might have been different and I think they could have been had we but communicated better . . . ."

The pink scarf. Why didn't he think of it before, he wonders. He feels almost giddy, as if he's found the lock to the door of the secret reaches of his mind. The second one. She had pink shoes. Like the shoes Margo wore that summer at Bear Lake. And the third wore a pink slip that showed just a sliver beneath her skirt. He feels sweat forming on his forehead. It's all opening up like a flower and he feels it welling up in him again, the old feeling of power that came before the madness, the way a strong, clean wind sweeps over a plain before a storm.

His mouth waters as the old warmth spreads to his groin and up his torso. The madness is overtaking him, awesome and terrible, a force of nature that nothing can stop.

Margo says, "In court, you swore an oath to God that you didn't do it. I been telling all my friends how you didn't do it, that you was framed. I believed you. Well, half-believed you, to be perfectly honest. I wanted to believe you like you was my actual blood son. Was there ever love between us, Danny? I've asked myself that a thousand times. Really, I want to know." Her glancing at the assistant warden, trying to impress him, Danny thinks. Like she always wanted to impress the neighbors.

Danny says, "Kiss me, mother."

She stops talking.

"A mother's kiss," he says softly, sounding earnest. The madness has him now. Controlling him.

She turns to the assistant warden, "Might I kiss my son?"

The assistant warden looks at the guards; they consider the proposition. Danny smiles meekly at them, trying to look like a poor slob, even though the madness is bestowing on him the strength of a dozen men. He's a Samson. He could kill them all with the jawbone of an ass.

Danny says, "A kiss, what can be the harm? How will it look on the TV news tonight if you didn't let my mother kiss me good-bye?"

The assistant warden nods to the guards.

Margo stepping forward now.

"Keep you hands behind your back," the assistant warden says to Danny.

Danny hearing himself say, "Oh, I will sir."

Margo close now. Danny puts his hands dutifully behind his back. Her leaning towards him, puckering, his eyes on the sheer white skin of her throat. *Leap now*, he tells himself, *crush her throat quickly*.

But his body does not move; it's frozen in place. He feels her warm, wet lips upon his cheeks and a tremor of revulsion goes through his body. The kiss of a slime monster.

Do it now! But still his body will not react to his command. He starts shaking, in the grip of the madness. His damn body refuses to budge. Closing his eyes, he sees her face bloat and turn purple. A soft moan escapes his lips. *Kill the bitch!*

But he does not move. Can't move. Instead he stands frozen and dizzy, rocking back and forth, hearing a faint voice in his head. *I love her, Danny, don't ever hurt her.* And in a kaleidoscope of fractured memories, it's like a thousand other times he had moved on her to kill her and had been frozen by that voice in his head.

She steps away from him and he falls back on the coarse blanket on the cot, the strength quickly gone out of his limbs, the madness and the power draining from his body.

"I guess I better be going now, Danny," she says. "I hope this isn't good-bye. I hope the governor comes through for you, honestly I do."

Warm tears run down Danny's face. The moment has escaped him again. His last possible chance.

"Oh, Danny, you poor boy," Margo says. "You poor, poor boy. I love you as if you were my own son. I've always loved you. If only your father had not been so difficult . . . ." She starts towards him, but the assistant warden holds her back. "I do love you, Danny. Honest. I love you with all my heart."

"Love?" Danny says. He stands on his shaking legs and shouts: "Love! You love only yourself and that monstrous little cretin you gave birth to. Love! You selfish bitch! God, I want you dead! I want to kill you! I want to sink my teeth into your throat and rip out your jugular!" He bursts into sobs, then screams: "Even now, with him long dead, Dad's still protecting you. Oh, God, I want you dead!"

The priest puts his hand on his shoulder. "Please, Danny, you can't mean that."

Danny pushes the priest's hand off his shoulder. "All them girls," he says to Margo, "they all died on account of you."

"How dare you say that? How dare you try to implicate me in your foul deeds?"

"I was not born evil! I wasn't. Ask Aunt Agnes. She said I was a regular Paddington bear. It was you who changed me. You put the madness in me!"

"No, Danny. I knew by the way you looked at me you had a filthy mind. I was your father's wife, not yours. You could never stand that."

"You're a damned liar! You prancing around half naked all the time! You in that pink robe, your tits hanging out. You're the evil one. Oh, God, why didn't I do it? Why didn't I do it?"

"This is going to be on TV and the governor is going to hear of it," Margo says. "I'll have to tell the truth, you know. You're a horrible person. You deserve what they're going to do to you today."

"No I don't—you do!"

She turns to the assistant warden. "His father was a weakling, and the son is a coward who can't stand up to what's his own doing."

"Yes, ma'am," the assistant warden says.

She turns and steps out into the corridor.

"Let me finish her!" Danny screams. "She's the devil!"

He starts for her, but the guards hold him, forcing him back onto the coarse gray blanket. He tries to shake them loose, but, seeing she's gone, he stops struggling and the guards back off.

The priest mumbles a prayer to the Virgin under his breath.

"Don't you see?" Danny says to the priest. "It was the pink. That was it all along."

"The pink?" the priest says, not comprehending.

"It brought the madness. I wasn't born evil, don't you see?"

The priest nods, but it's clear by the perplexed expression on his face that he doesn't understand.

Danny sees pity, too, on his face. Because it's over now. The governor won't give him clemency and he'll have to suck the gas. He feels a wave of panic and goes rigid.

But then he thinks: *At least the agony of waiting is over.*

Danny sits back on the cot and lights a cigarette, calming himself, thinking that somehow, by nailing the bitch, he'd struck a blow for himself. And it was starting to make sense—all the ragged, jumbled-up pieces of his screwed-up life were falling into place. He wasn't evil by nature, that was the most important thing. His heart beats fast.

When Danny hears the cart coming with his steak and fries and two cans of stout malt liquor, he asks the priest to go. He thanks him for trying his best to help make things easier. The inmate who brought the food tray takes the towel that was covering it off. The French fries are golden brown and piled high. The steak is blood red, just as he ordered it. And they did bring two cans of stout malt liquor. He digs in with relish, carefully chewing each piece of meat, washing it down with the cold brew that slides so smoothly over his tongue.

The assistant warden tells Danny he's never seen a man enjoy a meal so much.

Duty
James N. Frey

It was the day shift's turn to participate in the lottery. It took place at 16:10 hours in the staff coffee room at the far end of the row just after the shift was over. The nine men and one woman filed in with the quiet solemnity of monks at vespers and stood around the long, narrow table. Yellow light filtered in past the curtains that showed gray shadows from the bars on the outside of the windows. No one sat down. No one spoke. The air was stale. They all knew why they were there, even though the memo that had summoned them didn't state the purpose. Some glanced at each other, suppressing nervous smiles. A few lit cigarettes.

The day shift leader, Sergeant Bill Martinez, came out of his small office with a yellow riot helmet tucked under his arm and stood at the head of the table. His lips were drawn tight over his teeth. He removed his ID badge from his pocket and dropped it into the upside-down riot helmet. He passed the helmet around and each of the officers dropped their ID into it. When it got back to him, Martinez put his hand in the helmet and stirred up the badges. The clips made scraping sounds against the metal helmet.

"Everybody in?" he asked.

Everyone nodded.

"Who wants to do the honors?" Martinez asked. No one volunteered. "Okay," he said. "Guess I'm elected."

He held the helmet high and reached in and took out one of the badges and dropped it on the table. Everyone seemed to hold their breath. The badge landed upside down. No one moved to pick it up for a long moment. Finally, Old Gus Handly, who had worked on the row longer than anyone, reached for it and flipped it over.

It was Billie Sue Dodds', the only woman who worked the row.

A few sighs of relief were heard. One of the men whistled.

"Nice going, Billie Sue," Old Gus said. "You win a day's leave and a hundred-dollar bonus."

Charlie Stephens said, "Let's see if she's got the balls for it."

"Enough of that!" Martinez snapped. "Billie Sue knows her duty and she'll carry it out like any other officer."

They picked up their ID badges and started filing out. Martinez gave Billie Sue a reassuring, tentative smile and went into his office. One of the men, Randy Walsh, a florid-faced Irishman, stayed behind with Billie Sue, who was still holding her badge in her hand, staring at it, her cheeks flushed.

Walsh said, "You only been up here three months, nobody'd fault you if you said nay."

"Wouldn't they?" she said.

He clipped his badge on. "I guess maybe they would at that."

She clipped her badge back on. It felt strangely slippery to the touch. "I guess with forty-seven officers assigned to the row, I figured I'd be up here a while before my number came up." Under her uniform she felt goose flesh on her arms.

"You never know," Walsh said. "Jennings walked the row for twenty-one years and his badge never popped out of the helmet. He used to say he just weren't lucky."

"Yeah," she said. "Not like me."

"Nothing to worry about, Billie Sue," Walsh said. "It's a matter of pulling a lever when they tell you."

"Seems simple, don't it?"

Billie Sue got her purse from the small locker near the time clock. Some of the other lockers had pictures of little chairs with straps on the arms to mark when a correctional officer had won the lottery and carried out his assignment. It wasn't professional, doing things like that, she thought, and Billie Sue prided herself most of all on her professionalism.

But then what of her professionalism if she couldn't go through with it? she wondered.

Suddenly she could see in her mind's eye a man in the chair, strapped down, and the pellet falling into the pail to make the gas. It gave her a queer feeling deep inside, a tingle that she hadn't felt since she was a kid daring to go too high on a swing, higher even than the boys.

Sam, Billie Sue's husband, looked across the dinner table at her and said, "You ain't talking much tonight."

"Got a lot on my mind, Sam." She glanced at her eleven-year-old daughter, Jennifer, who seemed absorbed with moving peas around her plate. Billie Sue passed the fresh-from-the-oven cornbread to her, but Jennifer declined. Her daughter was at the awful stage, Billie Sue thought, acting just as surly as she had at that age.

Since there was a good chance the condemned man would get a reprieve and the assignment would be rescinded, there was no use telling her daughter about it. Billie Sue knew deep in her heart that her daughter would react emotionally to it. She seemed to be getting emotional now at most everything.

Sam cut into his Salisbury steak and shoveled a juicy hunk into his mouth. He was a wrought-iron worker by trade. A big man, with round, brown, friendly, curious eyes. They were eating in the breakfast nook of their nearly new, double-wide modular home. Out the bay windows, the summer sun was setting over the mountains on the other side of the valley. The gray stone prison across the valley was gradually disappearing into the shadows.

"I've got my Bible group tonight," Sam said. He was a lay preacher at the Christian Fellowship Church. "Want to come, girls? We're doing Luke."

"Got to study," Jennifer said. "Big test tomorrow in history."

"I'm kinda tired," Billie Sue said. "Hope you don't mind, Sam." The truth was, she never could get too enthused about Bible studies. She was sure it was good—she just didn't see where it applied to her personally. The way she looked at it, as long as you were a good person, you were Christian enough.

"Maybe you ought to quit the row," Sam said suddenly. "Go back to work on the main line. Working the main line didn't seem to wear you out."

"It's getting better, really."

"I don't like seeing you look this tired."

"I'll go to bed early."

Sam stuffed his mouth with cornbread, chewing slowly. "The other officers, they still giving you a hard time?" he asked.

"I can handle it."

"They're just against a woman getting something after nine years they had to wait twenty years to get. They don't understand that they should have women up there on the row, and they would have had if women had been allowed to be correctional officers twenty years ago. It's only right."

"They'll get used to the idea. They can't go on acting like four-year-olds forever."

"Makes me mad as hell you got to put up with them being mean to you."

"So they hide my time card and they make cracks. They'll get tired of it after a while. When women first started working on the main line they had to put up with worse. Let's not talk about it, okay?"

"Okay."

"Tell me about your day," she said, trying to look interested.

Sam told her he spent the day making a fence around the pool at the new Motel 6. He told a joke he heard about space men. Billie Sue didn't pay much attention, but she smiled and pretended she thought it was cute.

After dinner, Sam helped his daughter clean up the dishes, then he hurried off to church. Billie Sue started in on the laundry that had been piling up, trying to keep her mind off things at the prison, but it kept flashing in her mind how her badge looked when it was flipped over and the strange sensation she'd felt. Her mouth felt dry thinking about it.

$\bullet$

It was after ten when Sam got home to a darkened house. He put his large, leather-bound King James Bible in its honored place in the cabinet at the end of the bookshelves in the entryway. He found Billie Sue wrapped in her old flannel robe, lounging in the La-Z-Boy by a crackling fire, staring into the flames.

"Thought you'd be in bed, hon," Sam said.

"Couldn't sleep."

"Somethin' real bad happened out there today, didn't it? One of them do something nasty to you?"

"Not this time."

"The Lord sent me to you so's you'd have somebody to care for you. I can't do nothing if you don't tell me."

She took his hand. "You're so strong. Sometimes I wish I was a man. My female feelings sometimes get in the way."

He pulled up a footstool and sat next to her.

"Whatever it is, we can work it out."

She stared into the flickering flames. "I'd have said something at dinner, only I didn't want Jennifer to hear. They got an execution on July 29th at noon. The condemned man's name is Walter Michael Jones. Maybe you read about him in the paper. He's a black man, killed them two police officers over in King City about ten years ago. Tied them up, shot them each about

232

fifteen times with a shotgun. They said on one of them TV crime shows you couldn't even hardly tell the victims was human."

Sam bowed his head. "The devil was surely working on that man's soul that day. Why does there have to be that much hate in the world? The execution, that what's troubling you? I guess this will be your first one since you been on the row."

"It's not just the execution. We hold a lottery on the row to see which of us got to pull the lever that lets the cyanide pellet into the chamber."

"Oh, my God, it was you was the one picked, Billie Sue?"

She nodded.

He stared at her, shaking his head in disbelief.

"Somebody's got to do it," she said. "We're only carrying out the law."

"Ain't there no way to get out of it? You only been working on the row three months."

"It's my job. I got to take the good with the bad."

Sam stood up and paced around the room for a moment, rubbing his head. "I don't know about this, Billie Sue, I just don't know. I had no idea that they'd make you do something like that. I always figured they had professionals for that kind of thing."

"There's nothing in the Bible against it, is there?"

"No, no, of course not. The Lord says you can execute murderers. Send them to him."

"Then I got to do it."

"Not if you was no longer on the row. You could always go back to the main line. They'd have to pick somebody else."

"And then what would they say? A woman can't hack it on the row?"

"That wouldn't be the end of the world, Billie."

She said nothing for a long time. They sat holding hands until the log burned down to glowing cinders.

Finally Billie Sue said, "I'd just be doing my job."

He nodded, but she could see that he didn't understand the importance of it.

﹏

Billie Sue took the lunch tray off the cart and put it into the slot of the door on cell number 24. Usually, she didn't look through the peephole. She respected the inmates' privacy. But this time, she pulled open the cover over the glass peephole and peered in.

The cell, like all the cells on the row, was twelve feet deep and five feet wide. On the far wall of this one, sagging bookshelves were piled high with papers. There was a toilet, a small desk, a stool, a cot.

Walter Michael Jones was sitting on the cot with one leg up, reading a thick book. He was thin and almost bald. He wore wire-rimmed glasses and looked like a bookkeeper or a librarian. His prison blues were neat and clean. There were dozens of pictures of black men on the walls. Some were wearing funny round hats, and she took them to be Black Muslims. One of them, she thought, was Malcolm X. She'd seen the movie.

Billie knew Walter Michael Jones was now 42 years of age. He'd been in this cell for eight years straight, except for a few months spent down in the county jail while his case was being appealed.

He suddenly looked up, slid off his cot, and came over to the door.

"Mrs. Dodds? Is that you out there?" His voice was muffled.

She stepped back, letting the peephole door slip closed.

"So you're the one who'll murder me," he said, his voice cracking.

He knew, she thought. One of her so-called fellow officers had told. She burned with anger for a few moments, trying to figure out which one did it. Which one hated her the most. Stephens or Peters. It was one of them. Or maybe even Cykech, the quiet, sneaky one.

"Will you enjoy murdering me?" Jones said.

She grabbed the lunch tray cart and hurried away, her heart pounding. She felt a strange clamminess come over her. The word *murder* rang in her ears. Yes, she thought, that's what it was. Murder. No matter how else you thought of it, she was going to pull a lever and a man was going to die. The lever might just as well be the trigger of a gun.

A Utah highway patrolman had lost his mind and had to be put away in a hospital after being on a firing squad last year. She remembered reading about it in the paper. He started babbling that he was Ivan the Terrible. His name was Ivan something. She shuddered.

Billie Sue's dream:

A black man in a slave camp is being chained by two white men. One looks like Randy Walsh, the other like Warden Anderson. Everything is gray. The slaves come out of their shacks and watch, their eyes full of fear.

The men take the chained man up a hill to a scaffold. They bring him up the steps and force him to kneel next to a chopping block. The black man looks up at Billie Sue, who has a chain saw in her hand. She pulls the cord to start it up. The two men push his head down onto the block. Billie Sue holds the chain saw over the man's neck.

Sam appears reading the Bible, "Ashes unto ashes, dust unto dust, flesh unto sawdust."

Billie Sue feels the chain saw moving downward and suddenly the man's head falls into a basket at her feet, his eyes looking up at her.

Sam was shaking her awake.

"What's the matter, hon? You've been thrashing around something awful."

She held him tight, feeling her nightgown wet with perspiration.

"Just a dream," she said. "Weren't nothing but a silly old dream."

ﾞ

Sunday morning.

Jennifer had spent the night at her girlfriend's and Sam and Billie Sue had spent a wonderful, romantic evening together giving each other back rubs and making love on a pile of blankets in front of the fire while rain and hail pelted the roof. God's own symphony, Sam called it. They'd even had a little wine, which Saint Paul had said was good for the stomach. Good for lovemaking, too, Billie Sue thought.

Now she was making apple fritters for breakfast, Sam's favorite. Sam came out of the bedroom with a big smile on his face, still in his pajamas. He gave her a hug and a kiss on the neck.

"The Lord done good when He gave you to me."

"And you to me," she said, giving him a big squeeze. His muscles were hard under his pajamas and he smelled of sleep and fresh cotton.

They opened the drapes over the bay windows and looked out on a bright, clear, summer morning. Sam said he was feeling so ambitious that he was going to fix the fence where dry rot had set in as soon as they got back from church.

The phone rang.

Billie Sue answered it. It was her neighbor, Maggie, down the street, where Jennifer had spent the night.

"Jennifer's on her way home. She's madder than hell, Billie Sue. I just wanted you to know it wasn't me that let the cat out of the bag."

"What cat?"

"Hector didn't even know himself, honest." Hector was her husband. He worked at the prison, too. Only he was an accountant.

236

"Didn't even know what?"

"You know, about you getting the assignment to kill that man . . . "

Just then the front door banged open and Jennifer came racing into the room, her face awash with tears.

"Mother! How could you?"

"How could I what?" Billie Sue hung up the phone.

"Be an executioner!" Jennifer screamed.

"You best not talk to your mama like that," Sam said. "You don't ever raise your voice to her, young lady!"

"But Daddy, it's all over town! Marcie says Mama's gonna wear a hood and everything—it's too horrible! I can't ever show my face again!"

She turned and ran from the room. Sam looked at his wife, shaking his head hopelessly.

"I'll talk to her," Billie Sue said.

She went to her daughter's room and entered. The drapes were drawn. Jennifer lay on her lace-fringed canopy bed, sobbing, her face buried in her heart-shaped, red-velvet pillow.

Billie Sue sat down next to her and gently rubbed her back. Jennifer pushed her hand away and turned on her side.

"How could you do this to me?" Jennifer sobbed.

"Can I explain something to you?"

"What?"

"Sometimes we have to be brave."

"I don't want to be brave."

"Sometimes we have to do something we don't want to do. I took an oath when I took my job to do my duty."

"But to be an executioner . . . oh, Mother, how could you? Tell them you won't do it!"

"I can't do that. I work on the row, you know that. Along with that come certain privileges and obligations. If I expect to have the privileges, I've got to perform the obligations."

"Nobody's going to invite me to a party forever. The executioner's daughter! My life is ruined!"

"You tell your so-called friends that the judges and the juries have ordered the execution and we at the prison are only doing our duty, just as a soldier does his or her duty. When you're grown up, Jennifer, you have to do grown-up things. Understand?"

"Please don't do it, Mother, please! For me. I'll never ask you for anything else. Please."

Billie Sue patted her daughter's hand. "When you grow up, you'll understand."

Jennifer burst into sobs again and rolled away from her mother.

"I might not even have to do it, Jennifer. But if I do, I want your support."

"Never!"

"Your friends will forget it soon enough."

"I'll never forget it!"

Billie Sue reached out for her hand again, but her daughter pulled it away. Billie Sue got up and went back into the kitchen. Sam was looking out the window, sipping coffee.

"She's got a point, you know," he said.

"He's making his case based on racism in the jury. He'll get the reprieve and everything's going to be okay. The Supreme Court surely will be favorable."

"I'll keep praying on that."

"I will, too."

At the end of the shift the next day, Linda Askew, the sergeant in charge of the gate, stopped Billie Sue and took her aside. Linda Askew was head of the local chapter of the women's officers' association. She was black, fifty-ish, strong-jawed, wearing dark brown lipstick.

"I just wanted you to know, Billie Sue," she said, "that we're all pulling for you."

"What do you mean?"

"I mean, we know that dropping the pill is not an easy thing to do. Even some of the macho butt-heads have trouble with it. They puke, some of them. Bawl. I mean, it's not easy. I know you got what it takes to do it, Billie Sue. You show those jerks that a woman is as good at doing what has to be done as any of them. Better."

"The last I heard, Jones was going to get a stay of execution, which is okay by me."

"You didn't hear?"

"Hear what?"

"It was on the news a while ago. The Supreme Court turned down his appeal. The execution is going ahead as scheduled."

Billie Sue felt flush.

"I'm sorry, Billie Sue. I thought you knew."

Billie Sue drew a deep breath. "I wasn't expecting it, is all. I'll be fine."

"All the women are pulling for you, Billie Sue."

"What if I can't go through with it?"

Linda Askew shook her head. "But you got to, Billie Sue. They won't send no women up there and it's the best job in the facility. You got it in you, Billie Sue, I know you do."

Billie Sue began X-ing out the days on the calendar for the first time in her life. Jennifer came home later every night, moped around the house, stayed in her room, hardly spoke.

"She'll get over it," Sam said. "You don't worry about it."

But Billie Sue did worry. It was keeping her awake nights. Thirteen days to go.

Friday evening:

Billie Sue and Sam sat at the picnic table at the back of their lot under some pine trees and watched the hills beyond the valley turn pink, then gray, then melt with the darkening sky of an approaching storm. A cool, fresh breeze blew up from the valley and it felt good in Billie Sue's hair.

A flash of lightning lit the horizon.

Sam said, "I love you, Billie Sue." He said it suddenly and quickly, and it gave Billie Sue a strange feeling that something was deeply troubling him. She waited. She knew Sam had difficulty sometimes putting together the right words. He got up and paced, facing the coming storm.

"I been feeling the whisper of the Lord in my ear, Billie Sue."

"What's He been whispering, Sam?"

"That it ain't a good thing, what they want you to do."

"How do you mean?"

"There's something not right about it. It ain't in the nature of a woman to be doing things like this."

"But it's part of the job."

"It's your soul I'm speaking about."

"You don't know what it means to me, Sam. I grew up in a trailer park, my daddy was a drunk, and then he disappeared out of my life. My mama was only half there, you know what I mean."

"Indeed I do. The devil and his alcohol did some bad things to her mind."

"I never had decent things. You know that. The best I had was hand-me-down clothes from my cousin Claire. Never had no money for anything nice. In school I wasn't no genius. Heck, I barely passed the test for correctional officer after studying the book for near a year."

"We do the best with what God gives us, we can't do no better than that. Still, I don't like what they want you to do."

240

He was pushing her hard, she thought, as hard as he ever had. "Look around, Sam," she said. "We live good. Got good cars, nice house here. We even got some savings. We got it good, mostly because the prison pays me well and it's steady."

"I don't deny that."

"I like being a correctional officer. I got a profession. The other officers respect me—least they did on the main line. And they will on the row."

"That why you're going through with it? To get respect. Something not right about that."

She felt anger flash to her cheeks. She said nothing.

"Well, is it?" he said, raising his voice.

"It's my job!" she snapped.

She got up and went into the house. Sam stayed outside. He didn't come in until after the rain started.

Sergeant Martinez unlocked the door with a big brass key and stepped inside the hallway and turned on the light. It had a dank, closed-up smell like an old basement. Billie Sue followed him in. Her mouth tasted sour.

Ahead of them was a wide room and, in it, the chamber itself: squat, round, with huge rivet heads showing. Painted dull green. It had three wide, oval windows. Inside she could see the chairs, two of them, with straps on the arms dangling down.

To their right was the gallery, where the hundred or so witnesses would be seated, and, back of that, the smaller press gallery, where dozens of reporters would be packed in.

"You okay?" Sergeant Martinez asked.

She nodded.

"You seen it before, haven't you?" he asked.

"Once, when Captain Farley was giving me an orientation. But they passed through quickly because they were getting it ready for an execution."

241

"Okay, take a look on the other side of the death chamber," Martinez said. "You see that window?" It was around the corner from the chamber, small and dark.

She nodded.

"You and me, we'll be in the room on the other side of that window."

"You'll be with me, then?"

"That's right. If you fail in the performance of your duty, I'll take over."

"You think the little lady might faint?"

"It's not just you, Officer Dodds. Men sometimes don't go through with it. One guy who fainted was a Vietnam vet with a pile of medals."

The thought of fainting made her dizzy. Fainting would be the most terrible thing that had ever happened to her, she thought. How could she ever face them if she fainted? She remembered once seeing a man's arm cut off in a wreck. Her head had started swimming and she'd almost fainted.

"This way," he said.

He showed her where the warden would be standing, assuring her that nobody else could see her from there, none of the reporters. Then he took her back out and down another corridor to the little room where the two of them would be standing. There was a large red lever with a padlock on it.

"Go ahead and touch the lever," he said.

She put her hand on it. It was cold to the touch. A shiver ran down her spine.

She peered out the window and saw the small platform where the warden would be standing. Beyond, she could see a big clock.

"We can't see the condemned man from here," Sergeant Martinez said. "They designed it that way."

"I see," she said, trying to sound conversational. The room seemed to be closing in on her. She heard the voice of the

242

condemned man ringing in her ears: *So you're the one who'll murder me.*

"The warden, he don't like to watch. He'll keep his eyes on the clock, then he'll raise his arm. I'll unlock the padlock. When he lowers his arm, you pull the lever. Inside the chamber, a pellet of sodium cyanide will drop into a pail of water, which will produce cyanide gas. Got it?"

"Yes, sir."

"On the day, you don't have to come in until it's almost time."

"I understand," she said.

"Then after it's done, you get the rest of the day, and the next day off."

"I understand."

"You're sure you can do it?"

She licked her dry lips and nodded. "I have to, sir."

He gave her a pat on the back. "I have full faith. In case you change your mind, Charlie Stephens said he'd be happy to take over."

She cleared her throat. "My old daddy told me if you want to ride the horse, you got to shovel the manure."

"My dad told me the same thing," he said with a grin. "Only it was a burro."

They both laughed, but she was sure he knew she'd faked hers.

☙

The following day before her shift, with three days to go, she found an envelope with her name on it lying next to the doughnuts on the counter in the coffee room.

It was light, but thick. She opened the envelope and inside were chicken feathers.

Some of the men chuckled.

She threw the feathers into the basket and, without saying a single word, marched out of the coffee room. Peals of laughter echoed down the hall after her.

At noon, Billie Sue was passing out the lunch trays.

As she slipped his tray into cell number 24, Walter Michael Jones said, "That you, killer?"

"Officer Dodds," she said.

"You gonna kill me, are ya?"

She didn't answer.

"Afraid to speak to me?"

"No."

"Sure you are."

"No, I'm not."

"I'm a human being, I want you to know that. I got feelings, same as you. You afraid to look at me?"

She opened the small access door beneath the peephole and stared at him through the wire mesh. His face was close up. She could smell his toothpaste breath. She felt her own breath catch in her throat. His eyes were rheumy. "You don' look like death, but you surely is," he said.

She shut her eyes for a moment. She didn't want to look at the man, or speak to the man, or even know anything about him. She opened her eyes and stared at him.

"You're just making it harder on everyone," she said. "Especially yourself."

"So how's it going to feel?" he said. "I hear some of the boys really get off on it. Gives them a real thrill. You gonna have a big thrill, Officer Dodds?"

"Mister, the state is executing you because of what you did in King City ten years ago. This is not a personal thing with me."

"Murder is always personal. Very personal."

"Execution is punishment, not murder."

"Doing it for the hundred dollars?"

"I should think you'd be better off, sir, to spend your time praying to your God for forgiveness."

"I executed those cops, same as you gonna execute me. Only thing, they was evil men and I'm not."

"I'm sure, in some twisted way, you had your reasons."

"They was gonna work me over 'cause I was fightin' for the rights of black folks. Executing them was no wrong in the eyes of my God."

"I'm sure."

"By refusing to go along with killing a man for doing what was right, you could strike a blow for justice in this land where injustice clings like leeches on the backs of black people."

"I have other lunches to serve, Mr. Jones. I'll leave the worry over injustice to other people."

She found her hands were trembling. She had to grasp the lunch tray cart firmly to make them stop.

＊

"I remember the case," Linda Askew said, pouring a beer from the pitcher. They were sitting at a table at the Lockup, the bar nearest the prison.

"He says he was defending himself," Billie Sue said.

"You ever hear a con say he was guilty of anything?"

"No."

"Listen, Billie Sue, these black cons have given me shit ever since I started working here about how damn oppressed they are. Christ. They got more piss-ass excuses for their killing and robbing than Georgia has goobers."

"King City does have a reputation for tough cops."

"That don't justify killing, my friend. He's pulling con jive on you, believe me. Don't let him play with your mind. You ain't the judge, you ain't the jury, you ain't the Supreme Court. You just do your job."

"Thanks, Linda."

After having a couple of beers, on the way out they passed a half dozen of her male colleagues sitting at the "row" table. She'd not presumed to sit there; no telling what insult she'd have to endure if she tried. Charlie Stephens looked up at her as she passed and winked.

Billie Sue was going to ignore him, but Linda Askew stopped and said, "You sure are having your fun, aren't you, boys?"

"Guess we are. We know what it takes to pull that lever. We've all been there."

"And you all liked it, didn't you?" Billie Sue found herself saying. "With me it's a duty, but with you scum, you get your jollies off doing it."

"Listen to her talk, and she ain't even been up to bat yet," Charlie Stephens said. "But if you decide it's not for you, little lady, I'll be happy to take over. And yes, I do enjoy my work."

"You're a weirdo creep, Charlie Stephens," Linda Askew said. "To like doing something like that, that's a perversion."

They made a toast: "To perverts."

Linda Askew took Billie Sue's arm. "Let's get out of here. It's beginning to stink real bad."

⤝

Jennifer called it E-day.

She sat glaring at her mother while Sam hid behind his newspaper. A drizzling rain streaked down the bay windows. Billie Sue was feeling tired. The nightmare of the black man and the chain saw repeated itself over and over in her sleep, waking her up in a cold sweat a dozen times.

"Nice day for it, isn't it, Mother?" Jennifer said suddenly, her voice brittle.

"Speak with kindness, Jennifer," her father scolded.

"Oh, kindness? Is that the proper etiquette when speaking to an executioner?"

"I'm a correctional officer," Billie Sue said. "As you well know."

"Know what I think, Mother? I think you'll love it."

"You're being dramatic now," Billie Sue said.

Tears started bubbling up in Jennifer's eyes. Billie Sue reached across the table for her hand. Jennifer pulled it back. "I don't want you ever touching me again."

She got up from the table and ran out the back door, slamming it behind her.

"She'll grow up one day," Sam said.

Billie Sue stirred her coffee. "Women, if they want equal rights, they got to be willing to take responsibility. If you're gonna have a good life, the doors got to be open, which means that the women who went ahead of you did the job. They didn't wimp out or whine or nothing. They got to prove they can do it. They got to reach deep inside themselves and find the strength. I'm trying mighty hard to do that, Sam. Mighty hard."

"I been doing some mighty hard thinking about this thing, Billie Sue. You want to know what I been thinking?"

"Sure, Sam, I want to know your thinking."

"I'm scared, Billie Sue."

"Scared of what?"

"Scared that somehow when you do this, you won't be the same. Scared it's somehow going to change you."

"You mean that things between us won't be the same?"

"Will they?"

"There ain't nothing on God's good earth could change things between you and me, Sam. Only one thing, Sam. I need you behind me on this one hundred percent. You got to say I'm doing what's right."

He stood up from the table and went over to the window. "I'm sorry, Billie Sue. I love you, but I don't want you doing this thing and that's all there is to it."

"I guess there's nothing more to say, then," she said, feeling a terrible ache inside.

She put away the breakfast dishes. That was the first morning she could remember he didn't kiss her good-bye before leaving for work.

⚓

Billie Sue drove her Toyota Camry through the front gate of the prison and turned off toward the employees' lot. She was feeling a heaviness now inside. Feeling like she was all alone on a desert island.

She glanced toward the prison, looming huge and gray like a medieval fortress of stone. Her eyes shot up to the row, to the window of the good-bye room where they'd be getting Walter Michael Jones ready. *So you're the one who'll murder me.*

She was suddenly cold, even though it was a mild day. She got out of the car and felt the wind in her hair. Perspiration was making her uniform shirt cling to her. She started walking toward the row. She seemed to notice every smell, the plastic in the car seats, the grass, the faint smell of metal from the smelter to the east. And she heard every sound, the voices of the reporters more than a hundred yards away. Insane people could hear and smell everything, she once read. That thought frightened her.

A few dozen protesters had been marshaled into the visitors' parking lot. She could see their signs: STOP STATE MURDER. LOVE NOT KILLING IS THE ANSWER. Silly stuff, Billie Sue thought. When so much was wrong with the world, why did these people worry about cop killers getting what they had coming?

She remembered her father saying once that people made their own lives whether they knew it or not. Somehow, some way, we all get what we got coming.

How was it she made her badge be the one that got picked? Wasn't it just dumb, blind luck? Or was it the will of God?

Nothing on earth happened that wasn't the will of God, Sam always said.

So you're the one who'll murder me.

Her throat was scratchy as sandpaper. She couldn't make spit. Her hands trembled. She hadn't felt like this since she'd had surgery on her hand when she was a kid. She was feeling sick. Surely if she were sick she wouldn't have to go through with it.

But then they'd say she had PMS or some damn thing, another reason why women couldn't do the job. Couldn't measure up. Damn it, she'd earned the highest rating in her unit on the ward. She could do this damn job better than any of them. Even this she could do. Simply a matter of pulling a lever.

The TV remote trucks were lined up along the gate unloading cameras and microphones. They were always there on execution days.

She went inside, showed her badge to the guard behind the Plexiglas, and was buzzed into the sally port. She entered the row and went up the back stairs—smelling the dust, the floor polish, noticing the tiniest cracks in the wall and how they looked like spider webs. Everything seemed so different, so new. Suddenly she felt dizzy. She stopped and held her head down, counted slowly to twenty, then straightened up and took a few slow, deep breaths.

Don't let them see you like this, girl, she thought.

At the top of the stairs she used her key to open the metal door and went into the coffee room. Charlie Stephens, his fat buddy Peters, and Randy Walsh were having a cup of joe and munching on donuts.

"Morning, gentlemen," she said, steadying herself.

"Good morning, Billie Sue," Randy Walsh said. The other two grunted.

She poured a cup of coffee and grabbed an old-fashioned donut and sat down and started leafing through a newspaper somebody'd left on the table.

"You okay?" Randy Walsh asked her. He said it low.

"I'm fine, and you?" she said.

"I'm fine, and you?" Charlie Stephens said to Peters.

"I'm fine, and you?" Peters said to Charlie Stephens.

The two of them laughed.

"Don't pay no attention to them," Walsh said.

"I don't."

"She's too busy holding her asshole tight," Charlie Stephens said.

"Blow it out your ear!" Walsh snapped.

"Boys, boys," Billie Sue said, "I'm trying to read here."

Charlie Stephens guffawed.

Billie Sue raised the paper, leafing through the pages idly.

Charlie Stephens and Peters got up and dumped their paper cups in the trash. "You feel like fainting, put your head between your legs," Charlie Stephens said.

"That what you did when you had your turn?" she said, grinning at him.

Charlie Stephens glared at her, but Peters roared, slapping him on the back. "She's got a sharp tongue on her, ain't she now. She's talking good, let's see how she does when push comes to shove."

"Yeah, we'll see if she needs diapering."

The two of them left, laughing and slapping each other on the back.

"Don't pay them no mind," Randy Walsh said.

Billie Sue nibbled on a donut and read the paper. "Supposed to rain today again," she said. "Sure been a wet summer."

Neither of them spoke for a few minutes. Then Randy Walsh said, "You want to talk about it? Sometimes helps to let it out, how you're feeling."

"What's there to say?"

"I don't know. Me, when I'm upset, I talk."

"Tell you the truth, Walsh, I'm not feeling all that upset."

"Hasn't hit you yet. It will, believe me."

"Could be."

He crushed his cup. "Got to go. They got me on lunch tray duty."

"See you around."

"Okay."

"And Walsh . . . thanks."

"For what?"

"For not being like the rest of them."

He smiled.

As soon as she was alone, she watched the hands of the clock spinning toward noon. Her daughter's words kept repeating in her head: *You'll love it.*

Her throat closed up. She must be coming down with something, she thought. The flu. She felt flushed. She was running a fever, perhaps, she thought. She did feel chilled.

So you're the one who'll murder me.

She went to the sink and wiped her face with a wet towel and went back and sat down and gulped coffee. Yes, it definitely was the flu. She had every symptom . . .

Suddenly the door to the back stairs opened and Linda Askew came in. Marlene Parker was with her. Marlene was a social worker, a forty-ish redhead.

Linda Askew said, "We just come to lend our support."

"And to say how much we admire you," Marlene Parker said.

Linda Askew pushed a couple of pills into her hand. "'Case you need a friend," she said.

Just then Sergeant Martinez came out of his office with a clipboard.

"It's time," he said.

"We're leaving," Linda Askew said, heading out.

"Our champion!" Marlene Parker said.

As soon as the door closed, Sergeant Martinez said, "Warden Anderson just phoned. They're moving the condemned to the chamber. The cop-killing prick refused to be sedated and he's giving the men a tough time. Christ, I hate it when it goes down like this."

"He's just making it harder on himself," Billie Sue said. "And everybody else. I told him that myself."

"You ready?" he said.

"I'd like to have a little water." She went to the sink and washed the two tablets Linda Askew had given her down the drain. She wanted to be in full control.

Sergeant Martinez showed her a form he had on the clipboard: *Official Procedures for Carrying out a Death Warrant.*

"I go straight by the book," the sergeant said.

"Always the best policy," Billie Sue said. "If I don't go through with this, would everybody have to know about it?"

"I'd have to file it in my report."

"Of course."

"Charlie Stephens will be glad to do it in your stead. He said he was ready."

She shut her eyes. Having him do it for her was more than she could bear.

"I'll do it," she said.

"Okay, let's go."

She followed him down the hallway to the booth behind the death chamber, her heartbeat quick in her ears. She could smell Martinez's after-shave, the spit-shine of his shoes, the faint odor of dry cleaning. Everything was magnified. She could hear the hum of the air conditioning system two floors below, the tiny squeak of her shoes on the floor.

They entered the small room. It was dim. The red-painted lever seemed huge in front of her. Her heart now thundered in her chest. For a moment she experienced a strange, buoyant sensation.

She heard a muffled scream: "You bastards will roast in hell for this!"

"The sound proofing is the pits," Martinez said. He wiped his sleeve on the glass to clear the view. The warden was not in position yet.

More muffled voices. Screaming.

"We got ourselves a real tiger," Sergeant Martinez said. "Most of them go down like sheep."

"My husband says men let the devil in, that's why they do horrible things. You believe that, Sergeant?"

"I'm not religious. I think they're just stupid."

The warden came into view, facing the clock just as Martinez had said he would. More muffled cries and curses came from the chamber. Billie Sue noticed how the red lever seemed so much larger. Everything was so strange. She remembered the time she was going to have a root canal, how scared she was, how she had to force herself. She thought this would be like that. But now, she felt . . . *light*. It was almost as if she could float in the air. Do anything. As if for the first time in her life she knew what it was to be 100% alive.

For a moment she felt as she had on the swing as a child, going higher and higher. Twice as high as the boys.

Another muffled scream came from the chamber. One word was clear: "Racists!"

"The news media will be chewing this up good on the TV tonight," Sergeant Martinez said.

She said nothing—she was staring at the warden, who was shuffling his feet nervously, looking at the clock, then toward the chamber, then toward the gallery.

The door of the chamber slammed shut.

"Won't be long now," Martinez said. "They got him strapped in."

Billie Sue could see sweat on Martinez's lip just above his graying mustache. He was scared, she thought. The macho sergeant was scared she might pass out and he'd have to do it. Knowing it gave her a strange feeling of power over him.

Sergeant Martinez gave her a reassuring nod. He took out a key and unlocked the padlock on the red lever, but he kept the key in the retaining slot and his hand tight on the lock.

The warden raised his hand.

In her mind Billie Sue could see Walter Michael Jones in the chair, and she knew he could see the warden too and his raised hand and, for him, this was the last thing he was going to see.

Murder is always personal.

She put her hand on the lever. She knew her face was flushed red. Martinez was watching the warden. The warden's hand was going up; he was slowly turning toward them.

The incredible clearness, the sharpness, had grown even greater. Billie Sue was aware of her toes inside her shoes, the pulse at her temples, and then it was as if she could see through the wall, see the gallery, the press, and the man strapped in the chair.

The warden's arm came down.

Sergeant Martinez slipped the lock out of the slot and for a moment Billie Sue froze, as if time itself had stopped and she was standing before the door to eternity.

Sam's words, *It's going to change you*, rang in her ears.

She pulled the lever. It seemed to resist for a moment, then sprang toward her breastbone. She held it there for a moment. Through the window she could see the warden looking toward the death chamber. Billie Sue knew what was happening. The pellet had surely fallen into the pail of water and now the chamber was filling with gas and Walter Michael Jones was probably still holding his breath.

She watched the second hand sweep around the clock. Ten, twenty, thirty, forty, fifty . . .

Martinez took a deep breath and let it out slowly. Then he said, "We'll be getting the signal to evacuate the chamber in a minute. The doctor always waits a while after he hears the heart stop."

Martinez made some check marks on the paper on the clipboard, looked at his watch, and wrote down some times.

Billie Sue leaned against the wall with her hands in her pockets, still feeling that wonderful, tingly sensation she'd experienced as a girl on the swing, soaring higher and higher into the sky.

Finally the warden waved his arm, giving an all-clear signal. Sergeant Martinez turned the switch to evacuate the gas.

"That's it," he said. "Good job, Officer Dodds. Very good."

"Thank you, Sergeant Martinez."

"Remember, you don't have to report tomorrow."

"They got a big sale at Sears. I'm planning to shop till I drop."

Billy Sue and Sergeant Martinez went back down the hall to the coffee room, hoping there was a donut left. Charlie Stephens, Peters, and Cykech were there monkeying around with her locker.

"Hey!" she said, "What the hell are you doing?"

They stepped back to show her they'd etched a chair onto the door.

Charlie Stephens said, "Don't want it? We can have it painted over."

She stepped closer and ran her fingers over it. "No . . . it's okay."

"Hey," Cykech said, "look at her face. Man, she not only did it, she got off on it!"

"Well, I'll be damned," Charlie Stephens said.

Peters said, "How about we buy you a brew after the shift down at the Lockup? Fill us in on all the gory details."

"Yeah, sure, so you can put Krazy Glue on the seat, something like that."

"Hey," Peters said, "we're being straight here. Tell her, Sarge."

"They mean it, Billie Sue," Sergeant Martinez said. "You got your chair."

He was looking at her with narrow eyes, as if seeing her for the first time.

"Yeah," Peters said, "you didn't wimp out, we got to respect that."

"So how did it feel?" Cykech said. "You get the rush? That's how it was with me. Like somebody shot some cocaine or something right into my brain."

"Something like that," she said. "But before, there was this incredible . . . "

"Wait," Charlie Stephens said. "We got to hear every last detail. Blow by blow. See you after the shift at the Lockup? What do you say, Billie Sue? Let us buy you a beer."

"Gentlemen," she said, "I accept."

Sometime after eight that evening she called Sam to tell him she'd be coming home late and, no, she didn't know exactly how late it was going to be.

Reflections on the Absurd

Bread and Circuses
Lester Gorn

The gods, it seemed, had conspired to help make the Presentation a success. Solar flares had done freakish things to T.V. reception, so a greater proportion of people outside the Los Angeles blackout area could be counted on to make the trek to the city. Yesterday's shark scare at Santa Monica had kept many people from the beaches. The smog had lifted by 11:00, and now a breeze gave the lie to oppressive heat and nudged limp flags and banners flutteringly horizontal.

The new crowd-processing plans were working beautifully, too. Bulldozers and condemnation proceedings had created seventeen huge parking lots at key points throughout the city. Patrons were whisked from the lots to the stadium by monorail. People movers took them the rest of the way.

The crowd was well behaved and tastefully dressed, as befitted the occasion. There was little jostling even when the monorails and escalators carried peak loads. Despite the heat, few men had removed their jackets or loosened their ties. The new hemline (six inches below the knee) was seen as often in the bleachers section as in the grandstand or the boxes. Many of the younger set carried pennants reading "McCoy" (in blue and white) or "Pardell" (in red and white).

From the Operations office cantilevered out over the field, Paul Sanks and his visitor—Walter Holsinger, a State field supervisor—

commanded a panoramic view of the Coliseum's interior. The brass band, resplendent in red and blue, marched through its paces on the greensward. Pennants winked in time to the music, and vendors caroled homage to beer, Red Hots and souvenirs. What Sanks called the crowd sound was friendly.

Yet the impresario brooded. "Seventy-five thousand."

Holsinger scanned the crowd. "I'd say closer to eighty."

Sanks punched the intercom with a forcefulness that seemed out of keeping with his slightness of body and quietness of dress. He could not have weighed more than a hundred and thirty pounds. His blue serge suit was set off by a dark gray tie. "Seventy-four and a half," said the intercom voice.

Sanks grimaced.

"They're still pouring in, Paul." Shoulders hunched in a golfer's stance over an imaginary ball, Holsinger simulated a drive. Swinging easily, smoothly, he gazed down the imaginary fairway. "It ain't over till the fat lady sings."

Sanks declined reassurance. "The final tally will be eighty-two, tops. Last year this time, we consistently racked up ninety-one, ninety-two. Not that I'm surprised. Last year, I ran an independent operation. I didn't have you people on my back."

Holsinger smiled indulgently.

"Factors beyond my control. That's what you should say in your report."

"My report cuts no ice," Holsinger said. "I'm not here to assess blame. All the boss wants from me is verification of the final tally."

"I hear different."

Holsinger lit his pipe. "You hear different."

"Yes."

"You're a little mixed up on the concept, Paul. Either ask me to bend the facts a little or attack me as a spy. Not both."

"Concepts be damned. I say what's on my mind and let the chips fall." Sanks turned to the monitors. One surveillance camera, panning the stands, held unexpectedly on a skybox where his wife, Millie, chatted with friends. Sanks' heart lurched. For the moment, Holsinger and the bureaucrats in Sacramento ceased to exist.

Vivacious was the word for Millie. Enchanting.

Once, Sanks had seen her from afar, as if with the eyes of a stranger, and he'd been shocked to realize she was no beauty, but the realization faded almost immediately and he again had fallen captive to the light dancing on brow and cheekbones, and the delicate hands dipping and soaring to express delight and fascination and concern.

Rousing, he pushed back to the business at hand.

"Six years I've been running the presentations, and never before a watchdog. Why now?"

"There you go again." Smoke eddied from Holsinger's pipe, blurring his features, softening the solid mouth and jaw line. "When you get something in your head, Paul, you just won't let go."

"Like the kiss at the cookout?"

Holsinger flushed. "Millie stumbled on a loose brick in the patio. I grabbed her to prevent a nasty spill and she planted a thank-you kiss on my cheek. Why make an orgy out of it?"

Sanks' gaze remained fixed on the field. The band had concluded its scheduled maneuvers and was using an encore to fill in the lull. Not too successfully. The rhythmic stomping of feet signaled the crowd's restiveness. For the moment, the stomping was ragged, good-natured, confined to one grandstand section, but soon it would spread, become insistent.

Time for Phase Two, Sanks decided. He pressed a button on the console. Within seconds, the band began marching into the stand. Simultaneously, the hydraulic lifts went into operation. Majestically, a courtroom—minus walls—rose out of the turf at the amphitheatre's center, a staid judge seated at the bench, twelve jurors good and true in the jury box; court officials standing in place with hands clasped loosely behind their backs.

The stomping stopped. The audience applauded as the trumpets sounded a fanfare and the opposing attorneys made their entrances from opposite ends of the field. McCoy wore a blue toga, Pardell a red one. Blood red. Marching to the courtroom, the two bowed to each other. Pardell's bow was courtly. Young McCoy, in contrast, bobbed his head as if he thought the gesture excessive.

Sanks' attention shifted back to his visitor. Up to now, he'd attacked Holsinger at every opportunity. Now the man was softened up, vulnerable. A conciliatory tone might turn the trick.

"Ole Pardell, he's a crowd pleaser," Sanks said. "None better. He'll make mincemeat of McCoy."

"I don't know." Holsinger kept his voice low and even. "McCoy may surprise you. What's his average now? Three for nine? Not bad, considering."

"Is that why you favored him for the assignment?"

"In part. The Judiciary liked him, too. They thought he did a nice job his last time out."

"He lost."

"Most do," Holsinger said wryly.

Sanks quashed irritation. "Too earnest. 'Youth vs. age,' that's not enough. By rights, it should be me picks the attorneys. The Judiciary—what do they know? Look at the judge they fob off on me. Solemn Sam. I need someone looks the part, grey at the temples, witty. Able to get off a quip without losing either his authority or his dignity."

Another fanfare sounded. From the north dugout stepped the defendant. With firm tread he made his way across the turf to the boxes. He was about 40, medium height, with a lean, photogenic face and thin, graying hair. To tumultuous applause, he made his bow to the dignitaries and, wheeling, walked to the chair at the defense counsel's table. There he stood waiting, his hands at ease, his eyes—as seen through binoculars—calm, almost placid. He blinked but did not move as two smoke bursts

262

rocked the stadium. Nor did he stir as the smoke dispersed and the two symbolic figures—Innocence, clad in white, and Guilt, in black—took their places beside him, the one lightly, the other with stealth.

"Cool," Holsinger said. "Good form."

"Too good. No visible fear. Grace under stress would have greater impact."

Holsinger thumbed fresh tobacco into his pipe. "You have to think of everything, don't you?"

"It'd be nice if the big brass realized that." Sanks nodded toward the courtroom, where the defense attorney was making his preliminary remarks to the jury. "Take the opening defense statement. Why twenty minutes for a formality? Time for the audience to settle in? The audience can get settled during the prosecutor's opening statement, and the time saved could be used to exploit the trial's more exciting phases. You want to draw a full house, you've got to heighten the drama—that's what I keep telling your associates in Sacramento. Do you listen? Hell, no! You sit up there on your backsides and criticize."

Holsinger watched a fly move up and down the plate glass window.

"Oh, yes, you'll make a concession here and there, but when it comes to fundamentals you throw jurisprudence at me and the need to preserve decorum." Despite the impatience in Holsinger's blue eyes, Sanks felt impelled to follow through. "Now I ask you! How can trimming an opening statement foul up the decorum?"

"Speaking strictly as a layman—"

"Increase it, actually. What increases interest increases decorum." Sanks' grin, though genuine, lacked staying power. "Another thing—the huge tax bite this year forced a hike in ticket prices. Naturally, the fans resent it. Attendance figures suffer."

In the courtroom below, Pardell was into his William Jennings Bryan act—posturing, parading, preaching, tossing his mane. That the defendant was guilty of a Class B affront to the State, he said, could not be gainsaid. The man had publicly denounced the presentations, picketed the stadium, gone limp when arrested. Passive resistance, Pardell pointed out, had long been discredited. It flouted the very law that kooks used as a shield.

McCoy was putting on a good show, too. Technical objections were sharply phrased. The swirling blue gown set off his suntanned face and balletic movements. The underdog role might well be helpful if the verdict proved close.

"What's needed," Sanks said, "is a twilight double-header."

Holsinger started.

"Hey!" said Sanks. "Something wrong?"

"No."

"You seem shook up."

"It's just I was startled. You may find it hard to believe, Paul, but this morning in Sacramento we discussed that very idea."

"Really?"

"Really. A semi-final, so to speak, and a final. One felony, one capital crime."

Sanks nodded. "Sometimes the special added event could be sprung as a surprise."

"That occurred to us, too. A feel-good bonus."

"Same wave length for a change." Stepping to the liquor cabinet, Sanks swung open its doors. "Join me?"

"Don't mind if I do."

"What'll it be?"

"Bourbon, please. A little water."

On the field, the trial was moving toward its climax at a satisfying clip. Despite his limitations, Solemn Sam had not hesitated to constantly remind witnesses and attorneys that brevity was the soul of justice.

Sanks said: "I've been watching the defendant. Well schooled, as you said. How do you score him?"

Holsinger sipped delicately at his drink. "Nine point two?"

"That's about right, I'd say."

"For a man forty-one, a fine performance. If the jury finds him guilty, he may get off on appeal."

"No. Uh. I doubt it. Study the tables. Very little correlation between a nine point two rating and a successful appeal. He'll need at least a nine point four."

"Perhaps he and his family can bring it up to a nine point four by their post-verdict form."

`"I hope not. Not that I've anything against them, mind. But it's risky to pull the stinger from climactic justice. To be effective, a drama has to spin itself out. The audience wants to feel purged, pure, gloriously alive. One reason I love the idea of the double-header is that the audience gets a second chance at purgation."

Time passed. Pardell delivered his summation, segueing easily from folksiness to the urbane, playing every harp string and drum beat. So deluded was the defendant, Pardell said, that he could get no one—not even members of his congregation—to join him on the picket line. Listening, one tended to regard the man as already convicted.

When McCoy took his turn before the jury, however, it became clear he was far from beaten. To Pardell's hot virtuosity, McCoy opposed cool logic. Under control, his earnestness emerged cleansed of callow overtone. Nor did he lack technical skill. He had a trick of talking off the microphone's center when making points inherently weak, bruising the words in flight. The arguments inherently strong came through the sound system with fidelity. The indictment, he said, charged the defendant with participation in a picket line as well as resistance to lawful arrest. Webster's dictionary defined a picket line as "a line of people." A technicality, no doubt. But no matter how you sliced it, a solitary picket did not constitute a line.

Returning to the bar, Sanks brandished the bourbon bottle. "Another?"

"Don't mind if I do."

As the jury retired to consider the verdict, Sanks made an audio check of key sections in the bleachers and grandstand. Some of the more excited bleacherites so far forgot themselves as to give utterance to partisan cries for McCoy. The tote board atop the stadium wall showed the betting odds as close to even now.

Suddenly, nervous laughter rippled through the stands. A dog had run onto the field. It headed straight for the courtroom, an attendant in pursuit.

Holsinger, watching, smiled.

"Think the dog wandered out there by accident?" Sanks said. "Not on your life! In a Sanks production, accidents happen according to plan."

"Pardon?"

"Breaks the tension, gives it new impetus."

"Hey!" Holsinger said. "Neat!"

Having used up the ten minutes allowed for its deliberations, the jury filed back into the box. The defendant stood up, a muscle pulsing in his cheek.

"Have you reached a verdict?"

"We have, Your Honor."

"State the verdict."

"Your Honor, we find the defendant guilty as charged."

The symbolic figure of Guilt placed a proprietary hand on the defendant's shoulder. Symbolic Innocence retreated three paces. About half the audience violated protocol with excited whispers. In the family box, the defendant's wife reached out to her two children and pulled them close. Somewhere in the grandstand, an infant started to cry.

Sanks spoke into the intercom. "Get that baby out of there."

"Yes, sir,"

"The jury foreman," Sanks said. "You catch the way he blurted out the verdict? Ten times he was briefed! 'We find the defendant—pause—guilty.'"

On the field, the band swung into the Long March theme. The stands hushed as the defendant slipped out from under Guilt's hand and started his march. At the third step, he faltered. A medic ran to his side. Waving the medic aside, the defendant continued on.

He faltered once more as he neared the whipping post—actually a board—but the last five paces were magnificently done, establishing a stylized air of confidence, even abandon.

The crowd broke into riotous applause.

"Bravo!" Baseball caps sailed down onto the turf. The sky hailed money.

The judge lifted his hand and the applause stilled. From the family box stepped the defendant's family. The two children—a boy and a girl—clutched their mother's hands. Although the monitors exposed some tears, the woman kept her chin high as she reached the on-deck circle. A chic sports coat, loosely belted, enhanced her image. Sanks thought she bore a vague resemblance to Millie.

A splendid hush blanketed the crowd as the defendant made his appeal: his head turned left, then right, then (after a stately moment) fixed on the dignitaries. Symbolic Innocence raised her arms in supplication.

Sanks, in the office overhead, scanned the bank of skybox monitors.

"Ladies and gentlemen," the judge intoned. "What is your pleasure?"

Sanks couldn't help smiling when he saw Millie leap to her feet and join her shout to the multitude's. "Flog him!" Like a kid, sometimes.

Only the pallor of the convicted man betrayed his anguish. Stripping down to his shorts, he spread-eagled himself upon the board. Two uniformed guards stepped forward to strap his arms and legs in place. The condemned man's wife avoided looking at him, but her eyes were stricken. Twilight played tricks with her mouth, heightening her resemblance to Millie. The children, in a frenzy, clawed her skirt.

The final fanfare sounded. A gate opened. Onto the field strode Dan Dempsey, the renowned martial-arts master. Naked to the waist, skin oiled and gleaming, he crossed the field to the whipping post. The shaved, bullet head seemed anchored in his sinewy shoulders. He carried a rattan cane.

The condemned felon trembled.

Dempsey took up his position. Flexing his arms, he took a few practice swings. Satisfied, he waited for absolute quiet.

He readied himself.

The brine-soaked cane whipped down on its target with the master's full weight behind it. Its impact could be heard throughout the stadium. An ugly red welt appeared on the condemned's back. The man did not cry out.

The second and third blows slashed the buttocks. Blood and bits of flesh spattered on the board, painted white to enhance visibility. Still, the felon made no sound.

The microphones picked up a moan at the fourth stroke. The body sagged. Medics came running with water and smelling salts.

Breaking protocol, the condemned's two children vented gasping-sobbing sounds.

Observing the spectacle from his office, Sanks poured another drink. A flick of the speaker switch swathed the cries beyond the plate glass window in soundlessness.

The intercom buzzed. "Eighty-two, three-one-five."

"That does it." Holsinger gathered the spreadsheets on the desk and stowed them in his briefcase. "Official, now. Ten thousand short."

"As anticipated." Sanks fended off uneasiness. He'd discerned a new edginess in Holsinger's voice. Understandably, the man was upset. Reporting the official tally to his associates would not be pleasant. "Probably the last time we'll have a shortfall, Walter. With double-headers, we can pull in capacity crowds. All that's

needed is renewal of my contract. Five years, anyways three."
Sanks paused. "I'd appreciate your going to bat for me."

"Why should I?"

Sanks goggled.

"Just a little while ago, you went ape over a meaningless little
pass I made at Millie."

"Huh?"

"So righteous!" Holsinger eyed the fly climbing the window.

"You'd think Millie's, uh, reputation was the most important
thing in the universe."

Sanks winced. "I'm under strain, Walter."

"Cuts no ice. From here on out you'd better have your prior-
ities in order." Holsinger struck at the window with a folded
newspaper. A smear appeared at the spot where the fly had been.
"Millie's chastity ought to be pretty far down the list."

Sanks made a stab at the jocular. "No higher than second, I
assure you."

"That would seem to give us adequate leeway."

Sanks recoiled. For a second or two, he tried to misconstrue
the words and come up with a light-hearted rejoinder. In vain.
The rejoinder got stuck in his throat. He heard himself say: "If
you so much as lay a hand on Millie, I'll kill you."

"That tears it." Holsinger's mouth set. "You've forfeited
whatever sympathy I had for you. Now I can move on,"

"Move and be damned!"

"What I may not be able to pin down, Paul, is motive." His
eyes scanned the crowd. "You live in a tract house and drive a
compact car—greed can't be a factor."

"What am I supposed to have done?"

"Blowing smoke will get you nowhere, Paul. Today alone you
managed to contrive ten thousand empty seats." He waved to
someone in the stands. "Why, I wonder? Notoriety? Retribution?
Martyrdom? Hatred of the State?"

Sanks stumbled to the bar. He poured a fresh drink. The
bourbon spilled over the rim onto his hand.

As in a dream, he looked out over the field. Almost automatically, he turned on the speaker. The prescribed six strokes had been completed, and the felon was being carted off. Feeble movements could be detected in his hands and legs. The fans gave him a hearty round of applause. Apparently the flogging had satisfied them. The guillotine would be denied its nourishment today.

Sanks said carefully: "You think I deliberately devised ways to sabotage attendance. How?"

"Let me count the ways." Holsinger walked to the door. "Just between us, Sanks, I don't mind admitting that I take particular pleasure in bringing you to justice. It's not so much that I resent your constant attempts to manipulate me. What burns my ass is your certainty I can't see through you. All this hype about crowd processing and intensifying the drama. As if a mere eighty-two thousand at a Parnell-McCoy face-off could be anything but sabotage!"

Down on the field, an astonishing thing happened. As the fans began to leave, the hydraulically-lifted guillotine—normally under Sanks' control—emerged from underground. Its glass walls gleamed in the sun's dying rays.

The exodus stopped.

In the courtroom, Solemn Sam banged his gavel and the jurors returned to their seats.

Sanks gawked. What was happening? Who had authorized the elevation of the guillotine? Why had the judge recalled the jurors?

"Now you've got your wish," Holsinger said. "A twilight double-header. A surprise attraction." He smiled. "You."

Sanks sagged against the bar.

"Let's hope they don't blame you for the jump in ticket prices." With a wave of his hand, Holsinger was gone.

Less than a minute later, a monitor showed him joining Millie in her skybox.

As Sanks watched their embrace, two police officers arrived to escort him to the courtroom.

There's a Stranger in Town
James N. Frey

M aggie, who runs the cafe in our town, knew right away—
by the glint in his eye, she said later—that the stranger
was sane.

He'd just driven into town in an old gray Plymouth. It was
late in the afternoon. In May, it was. Warm, sunny, not a cloud in
the sky. None of us knew he was coming.

Maggie gave the stranger a menu and said she'd be right back
to take his order. She smiled her usual friendly smile and acted
like she didn't suspect a thing. She didn't want to spook him.

Maggie moved down the counter, topping off everyone's
coffee. When she got to Old Charlie Hand she whispered in his
ear that maybe he ought to take a look at the stranger. She didn't
say she suspected he was sane. She only said maybe Old Charlie
ought to take a look. Old Charlie was known to have a good nose
for sniffing out sane people. Once, when he was a much younger
man, he'd picked up a sane hitchhiker and knew the man was
sane even before the man got the door closed. Luckily, Old
Charlie had had his shotgun with him at the time, or we might
have been in deep trouble.

Old Charlie went up to the cash register and pretended to be
waiting for Maggie to come over to ring him up. He sat on the
first stool. The stranger was sitting on the third stool, so there

was only one stool between Old Charlie and the stranger. No more than a couple feet separated them.

The stranger seemed to be absorbed in reading the menu. Old Charlie looked him over good. The stranger was about forty, a little overweight, wearing gray slacks and a colorful shirt with a pair of sun glasses in the pocket. He had a stubble of beard. Old Charlie noted the way the man furrowed his brow, the look of concentration in his eyes as they scanned the menu. Old Charlie figured that only a sane person scans a menu like that. But he had to be sure and there was only one way to know for sure, and that was to talk to him.

Old Charlie took a deep breath and gathered up his courage. Finally he blurted out: "Nice day, ain't it?"

The stranger turned and looked at him and smiled one of those calm, chilling, sane-man smiles. "It is indeed a nice day," the stranger said.

Just the way he said it, with that calm, sane look in his eyes, told Old Charlie he was trouble. Old Charlie felt a bolt of terror, but he didn't let it show. He managed to find some words to keep the conversation going: "Gonna rain tomorrow, though, according to the paper."

"Doesn't feel like rain, though, does it?" the stranger said.

"Guess it don't at that," Old Charlie said, not wanting to argue with a sane man. "Well, guess I'll be seeing ya." He left a dollar on the counter for Maggie and, as natural and relaxed-looking as he could, backed toward the door.

Once outside, he hurried on his wobbly legs across the street for the sheriff's office. He burst in, out of breath. The sheriff was sitting at his desk playing checkers with Doc Beaumont, about to double jump into the king's row. Some of the other fellas were there, just hanging out.

"There's a stranger in town," Old Charlie gasped.

"So?" the sheriff said, concentrating on his game.

"Maggie had a weird feeling about him and asked me to check him out."

"And?" the sheriff said, taking his double jump.

"He's sane."

The sheriff kept his eyes on the board, like he was studying his next move, but his mind couldn't have been on checkers, not when there was the possibility that there was a sane man in town. Finally the sheriff said, "What makes you think he's sane, Charlie?" His voice was low, steady.

"It's the look in his eyes," Old Charlie said. "And the way he talks, like he said, 'indeed,' things like that. Words sane people use."

The sheriff glanced at Doc Beaumont, who looked worried. Three or four years before, a sane woman had shown up and nearly caused a riot and, as it turned out, she was only half-sane. Still, she'd given everyone a fright and Doc Beaumont didn't want to see a repeat of that.

"We'd better get the women and children off the streets," the doc said.

The sheriff nodded toward the deputy, who slipped out the back way. Nobody ever saw the deputy move that fast.

"You got to do something," Old Charlie said. "You can't just leave a sane man loose, there's no telling what mischief he might get into."

The sheriff stood up. He'd been a lumberjack in his youth, and still had a lumberjack's build: massive shoulders and large, strong hands. "I guess I better evaluate the situation." His face was gray. Going up against a sane man had him plenty scared. He walked to the door. Old Charlie moved aside.

"Shouldn't you go armed?" Doc Beaumont asked.

"All I'm going to do is talk to the man," the sheriff said. "If a sane man sees a gun, you don't know what he'll do. Just let me handle it, okay?"

"I better go with you," Doc Beaumont said. "In case you might need a professional opinion."

"Okay," the sheriff said. "But I can't guarantee your safety."

Doc said he understood. He was willing to take the risk for the public good.

The sheriff and Doc Beaumont went into the street. The sun was just above the horizon and the town had a pinkish glow to it. There were only a few cars on the street. The town looked deserted. A block away the deputy was hustling an old woman into her house. The sheriff walked to the cafe, paused, hiked up his pants, and went on in. Doc Beaumont was right behind him.

Usually about that time of day Maggie's would be packed, but there were only a half dozen people in the place, most of them toward the back, whispering to each other. Even if some of them weren't sure, most suspected the stranger was sane. They must have found a sort of perverse excitement in his being there, because they weren't about to go home. When they saw the sheriff, they stopped talking and waited, expectant.

The stranger was eating meat loaf, the special for the evening. The sheriff stood over him. The stranger put down his fork and looked up. Doc Beaumont stood next to the sheriff, studying the stranger's every move.

"I'm Sheriff Keller," the sheriff said.

"Something I can do for you?"

"Mind answering a few questions?"

"What's this about?" The sane man looked worried.

"No offense, mister," the sheriff said, keeping his voice calm. "I was just wondering if you plan to be with us a while, or if you were just passing through."

"Just passing through."

"Not visiting nobody in town then?"

"Don't know anybody in town. I'm heading up north, just thought I'd take the scenic route."

"The scenic route, eh?"

274

"Yes, I find the country around here charming."

"Charming, eh?"

"Is there a problem?"

"No, no problem. How long you plan on staying?"

"Till I'm ready to leave." He said this with a smile, but there was anger in his voice. Sane man anger.

The sheriff backed off and looked at Doc Beaumont, who nodded. He'd heard enough. They went back into the street.

"Well, what do you think?" the sheriff asked Doc Beaumont.

"You heard him say 'charming.' Who but a sane man would use a word like that?"

The sheriff glanced toward the setting sun. "Then we haven't much time. I better swear in special deputies."

The sheriff summoned a dozen of us to a meeting in the alley behind his office. We all had shotguns or hunting rifles, and we were plenty scared. The sheriff passed out deputy badges and he made us swear that we'd obey his orders. Then he said:

"Listen, all of you. We're a posse, not a mob. Nobody does nothing until I tell him. Got that?"

"We ain't gonna try to take him alive, are we?" Davy Sands asked. Davy ran the convenience store and had a couple of kids.

"Of course not," the sheriff said. "But there's no telling what kind of weapon he might have on him."

We all gasped.

Just then Mary Danskin, the manager of the feed store, showed up. A perky little thing. Mary was always opposed to violence of any kind, even boxing. Even football. A strange one, that Mary Danskin.

"Just what's going on here, Sheriff Keller?" she demanded.

"We've got a little problem. There's a sane man in town. No need to trouble yourself about it."

"And what's he done? Nothing. He's simply having dinner over at Maggie's."

"It's not what he's done," the sheriff said. "It's what he might do that's got us worried."

"Did you think to question him, find out what's on his mind? He might not be as sane as you think."

"Of course I questioned him. He's as sane as sane can be. Would you please keep out of it. It's going to be dark soon. You want to have a sane man loose in this town after dark? Think, woman."

That got her. She shut up and just swung around and walked off. The rest of us, we loaded our guns and the sheriff told us where he wanted us to take up positions. Some of us were to get up on roofs; others were to get behind cars; the rest were to stay in reserve.

The sheriff had us synchronize our watches. Then he said he'd be standing across the street from Maggie's when the sane man came out. When he raised his cap, we were to fire. That suited us just fine.

So we took up our positions, everybody keeping low and out of sight. The sun was just a sliver on the western horizon and the shadows grew long in the street. The streetlights came on. We took a look into Maggie's from time to time. The stranger finished up his dinner and had a piece of pie. Apple, it looked like. He ate it with a little vanilla ice cream.

And then Mary Danskin came strutting down the street. She paused for a moment in front of Maggie's and looked at the sheriff, who was standing in the doorway to his office. He waved at her to get her off the street, but she ignored him. Instead, she went on into Maggie's. A couple of us snuck a look at the front window. She went right over to the stranger and sat down next to him and they started talking.

The sheriff was stupefied. He paced up and down in front of his office, wringing his hands. Finally, Maggie's door opened and the stranger came out. We all got ready to fire. It was nearly completely dark by then, but most of us could get a good bead on him by the streetlights. We waited for the sheriff to give the signal, which we figured would be coming as soon as the man stepped off the curb into the street.

But then Mary Danskin came out. "Hope you come by again," we heard her say to the stranger. "You're right, it is charming country around hereabouts."

She stepped into the street with the stranger, and kept talking to him as he got into his Plymouth, telling him to have a safe trip and be sure to wear his seat belt. The sheriff, he couldn't give the signal for fear of hitting Mary Danskin. He had hold of his cap, but he didn't raise it off his head.

So the stranger started up his car and drove away without a shot being fired. Mary Danskin waved at the sheriff and went on home. The sheriff, disgusted, went into his office, slamming the door behind him.

Some of us got to talking later that night over at Jake's Beer Hall. That Mary Danskin! We decided she had been showing dangerous signs of sanity from time to time even before this— her being against football and boxing and fun things like that—and we unanimously agreed we'd better keep a close eye on her.

Lester Gorn

A native of Portland, Maine, Lester Gorn has lived and worked in every part of the United States. He has been at various times and in divers places a longshoreman, a cab driver, a news editor, a ghost writer, a teacher and a soldier. A combat veteran of World War II, he advanced from squad leader to staff officer assigned to the Defense Department. He taught for many years (story lab, world literature, world drama) at University of California Extension, Monterey Peninsula College and the San Francisco Black Writers' Workshop (its only instructor and sole honky). In the olden days, he put in a stint as book editor and daily columnist of the *San Francisco Examiner*.

A novel, *The Anglo Saxons*, was based on his experiences as the only American C.O. in the Israeli Army's ground forces during the War of Independence. Under the *nom de guerre* Ben Zion Hagai, he commanded the 5th Troop (Anti-Tank) of the Israel Army, which participated in every major battle of the Negev campaign. His command car was the second vehicle to enter Eilat (then Umm Al-Rashrash), on the Red Sea, the final objective of the Army's drive south. At that time, Eilat—now a resort city of 48,000—consisted of three huts and a flagpole.

The father of four sons, Lester Gorn now lives in Pacific Grove, California, with his beloved wife, Winnie.

Photo by Bill Coffin

James N. Frey

James N. Frey is one of America's leading creative writing teachers. For over fifteen years, he conducted the popular Open Workshop at the Squaw Valley Community of Writers and has run workshops and lectured at dozens of other schools and conferences, including the Oregon Writers Colony, the Santa Barbara Writers Conference, the Heartland Writers, the University of California Extension novel writing workshop, the California Writers Club conference, and many others, both in America and in Europe. He is the author of nine novels and five widely read creative writing guides: *How to Write a Damn Good Novel, How to Write a Damn Good Novel II: Advanced Techniques, The Key: Writing Damn Good Fiction Using the Power of Myth, How to Write a Damn Good Mystery,* and *How to Write a Damn Good Thriller.* He lives on a sailboat with his wife, Liza.